ChangelingPress.com

Ranger/Fox Duet

Harley Wylde

Ranger/Fox Duet
Harley Wylde

ISBN: 978-1-60521-821-2

Publisher:
Changeling Press LLC
315 N. Centre St.
Martinsburg, WV 25404
ChangelingPress.com

Printed in the U.S.A.

Editor: Crystal Esau
Cover Artist: Bryan Keller

The individual stories in this anthology have been previously released in E-Book format.

Table of Contents

Ranger (Reckless Kings MC 3)
Harley Wylde

Danica -- I followed in my dad's footsteps, chasing the rodeo. It's been my life, other than friends and family with the Dixie Reapers. Until now, no one's really noticed me. I've barely dated, and at twenty-three, I'm still a virgin. Then *he* walks in. Ranger. A Reckless King, and so far out of my league. But one kiss, and I know I'll remember him forever... even after he walks away.

I didn't think we had a future. Thought he'd forget I exist. But I was wrong. He wants me, every bit as much as I want him.

Ranger -- I saw her ride in a rodeo a year ago, and she held me spellbound. Running into her again at the Dixie Reapers, I'm not sure I can keep my hands to myself. She's Cowboy's daughter, and I should keep my distance. Too bad I've never been all that great at following the rules.

Only one thing is standing in my way. There's someone stalking her. A man who thinks she's his. He's wrong. Danica will be mine, one way or another. Anyone who stands in the way will wish they'd never heard of me.

Prologue

Ranger -- One Year Ago

"Why did I let you talk me into this?" I asked.

Scott grinned. "You'll like it. First time a bull stomps some poor cowboy, you'll be just as into it as the rest of the crowd."

"Your idea of entertainment is fucked up."

He ignored me and led us farther through the crowd. We ended up on bleachers halfway up, which gave us a decent view of the arena. I should have told him to fuck off and gone to a bar. Instead, I'd let him talk me into going to a rodeo. In my cut and motorcycle boots, I stuck out like a sore thumb. Scott had on his cowboy boots and a cowboy hat, which made sense seeing as how he worked on a horse farm outside Atlanta. My cowboy days were over. Long over.

"We just have to make it through the bronc riders and barrel racers before the bulls come out," Scott said. "Some of the barrel racers are good eye candy, though. A few of them compete all over the country."

Why did it not surprise me he'd be checking out the women, even the ones in the rodeo? The ladies had always loved Scott. Back when I'd served with him in the Army, I'd seen him walk out of a bar with two or three women hanging off him. I'd been leery of being with random women, unless I used a condom I'd brought with me. Even then, nothing was foolproof.

"Next up is Danica Adler on Windstorm," the announcer said.

"Oh, this will be good." Scott rubbed his hands on his thighs. "She's one of the favorites."

"Why?" I asked.

"Her dad is a champion rodeo rider. Last I heard, he was like you… a biker. They live down someplace in Alabama. Both his kids are following in his footsteps. Danica runs barrels and his son rides bulls. They're both damn good too."

I focused on the arena when a horse shot out of the gate. The slim rider on his back clung to him as he raced around the barrels. I couldn't see much of her, except long honey-colored hair and curves that made my mouth water. When she finished her run, the announcer whooped with excitement.

"She did good?" I asked Scott. I might have lived around horses most of my life, but I'd never really cared about going to a rodeo. I damn sure hadn't had a reason to watch anyone run barrels.

"Hell yeah! I bet she wins tonight." He smiled and nudged me with his shoulder. "Told you this would be fun."

Beast had sent me to Atlanta for a drop-off, so I'd thought I'd hang at a bar tonight before heading home. Nope. I'd decided to look up my old buddy Scott, and he'd nixed that idea almost immediately, so here I was at a rodeo. A *rodeo.* Although, I had to admit, watching Danica had been pretty exciting, even if it had ended quickly.

I spotted Danica making her way through the crowd. The smile on her face made my heart slam against my ribs. Fuck but she was pretty. Not gorgeous, but a sweet girl-next-door type. She just happened to be exactly the sort of woman I went for. Knowing she was a biker's daughter, and from Alabama, made me think she was most likely Cowboy's daughter and therefore the property of the Dixie Reapers. Which meant she was hands-off. Didn't stop me from wanting her.

One night of fun was one thing, but forever? I knew if I put my hands on her, one of two things would happen. Either her daddy would demand I claim her, or he'd make sure no one ever found my body. Hell, he'd probably string me up for even looking at her the way I was right now. If he was like the others, and like Beast, then I had no doubt he was overprotective of his daughter.

Scott jammed his elbow into my ribs. "Don't stare too hard. You know damn well her dad would have your balls."

Right. I scanned the crowd, wondering if there might be a willing woman, and soon realized they were all about the cowboys and boots and wouldn't want a damn thing to do with a biker. I may have grown up on a horse farm in Middle Tennessee, but those days were a thing of the past. I hadn't been on a horse in years and didn't plan to start now. Why the fuck did I let Scott talk me into shit like this? It wasn't the first time I'd listened to him instead of doing what I'd originally planned, and it always came back to bite me in the ass in one way or another.

"You owe me," I said.

"Oh, please. You may not be able to touch, but you can't tell me Danica won't be in your spank bank for a long while. The girl has legs for days, even if she is on the petite side. I'm not blind. I can appreciate all she has to offer. Doesn't mean I'm stupid enough to try and go there."

"I had plans for tonight. None of which included going to bed alone, so thanks for nothing."

Scott sighed. "We'll hit up a bar on the way back to the motel. You can find some easy pussy."

"Like you plan on abstaining?" I asked.

He shrugged and looked off in the direction

Danica had just disappeared. I narrowed my eyes at him and had the sudden urge to beat the shit out of Scott. Did he have a thing for the Reaper's daughter? I hadn't even spoken to her, and yet part of me wanted to blind any fucker who dared look her way. Scott included. What the fuck was wrong with me?

I definitely needed to get laid and put Danica out of my mind. No fucking way I'd ever be able to go there. Scott was right about one thing, though. She'd be starring in my fantasies for a long while.

Chapter One

Danica

Tears streaked my cheeks as I stared down at the freshly dug grave. My dad had promised to plant a tree over Champ's resting place. He'd been my best friend the last seven years, and it broke my heart knowing he'd never race across the pasture to greet me again. He hadn't been in the best of health when I'd rescued him, and the vet had warned he might not live long. Champ had surprised us all by lasting as long as he had.

"Rest in peace, my sweet boy."

My dad threw his arm around my shoulders and pulled me tight against his side. "Sorry, honey. I know it's hard."

"At least he's not hurting," I said.

Dad nodded. "Why don't you head over to the clubhouse? The Reckless Kings are visiting, and I know you want to see baby Madison."

"Are you trying to distract me?" I asked.

"Yep. Is it working?"

I sniffled and swiped at the tears on my cheeks, laughing a little. "Yeah, it's working."

Dad kissed the top of my head and helped me stand up. "Your mom should already be there. Your little brother too. Unless she dropped Langston off at Atlas's house."

After another hug, he sent me out of the pasture. I stopped in the house and splashed water on my face before heading to the clubhouse. I couldn't hide the fact I'd been crying. My eyes were puffy and most likely red. I wasn't a pretty crier. Pulling my keys from my pocket, I hurried out to my truck. I got in and heard something crinkle. Yanking a piece of paper out from under me, I cringed when I saw what it was.

I glanced at where I'd left my dad, thankful he wasn't paying me any attention. He'd seen the first one of these before I could hide it. While he'd been concerned, I'd blown it off as being nothing. Except I'd lied. It was definitely something. A chill skated down my spine and my stomach knotted.

We'll be together soon.

Like hell we would! I knew who'd left it, even if I couldn't prove it. I'd already spoken to the law in several states. Each had said the same thing. It was my word against his. Lewis Stevens was the golden boy of the rodeo. Champion bull rider, and ladies' man. Everyone treated his stalking like some sort of courting. I'd landed on his radar, and he wasn't backing down.

I balled up the note and tossed it onto the floorboard. It wasn't the first, and it wouldn't be the last. I put the truck in gear and drove to the compound. As much as I liked being around our extended family, I enjoyed having a house away from all the craziness. My dad had purchased a lot of land when we'd first moved here, and I wasn't ashamed to admit I still lived with my parents. The farmhouse was plenty big enough for all of us.

Dylan opened the gate when he saw me pulling up. I drove through and parked outside the clubhouse. Looked like quite a few people were already here. I yanked down the visor and checked my reflection. I took down my ponytail and ran my fingers through my hair, removing bits of hay. After I put my hair up in a messy bun, I grabbed my tinted lip balm from the console and smoothed some over my lips. Not perfect, but I looked a little less wrecked.

I got out and made my way inside, anxious to see

little Madison. Beast and Lyssa brought her to visit a few times a year, but I'd missed her last time. I'd been out of town at a rodeo. I'd needed the money, so not going hadn't been an option. Or at least, I knew some day I'd need it. I couldn't live at home forever. Thankfully, I'd won and pocketed a nice chunk of change. I might not ride broncs like my dad had, but I could hold my own in barrels.

Stepping into the clubhouse, I waited a moment for my eyes to adjust to the dim interior before tracking down Beast, Lyssa, and Madison. I found them at a table toward the back. Torch and Isabella were already there with their kids, and I noticed Leigha and Logan had claimed a seat nearby too. I scanned the room and saw their dad, Preacher, talking to one of the Reckless Kings.

"You may have to wait your turn."

I jerked my head to the right and smiled at Owen. "Yeah? I'd have been here sooner, but…"

Owen slung his arm around my shoulders. "I know. Your dad called and let me know you might need a friend. Sorry about Champ. He was a good horse."

"Where's your brother from another mother?" He snorted and pointed across the room. I spotted Foster talking to Lara. "Damn. If Preacher sees him chatting her up, your BFF might get neutered."

Owen was Rocky's son, and Foster was Bull's. The two were the same age and had been inseparable. I'd often joked they were in a relationship. At first, they'd been pissed when I teased them. Now they took it in stride. They were both also about three years older than Lara, who was only fifteen. Even though both boys were closer to Jackson's age than mine, they were still like family to me. With Farrah and Mariah gone, I didn't really have anyone my age to hang with when the club had gatherings. Leigha and Logan were two years younger than my brother, and a year younger than Owen and Foster. I was the oldest of the kids still at home.

As for the patched members, Viking was close to my age, but most were older. Out of the Prospects, Dylan was the closest in age to me, but I was still older than him. The only times I'd been able to go on dates, which was rare, had been with one of the guys from town. They hadn't ended well.

"Jackson coming?" Owen asked.

"You act like I keep up with my little brother."

He nudged me in the ribs and I relented. "Fine. Last I heard, he was heading to El Paso for an event. If his dumb ass doesn't die getting on the back of one of those crazy bulls, he should be home in a week. And if you want to know about my other little brother, I have no idea since I don't see him. Probably with Atlas."

The clubhouse door slammed into the wall right before I heard a deep, growly voice that sounded all kinds of pissed. "Let. Me. The. Fuck. Go."

I glanced that way and my jaw nearly hit the floor. The man had on a Reckless Kings cut, but I hadn't noticed him before. His hair was dark and windswept, making my fingers itch to smooth it back into place. When I saw why he was so angry, I ground my teeth together.

"What the hell is *she* doing here? This is a family event," I said.

I stalked toward them and didn't stop until I stood so close to the man I could feel the heat coming off his body. From the corner of my eye, I saw the name stitched on his chest. *Ranger*. We hadn't met previously, but I'd have to change that real soon. The man was gorgeous in that "I'm a badass" sort of way.

The whore sneered at me as she pawed at Ranger. "Danica."

"Get lost, LuLu." My hands fisted at my sides, and I knew if the bitch didn't back off, I'd end up swinging. I couldn't stand her! She'd already tried to sink her claws into my brother, Owen, and Foster. She didn't care whose bed she ended up in, as long as she had a permanent tie to the club. Since none of the brothers or Prospects were dumb enough to fall for her shit, she'd resorted to targeting their sons. I knew Foster and Owen had both talked to their dads about becoming Prospects. So far, they hadn't been allowed, and both were pissed about it.

"You have no say in where I go," LuLu said.

"Want to bet?" I narrowed my eyes and took a step closer to her. "You have until the count of three to remove your hand from Ranger. Otherwise, I'll take it as a challenge."

"You're such a bitch!" LuLu bared her teeth at me like a rabid chihuahua. "You're no better than me. You think your daddy being a Dixie Reaper gives you power here? You're nothing!"

I reacted before I even thought about what I was doing. My fist connected with her face, and she shrieked as she stumbled back on her ridiculously high heels, backing out of the doorway and onto the porch before she tumbled down the steps and onto the ground. I advanced on her, my boots clomping down the wood steps. Reaching down, I grabbed a handful of her hair and hauled her up long enough to punch her in the face again. I landed two more blows before a strong arm banded across my waist and hauled me off her.

"Stay away from me and my family," I said.

"And that includes my brother, Foster, and Owen. Everyone knows you're a whore. You don't have a chance in hell of ever ending up with one of them. You aren't fit to lick their boots."

The door behind me creaked open and Torch came down the steps, stopping next to me. He reached for my hand, lifting it to study my knuckles. When he realized I hadn't split them or broken any bones, he gave me a smile.

"Sorry for the disruption," I said.

"That's all right. You were just taking out the trash."

I felt the vibration of laughter from whichever man had grabbed me. I felt the scrape of whiskers along my ear and hot breath fanned across my skin. "Remind me not to piss you off."

I craned my neck to see who held me and my heart skipped a beat when I saw it was Ranger. His eyes were deep chocolate brown with flecks of gold. I'd never considered a man's eyes beautiful, until now. "I don't hit men. Unless it's my brother. He usually deserves a punch to the gut."

Ranger tightened his hold and took a few steps back, carrying me with him. Torch reached down and hauled LuLu to her feet, then gave her a shove toward her car. "Get gone, girl. I put the word out whores weren't allowed the next few nights."

"But I wanted to see your granddaughter," LuLu said with a whine to her voice. She poked her bottom lip out in an exaggerated pout.

"LuLu, I will kick your whorish ass if you don't leave," I said, spitting on the ground at her feet.

Torch sighed and eyed me. "I've got it handled, Danica."

"You and I both know you'll never hurt her," I

said. "That's not who you are. You might be the President of this club, but you're an honorable man, Torch. Always have been, always will be. I, however, have no qualms about knocking her on her ass."

"Ranger, get her out of here." Torch gave LuLu another shove. "I'll handle this one."

Ranger swung me into his arms and carried me back into the clubhouse. Instead of putting me down once we were inside, he walked straight through the main room and didn't stop until we reached the end of the hall. The shadows kept us mostly hidden from everyone else. Ranger let me slide down his body, then pressed me against the wall, caging me between his arms.

"So, little firecracker. Which Reaper do you belong to?" he asked.

I lifted my chin. "I don't belong to anyone."

His eyes lit up. "Really? Good news for me, then."

"Why is that?"

"Because no one will object if I do this." He crowded me, then lowered his head. His lips moved over mine, and when he flicked his tongue across the seam of my lips, I opened and let him in. I'd been kissed before, but never like this. My knees went weak, and it felt like my heart might beat right out of my chest. "Come with me."

"With you?" I asked. "I don't understand."

"I only rode this far with Beast so he'd have some extra protection on the road. I wasn't planning to stay. I rented a place a few towns over. Come spend the weekend with me."

I couldn't remember anyone ever asking me to spend a weekend with them. Then again, most people knew my dad and valued their lives too much to ask such a thing. But Ranger had no idea who I was. It was clear I was family or friend with the Dixie Reapers. Aside from that, I hadn't told him anything. If my dad heard him ask such a thing, I had a feeling Ranger would be missing a few teeth. Or he might go missing entirely, buried in pieces somewhere out back of the property.

"I'm not sure that's such a good idea."

The heavy tread of boots headed our way. The silhouette was enough to tell me it was one of two people. Either Bull or Viking. I wasn't sure I wanted either of them poking their noses into my business. When Viking stepped into the light, I gave him a slight smile.

"Hey, Viking."

He stared at me, his gaze missing nothing, then he faced Ranger. "Let her go."

"She yours?" Ranger asked. "Because she told me she didn't belong to anyone."

Viking folded his arms. "She's Cowboy's daughter, which makes her property of the Dixie Reapers. Since you aren't a Reaper, you need to step off."

Ranger leaned in closer. "That true, little firecracker? You the property of the Dixie Reapers?"

Was I their property? Eh. I never really considered myself as belonging to anyone. I loved my dad, and I had no problems with my mom wearing a property cut, but I wasn't sure it was the right path for me. Then again, I didn't know anyone who would go toe-to-toe with my dad, other than another biker. I didn't have a lot of options unless I wanted to die an old cat lady.

I shrugged a shoulder. "My dad is one of them."

"Didn't answer my question. You free to be with

whoever you want?" Ranger asked.

"You deaf?" Viking asked.

I sighed and eyed the big guy. "I'm okay, Viking. Really."

Instead of leaving, he came closer. "Danica, you've had a rough day. I don't want you doing something you'll regret later. You know you aren't thinking straight right now."

I felt Ranger tense and knew he wondered what the hell was going on. I didn't think the big, tough biker would understand I'd been bawling my eyes out over a horse. The guys here got it because quite a few had seen me compete, and knew I got my love of horses from my parents. My dad had been a champion bronc rider in the rodeos. I couldn't say I'd inherited the trait from him because he wasn't my biological father, but he'd been more of a dad to me than the man who'd been my sperm donor. Cowboy, as the Dixie Reapers called him, had been a good role model for both me and my brother.

"Maybe I need the distraction," I said.

Viking arched an eyebrow at me, knowing damn well I was still a virgin. Hell, everyone here knew it. As much as I hated to admit it, he was right. I didn't need to go off with Ranger for a few nights. I'd waited this long, wanting my first time to be special. Besides, if my dad found out Ranger had propositioned me, I had a feeling the club would make sure he never darkened the clubhouse doorstep again. He'd be run out of town within minutes.

"Come on, Danica." Viking held out his hand. "I'll sit with you at the bar. I think you need a beer more than you need someone trying to get into your pants."

I gave Ranger a gentle shove and he released me.

Taking Viking's hand, I let him lead me back into the main area and up to the bar. I took a seat while he got me a cold beer. I felt like I owed Ranger an explanation, but the truth of the matter was that he'd be gone in a minute, and the chance of me seeing him again was slim to none. If he did come back with Beast and Lyssa, it wouldn't necessarily be during a time I was in town. I traveled a lot, chasing the next rodeo.

"Thanks," I said, accepting the beer. "For this and also for keeping me from making a mistake."

"So I'm a mistake?" Ranger asked from behind me.

"She's not a club whore," Viking said. "If you only want a good time, you should have stuck with LuLu."

The tension rolling off the two men told me I needed to defuse the situation before they came to blows. While some girls might get hot over men fighting over them, it wasn't my thing. And if these two started swinging, then both clubs would get involved and it would become a huge mess. None of us needed that sort of headache.

"You're staying somewhere for the weekend, then you're going back home," I said. "It's not that you would be a mistake, but I'm not the type to have a weekend fling. I want more than a night or two with someone. Viking was right to remind me of that. I wouldn't have liked myself very much after you went back home."

Ranger shoved his hands into his pockets. "I don't have to take off right this minute. Would you consider going to lunch with me? Maybe spending part of the day just hanging out?"

I turned to face him fully. "Why would you want that?"

"I remember you," he said. "Saw you in a rodeo down in Atlanta a year ago. Thought you looked pretty great out there."

I knew which one he was talking about. I'd won the barrel racing event that day and taken home a decent cash prize. It just hadn't occurred to me any bikers were in the audience. Some of the Reapers had been to a few of my rodeos, the ones near home, but I hadn't had any other clubs come watch. I hadn't exactly been watching for anyone since I knew none of my family would be there. Why had the Reckless Kings been in the area? They weren't even from Georgia.

"You watched me ride?" I asked.

He nodded. "You were on a sorrel."

I bit my lip, wanting to know how he'd known the color of my horse. It wasn't something just anyone would know, which meant he'd either spent time around horses, or liked them enough to learn about them. He didn't seem like the type, but apparently I'd been wrong. "Her name is Sunny."

"So, want to grab some lunch?" he asked.

I shouldn't, even if the man did tempt me. He wouldn't be staying long, and I wasn't the one-night stand type. What would be the point in getting to know him better? By his own admission he'd be gone by tonight, off to some cabin somewhere, and there was a chance I wouldn't see him for years, if ever again. My thoughts must have shown on my face. He held up his hands and took a step back.

"No pressure, Danica. If you don't want to go, that's fine. Just say so."

"It's not that I don't want to. You're leaving tonight, and who knows when we'll see each other again. I guess I just don't understand what you're hoping to get out of this."

His lips kicked up on one corner. "I get to spend the day with a pretty woman. Who knows... maybe you'll convince me to cancel my plans and stay until it's time to head home."

My heart skipped a beat at his words. I didn't know why he wanted to get to know me. A man like him could have his pick of women. I wasn't anything special. The lack of boyfriends was proof enough. I'd been on so few dates, and I didn't think it was entirely because of who my dad was. Yeah, Cowboy could be intimidating, but not as much as say Torch. The President of the Dixie Reapers was getting up there in years. Didn't seem to matter. He was still scary as hell.

"All right. I'll go to lunch with you, and we can see where things go from there," I agreed. "But I'm not promising more than that."

He grinned, and my stomach tightened. "I can accept those terms."

Oh, holy hell. What had I just gotten myself into?

Chapter Two

Ranger

I shouldn't have been so excited to go to lunch with a woman. Especially after she'd eyed my bike, rolled her eyes, and tossed me the keys to her truck. There wasn't a damn thing wrong with my Harley Davidson Heritage Classic. I'd had it custom painted a charcoal gray with a tattered American flag on the tank. Being the daughter of a biker, I hadn't expected her to balk at riding behind me.

Viking had mentioned something about her having a bad day. No better cure than the open road. If lunch went well enough, maybe I could talk her into going for a ride. I hadn't been lying when I said I'd change my plans for her. If I'd known she would be here, I'd have never made arrangements to stay elsewhere.

"Turn left here," she said.

I followed her instructions as she guided me to her favorite Mexican restaurant. I found a spot to park not too far from the door and led her inside with my hand at her lower back. She didn't pull away, so I took it as a good sign. When we stepped up to the hostess stand, the woman eyed the two of us before lifting her chin a bit, putting her nose in the air. It wasn't the first time it had happened to me, and I knew it wouldn't be the last. But seeing her do that to Danica? I wanted to tear into the bitch.

"Table for two," I said.

She looked down at her podium and let out a huff before snatching two menus and walking off. I'd have to have a word with management before we left. I could have ignored her attitude had it just been me, but I wasn't about to let Danica be treated poorly. She hadn't done anything wrong.

"Sorry," Danica murmured.

"For what?" I asked.

She nodded toward the woman who slapped the menus on the table and walked off. "Marisa. She's hated me for a while now."

I pulled out Danica's chair and waited for her to sit before taking the spot across from her. She put her hand up to her hair, smoothing back a few flyaway strands, and cast a nervous look around the restaurant. I hadn't sensed any danger when we'd walked in, so my guess was she had a few enemies in town, like that Marisa bitch. And I wanted to know why.

I took my seat and folded my arms on top of the table, leaning toward her. "So what's the deal with her?"

"Her boyfriend asked me out in high school. I told him no, but she didn't care. Marisa has it in her head that I lured him away or something."

I arched my eyebrow and looked from her to the Marisa bitch and back again. The woman was still staring at Danica with pure hatred. "Wasn't high school a while back? Exactly how old are you?"

She smiled a little. "I'm twenty-three. Don't worry. I'm not jailbait."

Which meant there was more than a decade difference between us. I knew there was a lot more than that between Beast and Lyssa, and same for Hawk and Hayley. The question was whether or not Danica would have an issue with our age difference. I knew some women preferred guys closer to their age, or even younger. Although, for her to be a cougar, she'd be dating underage boys and I doubted that was her thing. If it were, she wouldn't be here with me right now.

"I'm thirty-six," I said, deciding to go ahead and put it out there.

"I figured you were a little older than me, although I'd guessed closer to twenty-seven." She shrugged. "Doesn't bother me. You've seen the couples in the Dixie Reapers. Most have a decade or two between them."

One hurdle down. A million more to go.

A server came over to take our order. He stopped about a foot away, glancing from Danica to me. "Do you need more time with the menus or are you ready to order?"

"I think we need another minute, Enrique," Danica said. "But I'll take a sweet tea and some cheese dip."

"And for you?" he asked me.

"Dr. Pepper. Can you bring out salsa when you bring her cheese dip?"

He gave a brief nod and hurried off. The fact Danica knew his name meant she really did love this place. I had to wonder how often she ate here. Did she bring dates here? Come with friends? I wanted to know more about her but didn't want to grill her with a ton of questions.

"You don't like cheese?" she asked.

"I do. I love it, in fact. However, my stomach hates me if I eat too much of it. If I were to eat the cheese dip, I'd have to order my food without cheese."

"That has to suck. We could have gone somewhere else."

I shook my head. "I'm good. I've learned my limits, and as long as I don't deviate, then I can eat pretty much anywhere."

I looked over the menu, knowing I needed to figure out what I was eating before our server returned, and since I'd seen him heading our way, I knew my time was up. Danica placed her order first, then I gave our server mine. He set the cheese dip, salsa, and a basket of chips on the table before unloading our drinks. Once he left, I wondered how I was going to get Danica to talk to me. I didn't want her to feel like she was being interrogated, and yet I needed to know more about her.

"Did you volunteer to come with Beast?" Danica asked.

"Yeah, I did." She stared at me, and I knew she wanted more than that. I was going to have to confess I always came when he needed an extra man just in the hopes of running into her. "Remember when I said I watched you at a rodeo in Atlanta a year ago?"

"Yeah. I still can't believe you were there."

"Well, I've come with Beast every trip since then in hopes of running into you. The last time we were here, you were off at a rodeo. This time, I decided not to take the chance and made alternate plans. Of course, it would be the visit where you *are* home. So here we are."

Her cheeks flushed pink. "You came here just so you could see me?"

I nodded. "I know we haven't met before. Maybe it's weird, and seems a bit stalkerish, but I really wanted a chance to get to know you. Watching you ride that day was amazing. You were so confident, and really damn good. Then you walked through the crowd, a big smile on your face, and I knew I needed to meet you in person."

"Why didn't you just come down and say hi then?"

"Didn't seem like the time. I was dressed the way I am now, at a rodeo of all places. Wasn't sure you'd want me approaching you."

She smiled and leaned in closer, dropping her voice. "You may not have noticed, but my dad is a biker. I'm used to men in motorcycle boots and cuts. I wouldn't have run away if you'd approached me."

"Did you start riding in rodeos because of your dad?"

She chewed on her bottom lip, and I wasn't sure she'd answer for a minute. "Actually, I've always loved horses. Cowboy isn't my biological father. He and my mom got together when I was in middle school. My birth father was a dirty cop who'd been abusing my mom. If she didn't fall in with his plans, he'd threaten me and my brother. When Cowboy decided to get us out of there, I was more than ready to. He's the best thing that ever happened to us."

I blinked, not knowing what to say. Her dad had been a dirty cop? When she said he'd hurt her mom, what exactly had she meant? Slapping her around? Or worse? I wasn't sure I wanted to know. Cowboy had likely buried the fucker, but if he hadn't, someone needed to.

"The shorter answer to your question is *yes*. I started out riding in local horse shows, and when my dad -- Cowboy -- said I had talent, I decided to try hitting the smaller rodeos. It just snowballed from there. Now I love what I do. I'm not in it for the money. Well, not *only* for the money. I've been saving for something, but it's also a thrill when I'm running barrels. I still live at home with my mom and dad, and Dad takes care of my horses. I honestly don't have any bills to worry about. The rodeo is my job. I've just been putting the money away. No clue what for, but the money will be there when I need it. Maybe I'll buy a house and finally move out, even if I'm not home all the time."

"It must be awesome to have such a supportive family," I said. "I joined the Army right out of high school as an escape from my home life. My parents weren't abusive or anything. I was just over small-town life, and my family didn't understand. Worked my way up to being an Army Ranger, hence my road name. I'm afraid the Reckless Kings weren't too original with that one."

She smiled and reached over, placing her hand on mine. "I like your road name. Can I ask you something personal?"

"Sure."

"I don't want to offend you."

I snorted. "Really? Danica, just ask."

"It's about your heritage. I just noticed you're darker complected than me, by quite a bit, and I didn't think it was a tan." Her cheeks turned a brighter pink. "It's a rude question."

"Dani girl, I'm okay with anything you want to ask me. That's part of why I wanted to take you to lunch, so we could get better acquainted. Can't really do that if we don't ask each other anything." I threaded our fingers together. "My dad was from Dubai. He came here for a business trip, met my mom, and ended up knocking her up. He's never wanted anything to do with me, even though he did relent and give me his last name. He also sent my mom child support. I doubt the courts would have been able to get anything from him if he'd decided to be a dick, since he lives in another country. I've only met him once."

"Do you look like him?" she asked.

"I do. Except I'm taller. I get my height from my mom's side. She's a little thing, but her father was six foot six, and her brothers were just as tall if not taller. I never met her grandfather, but I heard that he was six foot nine."

Her eyes went wide. "I don't think I've ever met anyone that tall. I'd feel like an ant."

My lips twitched as I fought not to laugh. "That's because you're a little thing like my mom. You're what? Maybe five feet?"

She straightened in her seat. "I'll have you know I'm five foot one. That's an entire three inches taller than people with dwarfism."

I rolled my lips into my mouth and bit down. I didn't think she'd appreciate me finding humor in the situation. But fuck was she cute!

Enrique returned with our food, made sure we had everything we needed, then disappeared again. The man knew how to make himself scarce. I'd have to make sure I left him a good tip. He'd taken care of us without hovering.

We dug into our food, and the chips we'd ignored so far, and I had to admit, Danica had good taste. The food was amazing.

"I grew up on a horse farm," I said. "In Middle Tennessee. My mom settled down with a man when I was still a baby. He raised me as his own. I helped with the horses until I left home at eighteen."

"Well, that explains how you know what a sorrel is. Most people just call Sunny a red horse with blonde hair."

Yeah, I'd run into those people most of my life. After I'd joined the Army, I'd knocked the dust off my boots and not looked back. When I went back to visit, I always stayed at a motel nearby and made sure I got there after the horses had been fed and stalls mucked and left before it was time to do it all again. Now I realized I'd been an asshole to my parents by doing that shit. I'd have to call and tell my mom I was sorry for being such a dick.

"I think my mom would like you. She's really into horses. I'm betting you'd live in the barn if you could."

She nodded. "I would. I talked to Dad about putting an apartment over the stalls when he had the new barn built. He considered it, then decided he preferred me being in the house. Something about it being safer."

"I know the Dixie Reapers aren't into much these days. Doesn't mean he's not right to worry about you. If someone wanted to get back at the club, a tiny thing like you would be tempting. They'd snatch you up and run, or worse."

"I get it. I really do. It's why I didn't argue and still live at home. Although, Dad did offer to put a tiny house out back. Close enough no one would think to mess with me, but far enough I'd have my independence."

I shoved a chip in my mouth and considered what I wanted to say. I didn't want to chase her off. At the same time, I needed to know if she'd ever consider moving away from Alabama. My home was with the Reckless Kings. I couldn't just up and move because I found a woman I wanted to keep. No, if I wanted an old lady, I'd need someone who either already lived in the area or would be willing to move.

"You ever thought about the future? Where you'll be in five or ten years?" I asked.

"Other than hopefully still riding? I'm not sure. I know I don't want to rodeo forever. I'll always have my horses. It's part of who I am. But I can do that without competing. I guess I'd like a family, a place of my own."

"Here in Alabama?" I asked.

She lowered her lashes and shrugged a shoulder. "Maybe. I guess it depends on who I end up with."

"So for the right guy, you'd be willing to move?" I pressed.

She nodded. "Yeah. Definitely. I want what my parents have. What Venom and Ridley have, Torch and Isabella, Bull and Darian. I see all the couples together, the laughter they share, the love, and I want it more than anything."

"I never thought I'd settle down. Didn't want anything steady. Just a good time for a few nights." I captured her gaze and held it. "But a year ago I saw a woman I haven't been able to get out of my head, and I realized maybe having more than that wasn't so bad. I've thought about you a lot, Danica."

"I'm not anything special."

"Yes, you are. If you can't see it, then I have my work cut out for me. Hell, Viking came to your rescue. I saw you with that other guy before that, the one who put his arm around you. It's clear the Dixie Reapers and their families love you. Do you think they care about just anyone?"

"I guess not." She smiled softly. "But they're my family. They kind of have to love me."

"You really believe that? Because I know a lot of families who don't give a shit about their kids, siblings, parents… or anyone for that matter. All they care about are themselves."

"You have a point. I know Ridley's mom was horrible, and my dad was just as bad. A lot of the Reapers' old ladies came to them because they were running from something, and quite a few were trying to escape their families."

Enrique brought the check, and I dropped

enough cash on the table to cover the bill and a twenty-five percent tip. I led Danica back out to her truck. Instead of going straight to the compound, I pulled off at a park we'd passed on the way in. She glanced my way, but didn't say anything. When she reached for my hand, everything inside me seemed to relax and settle. Almost as if this was exactly where I should be -- with Danica.

Suddenly, I wasn't looking forward to heading home in a few days. I wanted more time with her.

Chapter Three

Danica

I sighed and ran my hands over Sunny's neck. It had been two weeks since Ranger had left, and I missed him. Lunch had turned into so much more. He hadn't kissed me, not since he'd pushed me against the wall at the clubhouse when Viking had interrupted. Even when he'd left, I'd only gotten a hug. At first, I'd wondered if maybe he hadn't felt the same as me. Until I'd seen the longing in his eyes. For whatever reason, he was taking things slow. Too damn slow.

And with Lewis lurking in the shadows, I didn't have time for someone to drag their boot heels. Even when the man wasn't anywhere near my location, I still managed to find notes in my truck. I had no idea who was helping him, or how they managed to get into my vehicle even when it was locked. I knew time was running out. As much as I wanted to confide in my dad, or maybe even Tank, I didn't want the club to end up in the spotlight if something happened to Lewis.

I wanted to throw up, just thinking about the possibility of running into Lewis at the next rodeo. He didn't attend every event, but he went to enough that our paths crossed more often than I liked. The man always managed to corner me when no one else was around. One day, I wouldn't be able to break away.

My dad came up behind me and braced an arm on Sunny's stall door. "You about ready? Need to load up the horses."

"Yeah."

"You haven't been the same these last few weeks. Something on your mind? Or maybe some certain guy?"

I faced my dad and wondered how much he

knew. I hadn't kept it a secret I was spending time with Ranger. The entire club had known. But my dad had always seen more than I'd wanted him to, which meant he probably knew I'd started falling for Ranger during that short visit. He'd been so amazing. Sweet, kind, sexy…

"I guess my mind isn't in the game right now. I'm probably going to have my worst ride ever."

My dad tugged on a lock of hair that had escaped my ponytail. "Why don't you skip this one? Or at least stop by the Reckless Kings on the way. See Ranger and then decide if you want to ride or back out. You should have a decent nest egg by now. No reason for you to go to a rodeo when you don't really want to."

He had a point. Not to mention, it would keep me away from Lewis a bit longer. "Do you think they'd be okay with me just randomly dropping in?"

My dad rolled his eyes, something he'd picked up from my mother over the years. "Seriously? You think Ranger is going to tell you to get the fuck out? That kid couldn't keep his eyes off you the entire time he was here. I half expected you to tell me you were leaving with him."

"What about the horses?" I asked.

"Take them with you. If you decide you want to go to the rodeo, you'll have everything you need. Or you can stay and visit with Ranger. I'm sure Beast can figure out something temporary for the horses while you're there or find a local stable to take them in for a few days."

"Thanks, Dad." I threw my arms around his neck and hugged him. "Love you."

"Love you too, little girl. As much as I want to hold onto you forever, I know you're old enough now to be starting your own family and finding your own path. Until now, it's been right alongside mine. If you decide you belong with Ranger, I won't stand in your way. But if he ever hurts you, I'm kicking his ass."

I laughed and held on tighter before backing up. I hurried from the barn and up to the house. I'd packed my bag already for the rodeo, but on the off chance I decided to stay and visit with Ranger instead, I'd need a few more outfits. When I was finished, I carried two bags out to my truck and saw my dad had already attached the horse trailer and loaded Sunny and my black paint, Pharoah.

"All your tack, brushes, and anything else you need for the horses is already loaded. Including feed and hay," Dad said. "Call me when you get there."

"Shouldn't I at least let him know I'm coming? I'm not sure Beast will appreciate me just showing up on the Reckless Kings' doorstep."

"I'll handle it. Get on the road. I want you there before it gets late."

"Tell Mom I said bye," I said.

He gave a nod and took a step back. Normally, I'd have waited to see her before I left, but she'd gone on a shopping trip with Darian and Mara. I knew she'd likely be gone most of the day.

I got into the truck and waved at my dad. My hands shook a little as I started it up. Was I doing the right thing? Only one way to find out... And if I got there and Ranger didn't want to see me, then I'd continue to the rodeo. We'd exchanged numbers before he'd left, but I hadn't spoken to him in all that time. I'd gotten a few texts and nothing else. He'd claimed to be busy with personal stuff. It was possibly true, or he could have been trying to find a way to blow me off.

My stomach clenched as I hit the highway

heading out of town. My phone chimed with a message, and I swiped the screen long enough to see it was from my dad. It only said two words. *All Clear.* I took that to mean Beast didn't have an issue with me stopping by. And if he'd okayed my visit, that had to mean Ranger wanted to see me. Right?

"Don't second-guess yourself now, Danica," I muttered to myself and pressed the accelerator a little harder.

I made a few stops along the way. Gas. Bathroom. Food. By the time I pulled up to the Reckless Kings' gates, it was nearly dark, and I was tired as hell. My back hurt and I had a headache building. I rolled down my window and smiled at the Prospect manning the gate. "I'm here to see Ranger."

"Danica?" he asked, eyeing the horse trailer.

"Yeah. I haven't been here before, though, so I have no idea where I'm going."

He nodded and opened up the gate. "Turn left and look for the tan house with white trim. You'll see a small corral off to the side with a makeshift barn for your horses."

"Um, what?"

He grinned. "Ranger put up a corral today, with the help from some brothers. He wanted to make sure your horses had a safe place and didn't have to stay in the trailer. You can't miss it."

I thanked him and pulled through the gate and headed the direction he'd said. I passed a handful of homes before I saw it. The house wasn't overly large, but looked to be a decent size. I'd expected a small round pen. Instead, I saw what had to be about an acre fenced and a shelter big enough for two horses. He'd also provided water and feed troughs. Tears burned my eyes as I pulled up out front. He'd done all this for me?

I got out and Ranger stepped onto the small porch. A smile curved his lips and he hurried over to me. When he was close enough, I threw myself into his arms.

"I can't believe you did all this."

He held me tight. "Of course, I did. Couldn't have you bring your horses all the way here and not have a place to keep them. If you stay for a while, I'll expand the pasture."

"You're too good to me."

He tipped my chin up and leaned down, brushing his lips against mine. My heart felt like it was racing, and I clung to him. The kiss was soft and slow. Heat flushed through me, and I leaned into him.

"In case you were wondering," he said, his voice a bit raspy, "I'm hoping you decide to stick around a while. Beast gave me permission to fence another three acres and put up a real barn. There aren't any houses behind mine. Just lots of open land."

"That sounds like longer than a while," I said, feeling both happy and scared.

"A while. Forever." He shrugged. "Either one works for me."

My eyes went wide. Forever? Had he seriously just said he wanted me to stay forever and acted like it was no big deal? I'd wonder who the hell did that sort of thing, but I already knew. Bikers. They were a different breed and tended to go after what they wanted. If Ranger had decided he wanted to keep me, I had a feeling I wouldn't be returning home, unless it was just to visit.

"Forever seems like a big commitment after just a few days together," I said.

"Want to know how long Venom and Ridley

were together before he claimed her?" he asked.

My brow furrowed. "How do you even know the answer to that? They aren't part of your club."

"Fine. How about Lyssa and Beast?"

I sighed, knowing it probably wasn't very long. "Go ahead and tell me."

"He knew the second she walked into the clubhouse. All it took was one look, and she was his, even if she didn't realize it right then. I've heard it was the same for Venom and Ridley."

"What are you saying?" I asked.

He blew out a breath and looked up at the sky a moment before gazing down at me. "I want you. Not just for tonight, this week, or even this month. I want my name on your back, you in my bed every night, and everything that goes along with it. But I know you're used to chasing the next rodeo, and I don't exactly live near your parents. It's a big decision for you to make, so I'm willing to be patient-ish."

"That's not a word."

He winked. "Sure, it is."

"Let's unload the horses, give them some hay and feed, and I'll put my bags in the house. That's about as far as I can think ahead right now. The drive here was exhausting."

"Come on, beautiful. I'll help you." He kissed my forehead, then went to the back of the trailer. He unloaded Pharaoh like a pro and led him over to the pasture. The second the horse had been released, he galloped the length of the paddock and back, enjoying his freedom. I knew Sunny would do the same thing.

Ranger unloaded the second horse and helped me get them fed, then carried my bags into the house. He paused in the front entry, looking conflicted.

"What's wrong?" I asked.

"I have a spare room."

"All right." Where was he going with this?

"I don't want you to stay in it." He looked at me over his shoulder. "I want you in my room. I promise, I won't do anything you don't want me to. I'll be happy just holding you while you sleep. But if you're uncomfortable with that, I'll put your stuff in the second bedroom."

I chewed on my lip, knowing it wasn't something to take lightly, especially since I'd never slept with anyone before. I didn't know how he'd react to finding out I was a virgin. Although, since he'd already said he wanted to keep me, I had a feeling he'd be thrilled with the news.

"Before you put those in your room, there's something you need to know." I shoved my hands into my pockets, hoping he wouldn't notice I was trembling.

"You pregnant?" he asked, his eyes narrowing.

"No! What the hell, Ranger?"

"Then what?" he asked.

"I haven't shared a bed with anyone before," I murmured.

"I haven't either. Beds aren't necessary for anything other than sleeping. Even then you can sleep in a chair or a couch."

"Not what I meant." I felt my cheeks heat. "I'm a virgin. It's why Viking pulled us apart at the clubhouse. He knew I hadn't been with anyone before, and you were likely expecting things to go further than a kiss."

Heat flared in his eyes, and he gave a jerky nod. "Got it. I meant what I said. You can sleep in my bed, and I promise things won't go any further. I'd never take anything you didn't willingly give. You mean too much to me, Dani."

If I hadn't already been falling for him, what he'd just said would have cinched it. I didn't know men like him still existed, or how I'd gotten lucky enough to find one. He was like a damn unicorn. A biker who knew his way around horses, treated me like a princess, and respected me. I'd be an idiot to walk away from this man. The question was whether or not I was ready to go all in.

"You can put my bags in your room, but, Ranger, I don't want you to think it means I'm staying. Or that we'll do anything more than sleep in the same bed."

He folded his arms and stared at me so long I started to worry he'd ask me to leave. Had I pissed him off? There were times I couldn't read his expression. Like now. His face was a blank slate.

"I've already said I wouldn't touch you if you didn't want me to, Dani. Since you obviously trust me so little, maybe you should stay in the guest room."

A pang hit me right in the heart. I hadn't meant to make him feel untrustworthy. I didn't think he realized how scary this was for me. I'd traveled here, not knowing if he'd even let me into his house, and now he was asking me to share a room with him. It felt like I was walking through a funhouse tunnel and any moment I would fall on my ass.

"Ranger…"

He turned and walked off, leaving both me and my bags by the front door. I swallowed hard and picked them up before following him. I stopped in the hall, noting the guest room to my right. He'd pushed open a door farther down before disappearing into what I assumed was his bedroom. I looked inside the guest room and saw a queen-size bed, a nightstand with a lamp and remote, and a four-drawer chest. A

TV had been mounted on the wall. I assumed the remote went to the TV.

I placed my bags on the floor and sat on the edge of the bed. Had I made a mistake coming here? I had zero experience with relationships, or men. Being with Ranger definitely put me outside my comfort zone. He'd been with women before. Hell, he could probably walk over to the clubhouse right now and have any club whore he wanted. I didn't understand why he'd want me. I generally preferred horses over people. Well, any animal really, except bugs and snakes. Animals weren't complicated. If you hurt their feelings, it was easy to make up with them. People? Not so much.

I pulled my phone from my pocket and shot off a text to Viking, knowing he'd tell me what I should do.

I screwed up.

It took him a few minutes to answer. *That's vague as fuck.*

I rolled my eyes and started typing, knowing it would be a somewhat lengthy text.

I'm at Ranger's. I just showed up without calling, but my dad let him know I was on my way. He put up fencing and shelter for my horses. He said he wanted me to stay here. As in forever. Then I screwed it all up. I told him I'm a virgin. He'd already said he wouldn't touch me until I wanted him to, but I guess I made him feel like I didn't trust him when I said I'd share a room with him but only to sleep. Now I'm in the guest room, he disappeared into his room, and I don't know what to do.

I saw the little dots pop up, then stop, then start again. After a few minutes, the dots vanished and my phone rang. I answered, seeing it was Viking.

"What the fuck, Danica?" he asked the second the call connected. He didn't even give me a chance to say hi.

"I'm scared, okay? You know I've never had a boyfriend. I haven't even been on very many dates. He's so much more experienced than me, Viking. What if he wakes up tomorrow, or three days from now, and decides he's made a mistake? He can have anyone he wants."

"And you want to know why he'd want you?" Viking asked. "First off, take a good, long look in the mirror, Danica. You're beautiful. Add in how sweet you are, unless catty bitches are involved, and why the fuck wouldn't someone want you?"

I shrugged, even though he couldn't see me. "I'm going to mess it all up."

"Honey, if he doesn't want you because you're scared shitless and out of your depth right now, then he's a damn idiot and you need to run away."

"I just… I really like him, Viking," I said softly. "More than I should. We haven't spent much time together, and now he's talking about forever. Moving here would mean I wouldn't get to see my family all that much. And what if I want to keep riding in the rodeos? He said something that makes me think maybe he wouldn't want me to do that. It's part of who I am."

Viking sighed. "Only you can decide what you're willing to sacrifice to possibly find happiness with a guy who wants you for more than a quick fuck. But, Danica, ask yourself this. If you were to leave tomorrow, put Ranger in your rearview, how are you going to feel when he finally finds someone else? What if he comes with Beast, but he has an old lady with him? Will you regret walking away? Because if you will, then you need to cowgirl up."

I snickered. "That's not how that song goes."

"What-fucking-ever. You know what I mean.

You've let the club and your family take care of you ever since you came here with Cowboy all those years ago. I may not have been around back then, but I listen when people talk. You've been coddled. Never had to make a big decision without some help. It's time to put on your big girl panties and figure out what you want in life."

A throat cleared and I looked up, seeing Ranger in the bedroom doorway. He'd shoved his hands into his pockets. The look on his face made me pause. He jerked his chin toward the phone in my hand. "Hang up. We need to talk."

My stomach knotted at his words, and I fought back the stinging in my eyes and burning in my throat. Was this where he asked me to leave?

I had to swallow a few times before I could speak without breaking. "Viking, I'll talk to you later. I need to go."

I didn't give him a chance to respond before I hung up. I set the phone on the bed beside me and watched Ranger as he moved farther into the room, not stopping until he stood in front of me.

He hunkered down and reached for my hands, taking both of mine in one of his. I stared at our joined hands, marveling at how small mine looked in comparison.

"Why didn't you just say you were scared?" he asked, his voice low and husky.

"You're used to women with experience. I didn't want to come across as a stupid kid. I'm a grown woman, but I've never had a boyfriend. The thought of staying here terrifies me. Not because I don't want to. I do. So much. I just..."

"You're worried I'll decide I don't want you."

I nodded. "Everything is so new to me, Ranger.

I'm sorry I made you feel like I didn't trust you. I'm going to say and do stupid things. I can talk to Owen, Foster, or Viking without any trouble because I think of them like brothers. A guy I like? That's different."

"We talked just fine while I was visiting," he pointed out.

"Right. We did. But you were leaving, and I wasn't sure when I'd see you again. Dropping in like this had me anxious the entire way here. I show up and see you made a spot for my horses, and then you ask me to think about staying permanently. You're moving at warp speed."

He squeezed my hands. "Baby, I didn't mean to push too hard, too fast. I'm used to going after what I want. I heard your conversation with Viking. Moving here would mean leaving your family behind. It doesn't mean you can't visit, or that they can't come here. As for the rodeo… I have no problem with you still competing. I'd prefer you not chase every rodeo and be gone for weeks at a time, or longer. And if you get pregnant, I don't want you on a horse. The thought of you or our kid getting hurt -- that's what scares the shit out of *me*."

My lips curved into a smile. "Our kid? We haven't shared more than two kisses and already you have me pregnant?"

"One day at a time. I want you to stay, Dani. At least long enough to see if this can work. If you want to stay in here, I'm all right with that. If you decide you want to share my bed, I'm more than okay with that." He smiled. "You set the pace, beautiful. I'll follow your lead."

He seemed too good to be true. Before I could change my mind, I leaned forward and placed my lips against his. Ranger froze for a split second before kissing me back.

My toes curled in my boots, and I knew I wanted to stay.

He was right. I needed to see if things could work between us. If I walked away, I'd regret it later.

Chapter Four

Ranger

It had felt like my heart had been ripped out when I overheard Danica's conversation. Scaring her had been the last thing I'd intended. When she'd said she was a virgin, I'd been ready to throw her over my shoulder, carry her to the bedroom, and chain her to the bed. Instead, I should have taken a step back. She'd been right about one thing. The women I'd been with had been experienced. Didn't make them better than her. Just different. I hadn't ever dated a virgin, not even in high school. She thought she was out of her depth? I was completely lost with how to handle her.

Having her in the room next to mine would be good enough for now. She was here. It wasn't perfect, but it would do. I'd need to convince her to stay. Having learned she'd never had a boyfriend, I knew I needed to step up my game. I couldn't remember the last time I'd taken a woman on a date. Even then, it had been dinner or a movie, and a way to ease me into her bed for the night. With Danica, I wanted more -- wanted everything.

"I'm not much of a cook, otherwise I'd offer to make you something for dinner. You feel up to going out? If not, I can order and have a Prospect pick it up."

She ran her hands down her thighs and back up. The way she shifted foot to foot also belied her nerves. Since her dad was a Dixie Reaper, I knew she wasn't worried about going into town with a biker. So what bothered her?

"Am I dressed okay?" she asked. "For wherever we'd go? I mostly packed jeans and tees, but I have a few nicer shirts and two dresses."

I tugged her closer and wrapped my arm around

her. "Honey, you're beautiful no matter what you wear. If you're worried about your clothes, we can go somewhere casual like the diner. There's even one that sells breakfast twenty-four hours. They have great burgers too. Or you can get the steak and eggs to have the best of both worlds."

She gave me a slight smile. "That sounds really good. I think anywhere nicer, I'd prefer to have enough notice to do something with my hair and wear something better than what I have on now."

I eyed the cowboy boots on her feet. "You okay riding on a bike in those?"

"I've worn them on the back of a bike before."

I tried to contain my growl, not liking the thought of her riding with anyone else. It had likely been her dad, but the possessive side of me didn't care. I already thought of Danica as mine. She might need time and a little space, but she was it for me. I'd wait however long I had to.

"Need anything before we go?" I asked.

She shook her head. I took her hand and led her out to my bike. I got on and started the engine, then held out my hand to help her on. She swung her leg over and settled on the seat behind me, wrapping her arms around my waist. Having her snug against my back soothed the savage beast inside me. I liked having her thighs pressing against my hips. Feeling the heat of her body as she leaned into me.

I revved the engine and walked the bike backward down the driveway. Once I had it on the street, I pulled away from the house and toward the front gates. The Prospect on duty opened them before I had to come to a stop, and we rode straight through them. I enjoyed having Danica on my bike. So much I almost delayed our trip to the diner. I could have ridden with her for hours.

Instead, I went straight to the diner, knowing she had to be hungry. I parked as close to the door as I could, but the place looked packed. I only saw three open tables through the large windows. Danica got off the bike and I swung my leg over the seat. I took her hand and led her into the diner. Mina, one of the regular waitresses, waved a hand for us to take a seat wherever. I grabbed two menus off the rack near the door before leading Danica over to the booth near the window. It would let me keep an eye on my bike, and I thought she might like a view other than the people around us.

Danica sat across from me, and I handed her one of the menus. I didn't need to look at mine since I came here rather frequently, and instead decided to watch her. She tucked a wayward strand of hair behind her ear as she looked over the options. I couldn't help but smile. She was too fucking cute. The moment I'd spotted her at the Dixie Reapers, she'd held my attention. Hell, I'd been spellbound when I saw her at the rodeo, even before I'd known who she was. Just like now, she hadn't been all made up like most of the women I knew. I liked that she felt confident enough to go out while not wearing makeup. Or maybe it was the fact I'd already seen her without it, so she didn't feel the need to put any on. Regardless, Danica had me wrapped around her finger, and she didn't seem to realize it.

"Everything sounds good," she said. "Then again, all I've had is what I could get from the gas station or fast-food places. Hot food I can eat while sitting down will be amazing, no matter what it is."

"Can't go wrong with the burgers. Unless you want breakfast food. In which case, their omelets are great."

Mina stopped by the table. "Hey, Ranger. You want the usual?"

"That would be great, Mina. Thanks."

"And for you?" Mina asked, turning to Danica.

I leaned over toward her. "Get the burger. We can come back for breakfast if you want to try the omelets."

She smiled and nodded. "Sounds good. I'll take the bacon cheeseburger, no mayo, with onion rings. Oh, and a Dr. Pepper."

"You got it," Mina said. "Before I forget, we have apple and cherry pie tonight. The pecan is already gone and so is the chocolate cake."

"Damn," I muttered. I loved their cake. The pies were good, but nothing beats a slice of chocolate cake with thick icing.

"Can I go ahead and order a slice of cherry, but for after dinner?" Danica asked.

"Absolutely." Mina smiled. "And you, Ranger? Want to deviate from the cake?"

"The cake you're out of?" I sighed. "Fine. Give me a slice of apple."

Mina hurried off to put in our order with the kitchen. She came back a minute later with our drinks before scurrying away to check her other customers. It looked like Dana was the only other waitress on duty for the night, and I knew from experience, she was more about flirting than customer service. I couldn't have been more grateful that Mina was our waitress tonight. If Dana had flirted with me in front Danica, I wasn't sure what sort of reaction I'd have gotten.

"So you prefer the cake," she said. "Is it really that good?"

"It's amazing. You'll like the pie, though."

"You seem to come here often. Do you ever eat at home? The waitress even knows your order."

I leaned back in the booth. "Yes, I eat here a lot. And yes, I do eat at home. Sometimes. Like I said, I'm not a good cook. I can only eat so many hot dogs."

She put her fingers over her lips, but I could tell she was laughing. I enjoyed seeing her happy, even if it was due to my lack of culinary skills. "You can laugh. I know it's pathetic. I'm thirty-six and don't have the cooking skills of a teenage girl. But I haven't starved yet."

"Only because you're living off diner food," she pointed out.

"Not always." I smiled. "There are other places I eat, including the clubhouse. But if you ever feel the urge to make a home-cooked meal, I'll gladly eat whatever you make."

"Even liver and onions?" she asked.

I made a gagging sound. "Okay, anything but that."

"Noted. No liver and onions. Guess it's a good thing I don't like that either."

Mina delivered our food and the look on Danica's face had me laughing. I wiped at her chin. "Think you have a little drool right here."

She swatted me away. "Ass. I do not!"

I dug into my meatloaf while she bit into her burger. The way her eyes closed and her low hum of approval made my dick hard. Christ but she was killing me! I had to wonder if she'd make that sound in the bedroom too, while I was deep inside her. Hopefully, one day I'd get a chance to find out.

"Told you the food was good," I said.

She nodded. "Very good. We can definitely come back in the morning. Although, if we eat here all the time, I'm going to get fat. I hope you like extra padding on your women."

I liked how she said that. All the time. It made me hope she was seriously thinking of sticking around. I'd give her whatever she wanted or needed, as long as she stayed by my side.

"Dani girl, you're beautiful. Doesn't matter what size you are."

Her cheeks flushed, but I could tell my words pleased her.

We finished our food, but I wasn't quite ready to head home. I didn't want her thinking about the sleeping arrangements, or worrying how I'd feel if she didn't sleep in my bed. Instead, I took her to a quiet spot that overlooked a small lake. The stars were bright, and I knew the area would be tranquil. No one ever came here except me. I held her hand as we walked to the overlook. The lake lay beneath us, the moonlight refracting off the water.

"It's beautiful here," she murmured.

"I sometimes come here when I need peace and quiet. I always feel a bit more centered when I head back home."

"Thank you for sharing it with me," she said.

I watched the water ripple in the slight breeze. There was so much I wanted to say to her. Something held me back. I worried she'd bolt. After hearing her conversation with Viking, I didn't want to give her any cause to run from me. I couldn't convince her to give us a chance if she wasn't here.

At the same time, I needed to open up with her. Maybe if she knew she wasn't just another woman, some random hookup, she'd understand I was serious about wanting her forever. I'd had my share of women over the years. I'd hardly been a saint. But Danica was different.

"When your dad called Beast to say you were heading here, and my Pres gave me the heads-up, I couldn't believe I'd get a chance to spend more time with you. Your dad said you had your horses with you. I knew if there wasn't a spot for them, you'd likely be gone before morning. So I built a shelter for them, put up some fencing, and hoped it would be enough to show you how serious I am about you. About us."

I tightened my hold on her hand before lifting it to my mouth and kissing her fingers. She leaned against my side, and it felt like some of the tension melted away.

"I never meant to scare you," I said. "You said you were a virgin, but I guess it didn't really sink in how little experience you had. I've met virgins who had done everything but go all the way. I should have moved slower and given you more time. You're more than a piece of ass to me, Danica. I won't lie. I've been with more than my share of women, and they didn't mean a damn thing to me. They aren't you. I want to go on dates with you, watch movies together, share meals. Most importantly, I want to get to know you, for you to get to know me."

She looked up at me, her brow slightly furrowed. "No offence, but if you're such a great guy -- and trust me, you're saying all the right things -- why are you still single?"

I curved my arm around her shoulders and hugged her to me. "Because I was waiting for you."

She rolled her eyes and shrugged me off. "That has to be the cheesiest thing I've ever heard. Seriously? How can you expect me to take you seriously when you spout off nonsense like that?"

"It's true. Not once have I been tempted to keep a woman for more than a night. Hell, none of them have been to my house. I not only wanted you in my house, Dani, but in my bed. I gave your horses a safe place to stay. Do you really think I'd go to all that trouble for anyone else?"

Her shoulders drooped a little. "I'm sorry. You brought me to this amazing place, opened up to me, and now I'm ruining it. I guess I don't understand why you'd want me. I'm not like the other women at the Dixie Reapers. I'm not like Lyssa, or Farrah. They go after what they want and don't let anyone stand in their way. The only place I've ever felt confident is on the back of a horse."

I bit my lip. I wouldn't say it. I wouldn't. My jaw tightened and I knew I was going to lose the battle. "You can ride me anytime you want."

Fuck me. I closed my eyes and groaned.

I heard a faint snicker, and then she was all out laughing. I opened my eyes and watched as tears streamed down her cheeks. All right. At least she found the humor in my stupidity. I could work with that.

"I think I was wrong. You aren't giving me cheesy pick-up lines. You just suck at flirting," she said.

"Only when it counts, apparently." I folded my arms, glad she thought this was funny. At least she hadn't kicked me in the balls. I'd take whatever victory I could get, even small ones. With Danica, I wasn't worried about an instant win. I was in this one for the long haul.

Chapter Five

Danica

Being with Ranger left me off-balance. I never knew what to expect from him, and yet I looked forward to every second we had together. Despite his cheesy lines, I could tell he really did want me here. I might not understand why, but it was time for me to give him a chance. My dad had been right about one thing. If I walked away and Ranger found someone else, I'd never forgive myself. Not without knowing for certain things couldn't work between us.

Cowgirl up. I took a deep breath and let it out.

Ranger had gone to bed a half hour ago, but I'd heard his shower running. I'd paced my room and tried to work up the courage to go after him. The pajamas I'd put on were the sexiest I owned, which wasn't saying much. But the thin spaghetti straps on the delicate top didn't always stay in place, and right now, one of my shoulders had been bared. The shorts scarcely covered my ass cheeks and were trimmed with lace. I shook out my hands, took another breath, and opened his bedroom door.

My jaw dropped and my eyes felt like they were bugging out of my head as I took in the sight in front of me. Ranger had kicked off his covers and lay naked on the bed, his legs parted, and his hand wrapped around his cock. He grunted as he stroked himself, his eyes closed and head tipped back. I must have made a sound because he jerked upright.

"Um, I, uh..." Why did my throat feel so dry? I licked my lips, but it didn't help. My hold on the door tightened, and yet I couldn't seem to pry myself away. His fingers were still around his shaft, even if he'd stopped all movement.

"Danica, what are you… is everything okay?" He reached to the foot of the bed and yanked the sheet over his lap. "Shit. I didn't mean for you to…"

"Sorry." My cheeks burned. "I should go."

So why didn't I? My feet seemed rooted to the floor. The way he watched me made heat flare in my belly. My nipples hardened against my pajama top, and I squeezed my thighs together. Was it my imagination or were my panties getting wet?

"Danica, what's wrong?" he asked, reminding me he'd already asked me a question once.

"I, um…" My gaze skimmed over his chest. I let out a sigh and wished I had the guts to walk over and touch him.

"Dani girl, you have thirty seconds to tell me what you need before I get worried and come to you. And in case you forgot, I'm not wearing clothes. I don't want you freaking out and running from the house, especially dressed the way you are."

I jerked my gaze to his face and realized he really was concerned about me. I padded closer, not stopping until I'd reached his side of the bed. Before I could talk myself out of it, I sat on the edge of the mattress, my hip pressed against him. It didn't matter a sheet separated us. I could feel the heat of his body.

"Dani." His voice had become huskier. Deeper. A shiver raked over me, and I realized I wanted him to touch me, more than anything I'd ever wanted before. I didn't know why he had such an effect on me.

"I want more than just kisses," I said. "I don't want to leave tomorrow. Or the next day. If I run from you, from whatever it is between us, I'll regret it later."

"Honey, that doesn't mean you need to come crawling into my bed your first night here," he said, reaching out to take my hand. "I told you I'd be patient, and I meant it."

I swallowed hard, looking at our joined hands. I wasn't brave. I'd never been able to talk to guys easily. And I certainly didn't know how to ask him for what I wanted, or explain how he made me feel, but I realized I needed to try.

"I want to know what it feels like to be touched," I said softly. "By you. I want your hands on me. Your mouth. I…"

"You're killing me. Dani, as badly as I want you, I'm not sure I can only give you a little taste, then back off. I don't think I have that much control over myself."

My pajama top was hanging on only by one strap. I knew he was going to send me away, back to the other bedroom, and it's not what I wanted. Ranger was being honorable, which was sweet. And not what I needed right now. I gave the hem of my top a tug. The material slid over my breast, exposing me to his hungry gaze. Heat flared in his eyes, and it felt like my nipple pebbled even more as he stared at me.

"Jesus, Dani. You're so fucking perfect." His fingers clenched on mine. "You really want to do this?"

I nodded. I did. More than anything. I didn't want Ranger to become a regret. It had taken me long enough to get the courage to come into his room. If I left now, I'd not only chicken out from doing this again, but I'd likely run come morning. I'd be so embarrassed, and knew I'd never want to face him again.

"Show me the other one too," he said.

I reached up and pulled my strap down my arm and kept going until the material of my top settled under my breasts. He leaned forward and captured my nipple in his mouth, sucking on it hard. He gave the peak a nip, making me call his name. I thrust my breasts out, wanting more.

"Don't stop," I murmured. "Please. It feels so good."

My body ached and throbbed. My clit pulsed, and I wanted so badly to come. I squirmed, trying to alleviate the need building inside me.

"You're beautiful," he said, cupping my breast in his hand and rubbing his thumb across my nipple. "How far do you want this to go, Dani?"

"I want it all."

"Then show me how wet you are. Take those shorts off and let me see what's mine."

I shivered at his possessiveness but hastened to obey. I wiggled out of my pajama bottoms and panties. I'd never been naked in front of a guy before and felt a little self-conscious. Thanks to all the riding I did, my legs were muscular, which meant my thighs and calves weren't small. Ranger groaned and trailed his fingers over my legs, then gripped my hips and lifted me over him, only to lay me down next to him.

He rose to his knees and placed his hands on my inner thighs, spreading me open. I heard his mumbled *fuck* as he looked his fill. I squirmed, wanting to close my legs, and yet also wanting him to touch me. I'd never been daring or naughty, but with Ranger, I wanted to be all that and more. I'd once heard one of the single guys at the clubhouse say he wanted an angel on his arm, but a whore in his bed. At the time, I hadn't realized he meant it was two sides of the same woman. He'd laughed his ass off when I read him the riot act about cheating on his "angel" woman. Then Viking had explained what Thunder meant, and I'd been so embarrassed.

"You're mine, Dani girl. We do this, you can't walk away. I'll find you and bring you home every time. So if you have any doubts, even one, you say so now."

His. I would be Ranger's. His old lady. His property. I knew the Reckless Kings were like the Dixie Reapers in the fact their men were faithful to their women. I wouldn't have to worry about him cheating on me.

"I'm sure, Ranger."

He leaned down and lightly brushed his lips over mine. "My name is Parks. Parks Saeed. When we're alone, you don't have to call me Ranger."

"Parks." I reached up and ran my fingers over the five-o'clock shadow on his jaw. "Make love to me."

He shook his head. "I have no idea how to be all gentle and sweet, Dani. I'll do my best to make it good for you. But I like my sex rough. Think you can handle it? Handle *me*?"

I nodded. Honestly, I wasn't sure if I could or not, but I was going to do my best. I wanted him. Not just him, but a life with him. Rough sex wouldn't kill me. Maybe I'd even like it. The books I'd read made it seem exciting. Romances weren't really my thing, but the other girls had made me read a few. Now I was grateful to them.

"Put your hands over your head, Dani. Cross your wrists and don't move them."

I did as he said, waiting to see what he'd do or say next.

"If I hurt you, let me know. That's the last thing I want. Everything we do in here should feel good for both of us."

"All right, Parks."

He winked and stretched out on his belly between my legs. He hooked my thighs over his arms and the moment his mouth touched me, my hips bucked.

"Oh, God!"

He chuckled as he licked my clit. "You taste good, Dani. I'm going to make you come, and then I'm making you mine."

He worked my pussy with his lips and tongue, sending waves of pleasure crashing over me. Every flick and lick had me soaring higher and higher. I started to get dizzy and realized I was holding my breath. I sucked in a lungful of air right as Ranger brushed his tongue against the sensitive bud again. I screamed out his name as my body bucked. The orgasm rushed through me, leaving me boneless and out of breath.

The room spun and before I could come down from my high, Ranger settled over me. I felt the nudge of his cock against my pussy and spread my legs farther. He felt hard and impossibly big as he pushed inside me. It burned as he stretched me. The pain wasn't as bad as I'd feared.

"You're mine, Dani." He kissed me and I could taste myself on him. Without warning, he thrust hard, filling me completely. He didn't even pause before pulling his hips back and surging into me again.

"Don't stop. Please don't stop," I said, gripping his shoulders. Soon the discomfort eased.

"Never." His eyes seemed feverish as he drove into me. Ranger shifted so that on the next stroke, he brushed against my clit. Little sparks of pleasure danced along my nerve endings. Every push and pull of his cock made me plead for more. "Say you're mine, Dani."

"I'm yours. Only yours."

He kissed me long and hard as he claimed me. The bed slammed into the wall with every thrust, and I hooked my legs over Ranger's thighs. I felt the heat of his release and soon after I followed, coming so hard I saw stars.

"My Dani girl," he murmured, smoothing my hair back.

"Didn't you need to ask your club to vote on me being your old lady?" I asked.

He smiled. "They won't deny me. Soon as a property cut can be made, you'll have my name on your back."

I shifted my hips, feeling our mingled release seeping out around his cock and soaking the bed under me. "Um, Parks. We sort of forgot protection."

"No, we didn't."

I arched my eyebrows. "I certainly don't recall having that discussion, or seeing you put on a condom."

"You haven't been with anyone, so you're clean. I got tested after the last woman I was with, and I haven't been with anyone since then. I'm clean."

I sank my nails into his shoulders until he winced. "There's more to it than that, Parks, and you damn well know it. What if I end up pregnant?"

His eyes lit up and the smile that crossed his lips told me plenty. He'd been *trying* to knock me up. I couldn't exactly say I was surprised. I'd been around bikers long enough to know how they thought. He wanted me tied to him in every way possible. As angry as it should have made me, I couldn't find it in me to be upset with him.

"You want a baby?" I asked.

"With you? Yes." He kissed me. "I'm sorry, Dani. I should have talked to you about it before making the decision to not use protection."

"You're only sorry because I called you on it."

He shrugged a shoulder. "Truthfully? Yeah. I want you pregnant with my kid. Hell, I want several babies with you. I'm not exactly getting younger, Dani. I know there's a bit of a gap between us, and maybe you aren't ready for a family just yet, but I want it all with you."

"Just talk to me before making any more big decisions. If we're in this together, it means I should get a say in any life-changing plans."

"I will. Unless it's to keep you safe. If someone comes for you, I'll do whatever it damn well takes to protect you, whether you like it or not."

I cupped his cheek. "I understand, and I accept that part of you, Parks."

"How sore are you?" he asked.

"Not enough I'll be walking funny, but if you're wanting to go for round two, could we maybe wait a little? You're not exactly small down there."

He pulled free of my body and rolled off me. Before I could ask what he was doing, he got out of bed and walked into the adjoining bathroom. I heard water running and got up to investigate. Steamy water poured into the tub, and I saw he'd placed a folded towel on the counter.

"You sit in the tub and soak. I'll rinse off in the shower and make sure the club knows you're here to stay. I'll make arrangements tomorrow to expand the pasture for your horses and we can put in a better barn behind the house."

I sank into the water and flicked my fingers across the surface, splashing him. "Not too close if you want to have kids. They'll need space to play too. But make sure there's enough stalls and land for a pony or two. My kids are going to learn to ride."

He bent down, bracing his hands on the tub, and

kissed my forehead. "Yes, honey. They'll learn to ride. Maybe in a week or two, I'll take you to meet my family. After you've had time to settle in here. We need to call your family too."

I curled my hand around the back of his neck and pressed my lips to his. "Take your shower and do whatever you need to. After I get out, I'm crawling back in the bed."

"Better be the one you just got out of."

I smiled. "It will be."

Ranger got into the shower and washed quickly. I watched through the clear glass, admiring the strong lines of his body. When he'd finished, he gave me one more kiss before disappearing through the doorway. I wasn't sure what I'd gotten myself into. I only hoped I hadn't bitten off more than I could chew. My family would understand when I said I wasn't coming back home, but it would be a big adjustment. For all of us.

On the plus side, Lewis wouldn't be able to get into the Reckless Kings compound. I wouldn't find more notes in my truck, or worry about him catching me alone at home. No way he'd get through the gates. Of course, that didn't mean he wouldn't track me down in town. I needed to tell Ranger about him. Show him the notes. The ones I hadn't tossed out already. As much as I didn't want Ranger going after Lewis, I knew I couldn't keep this from him.

I only hoped he'd be reasonable about the situation.

Chapter Six

Ranger

Beast called Church first thing in the morning. I hoped the only thing we needed to cover was the vote for Dani to be my old lady. I wasn't up for handling other business. Not with my woman waiting at home. She'd still been curled up in bed when I'd left. I'd stayed long enough to check the horses' water and give them some feed. Not wanting Dani to feed them again, I'd left a note before heading to the clubhouse.

"Why the fuck are we having Church so damn early?" Brick mumbled as he practically fell into his chair.

"Sucks to get old, doesn't it?" Forge asked.

Brick flipped him off before groaning and laying his head on the table. Looked like he'd either partied too much the night before, or some woman had kept him up.

"As you all know, Cowboy's daughter, Danica, came here last night to see Ranger. The two of them spent some time together while we were at the Dixie Reapers' compound. Several of you helped put up the fencing and shelter for Danica's horses," Beast said. "She's decided to stay."

"And that means what, exactly?" Wrangler asked.

"It means I've claimed her as my old lady," I said.

"So we're taking it to a vote." Beast looked around the table. "She knows the score since she grew up with the Dixie Reapers. Hell, she's friends with my old lady. Raise your hand to vote yes for accepting Danica as Ranger's old lady."

Every hand around the table went up. A ball of

tension eased in my stomach. I might have told Danica the club would vote our way, but a small part of me had worried a few might say no. It was good to see my club had my back, even when it came to choosing my old lady.

"It's unanimous. Congratulations, Ranger. You officially have an old lady. I'll have a property cut made for her," Beast said.

"Thanks. I'm sure Danica would like the chance to get to know everyone better, but I'd like a few days to help her get settled. I'll be needing a bit more help with fencing and a barn, though. Since she'll be staying, her horses will need more room and better shelter." I smiled a little. "She's also mentioned getting a pony in the future for our kids."

"Damn. Already trying for a baby?" Brick asked.

Beast shook his head. "Of course, he is. At least our kids won't be too far apart in age. They can grow up together."

"Oh, hell. I think the Pres just jinxed the rest of us. Watch. One after another, we'll end up settling down," Snake said.

"Like anyone would put up with your cranky ass for a lifetime," Crow said.

"Enough!" Beast banged his fist on the table. "Church is dismissed. Get the hell out of here."

I stood, wondering if anyone would show up to help with the fencing. Forge stopped next to me, as did Hatchet and Satyr.

"We'll help with the fence," Satyr said. "Just tell us when you want to do it."

Beast paused in the doorway. "Figure out how much lumber you need. The club will foot the bill. Consider it a welcome gift for your woman. Whatever you need to make her more comfortable, make the place feel like home for her, let me know. Lyssa will like having another woman around, especially one she already knows."

"I'll get a list together in the next few days. Thanks, Pres. I'd like to have today with Danica without interruptions, but tell Lyssa she's welcome anytime from tomorrow onward. I'm sure Danica would like to see her."

Everyone filed out of the room, and I went out to my bike. In the past, I'd have lingered at the clubhouse for a drink. With Danica waiting for me at home, I had a good reason to leave. I pulled up into the carport and shut off my bike, listening to the horses in the small pasture. I hadn't realized until now how much I'd missed that sound. It had been a while since I'd been home to visit my mom. I couldn't wait for her to meet Dani. The two were going to get along great.

I walked up to the front door and let myself in. The sweetest smell greeted me, and I followed my nose to the kitchen. Dani stood in front of the stove, wearing my shirt. I saw a platter of cinnamon rolls on the counter, but it looked like she was cooking something else. How much food did she think we needed for breakfast?

"Morning, Dani girl."

She whirled to face me, a smile on her lips. "Hey. I woke and you were gone. Wasn't sure when you'd be back, but I didn't see breakfast dishes, so I figured you'd be hungry."

"Thought we were going to the diner this morning."

She waved the spatula. "We can do that any day. The cinnamon rolls should be cool enough to eat. The eggs and bacon are nearly done. Why don't you have a seat?"

"Where did you find all that stuff? I didn't think I had anything like that in the fridge."

She glanced at me over her shoulder as she worked on the eggs. "Lyssa stopped by with a bag of groceries. She said you most likely have the kitchen of a bachelor and thought we might need some food. There were a few cans of cinnamon rolls, two dozen eggs, a pack of bacon, and a few types of meat for dinners, as well as some rice. We'll still need to make a grocery run soon, but this should hold us for today and maybe tomorrow."

So much for the Pres' old lady not visiting just yet. I should have known she'd stop by while we were in Church. The question was whether or not Beast had known what she was up to. It had been a sweet gesture, and it seemed to have made Danica happy. That's all that mattered to me.

"Breakfast smells great, Dani."

"There's some orange juice and milk in the fridge. Lyssa brought those too. I also made a pot of coffee. I noticed it was the one thing you *did* have stocked."

I leaned back in my chair and watched her. "Yeah, I can't survive without caffeine. I usually have enough stocked to last a month."

"I'm a bear without my morning coffee. I had a cup while the cinnamon rolls cooked. Thanks for taking care of the horses."

"No problem. I didn't realize until I came home from Church how much I'd missed having horses around. I don't mind helping you with them. Are those the only two or do you need to go back and get more? What about the trailer? Do we need to return it to your dad?"

She scooped the eggs out of the skillet and into a

bowl, then placed the bacon on some folded paper towels. She blotted the grease before putting them on a platter. Danica carried everything to the table before pouring us each a cup of coffee, then she claimed the spot next to me.

"The trailer is mine. As for the horses, we buried Champ the day you came with Beast and Lyssa. The other horses aren't solely mine. My dad has more than enough land for them. If there comes a time when he doesn't want to take care of all of them, I'll need a place for a few more."

"All right. When I put in the new barn, I'll make sure we have at least four to six stalls. Better to overprepare than not have enough and need more."

She reached over and placed her hand on my thigh. "Thank you, Parks. No one's ever understood my love of horses. Well, not outside my family or my friends at the rodeo. I certainly didn't think I'd have a boyfriend who accepted that part of me. I can't tell you how much I appreciate all you've done for my equine best friends. They're my family."

"I've asked everyone to give us a day or two so you have time to settle in. The club will want to meet you. I know you've already met a few over the years, and you know Lyssa. Are you familiar with Hawk's old lady?"

"Not really. She was a few years behind me in school. I think she's friends with Mariah, though."

"I didn't see her during our visit," I said.

"The club sent her to the Devil's Fury. Savage agreed to claim her."

Agreed? As in Venom had asked him to? Something seemed off about the situation. My confusion must have shown because Danica gave me a smile and sighed before explaining.

"Mariah was hung up on a young cop. Venom didn't handle it too well. When the Devil's Fury needed assistance, Casper VanHorne offered to help if the club took Mariah. Savage said he'd claim her as his old lady. I haven't heard anything about it since. But knowing Mariah, she wasn't very happy about it."

The club's VP had a right to worry. The Dixie Reapers were pretty legit these days and not into many illegal activities but having a cop sniffing around wouldn't be good. Especially if they had any bodies buried on their property. I couldn't imagine having to deal with something like that. If we had a kid who fell in love with a cop, shit would hit the fan.

"Do we have plans today?" she asked.

"Nope. I don't have anything I need to do for the club right now. I'm yours to command for the day."

She arched an eyebrow at me. "Really? I'm in charge?"

"Well, within reason." I grinned. "Anything you'd like to do around here? Want to explore your new town?"

"If I ride on the back of your bike, I won't see much of anything. I'll be too busy enjoying the ride to look at the sights." She twirled her fork in her hand. "I should probably call my parents today. I'll need to make arrangements for the rest of my things to be sent here."

"You know as well as I do your dad will show up on our doorstep with his truck loaded down with boxes. He won't just mail it, or have a Prospect drop it off."

"Is there a problem with him coming?" she asked.

"No. Your family is welcome anytime. I'd prefer they stay in the guest house Beast put in when he claimed Lyssa. Might be a bit awkward for your parents to stay in the room next to ours."

Danica smiled. "I agree. I want to see them, and want them to feel welcome, but I'm more than fine with them staying in a different house. Except… what if Torch and Isabella decide to come too so they can visit Lyssa?"

"They'd bring the kids, and there wouldn't be extra room in the guest house." I leaned back in my chair. "Might need to talk to Beast about putting in another guest house. Or maybe a duplex."

"Your club is growing," she said. "I'd imagine it was like this for the Dixie Reapers when the first old ladies were claimed. They went from a club of bachelors to several men starting families. Before long, you'll be talking about playgrounds, picnic areas, and family events."

I couldn't help but smile at the thought. As much fun as I'd had since joining the Reckless Kings, I looked forward to starting a family with Danica. The things she'd just described sounded pretty good to me. I didn't think my club would feel the same, except Beast and Hawk who'd both already settled down. A few others, like Brick, I knew were eager to have a woman at home. The younger ones liked being single and having their choice of women.

"Let's call Beast before we call your family," I said.

I pulled out my phone and dialed the Pres, putting the call on speaker. He picked up almost immediately.

"I didn't expect to hear from you, Ranger. Shouldn't you be spending time with your woman?" Beast asked.

"You're on speaker and Dani is right here. We're

about to call her family, but I wanted to speak with you first. I have a feeling when she asks for her things to be sent, Cowboy will want to bring them to her. We'd prefer they not stay at the house with us, but if Torch and Isabella decide to visit at the same time, we won't exactly have the space for everyone. There's only one guest house right now."

"I discussed that with Hawk not too long ago," Beast said. "We'll work on more guest housing in the upcoming months, after your woman's horses are settled. For now, I'll ask Torch to not visit the same time Hayley's family, or Danica's, decide to visit. Although, with Hayley's dad being the Chief of Police, I prefer he not linger inside the compound for very long. He's sworn anything he sees while here will be forgotten. Go ahead and invite Cowboy and Jacey for a visit."

"Thanks, Pres."

"And, Danica? Welcome to the family. Let Ranger know when you're ready to meet everyone. I'll have Lyssa and Hayley put something together at the clubhouse."

"Thank you, Beast," Danica said.

I ended the call and slid the phone over to her so she could dial her dad's number. I'd need to program it in, now that he was family. Hell, I should probably add quite a few Reapers to my contacts. Danica might be a Reckless King now, but she'd always be a Reaper's daughter first.

She put in the number and pressed the call button. I reached over to put it on speaker. I didn't think Cowboy would let it ring for long, but I was wrong. It went to voicemail. I glanced at Danica to see her reaction. It didn't seem to bother her, which made me wonder if it was common for Cowboy to not answer his phone.

If I had a daughter, one who'd just went off to possibly move in with a man, I'd damn well answer the fucking phone. What the hell was wrong with him? I barely listened as Danica left a message, letting him know she'd be staying here and would need her things. After she ended the call, I took my phone back and added Cowboy's name to my contacts, saving the number.

"So… the town is rather small. We can take your truck if you're all right with me driving it. I'll back the trailer into the yard for now to get it off the road."

"And long-term?" she asked.

"I'll expand the driveway and add a covered parking area large enough to house your trailer."

"You know, you offered to take me on a tour of the town, but you haven't even shown me around my new home. I had to check things out on my own this morning. It's a bit bigger than it appears from the outside. I'd have never guessed one of the doors off the kitchen led to a sunroom."

"And you also noticed it's empty."

She smiled. "I did. Are you a vampire, Parks? Have an aversion to sunlight?"

I snorted. "No. I just don't particularly want to sit in a room with the sun beating down on me. It's only been me up to this point. The living room was sufficient. But if you want to put some furniture out there, you can. This is your home now too, Dani. Change whatever you want. Don't like the wall colors? I'll paint them. Hate my couch? We'll get a new one."

"I do want to decorate the sunroom. Maybe turn it into a room where I can relax and watch the horses out the windows. On one condition."

"What's that?"

"I use my money for it, and before you protest, you should know I've been saving up most of my rodeo money. Dad covered the expenses at home, and any vetting and food for the horses. I did take out some to buy Pharoah last year when I realized Champ wasn't going to be around much longer. Dad had bought Champ and Sunny for me. Other than that, I only use my money for clothes, motel rooms, and any expenses I incur on the road."

I wanted to protest, thinking she couldn't have made very much from barrel racing. I'd seen the big PBR events and knew bull riders could cash out quite a bit if they made it to the main event, but I'd always thought of barrel racing as more of a sideshow while everyone waited for the bronc and bull riders to come out. Maybe I'd been wrong all this time. I couldn't deny she had an athlete's body, and her horses were good stock. I didn't need to see their pedigree to know that much. Their conformation was damn near perfect.

She rolled her eyes at me, and got up from the table, only to return a minute later with her phone in her hand. She held the screen up in front of me, and I realized she'd opened her banking app. While her checking had a little under five thousand in it. Her savings had nearly three hundred grand. It seemed she'd made more than I'd realized. What the hell? Had she entered every rodeo available to her over the last several years? Or did barrel racers make more than I realized?

"Let me guess. You thought I was the fluff for the rodeo? The eye candy?" she asked.

I winced, thinking of Scott's words the first time I'd seen Danica. "I can admit I was wrong. I didn't realize you could make that much in an event like barrel racing."

"The average barrel racer can make anywhere from forty thousand to eighty thousand per year in prize money. Those of us who are better than average can top out closer to two hundred grand. I only rodeoed full-time for two years. The last year and a half, I realized it seemed more like work than something I enjoyed, so I backed off. I didn't really need the money."

"So you gave up the spot to someone who did?" I asked.

"Something like that." She smiled. "So, I have plenty to furnish the sunroom. No arguing about it. But I don't want to blow through my savings either. The horses are my responsibility now, and their vet bills and feed aren't cheap. I'll need to research the best place to get hay around here too. The small bales you have right now are fine, but they'll need a big round bale pretty soon."

"We'll get them everything they need, including the best equine vet in the area."

She leaned down and kissed me. "I'm going to shower and get dressed, then you can drive me around town."

I watched her sashay from the room and decided I'd give her a two-minute head start. Then I'd be joining her in the shower.

Chapter Seven

Danica

Instead of drying my hair, I'd braided it and left it wet. By the time I'd dressed, Ranger was waiting outside. The moment I stepped outside, I knew he'd found the balled up notes in my floorboard. He'd clutched them in his hand as he stared off into space. The tense line of his jaw told me how pissed he was right now.

"Parks," I called softly.

"Thought you didn't have a boyfriend," he said. The glare he cast my way nearly made my knees buckle. "What the fuck is this shit?"

I licked my lips and shoved my hands into my pockets so he wouldn't see how badly they were shaking. "It's not what it looks like."

"Really, Danica? Because they look like love letters."

I felt bile rise up the back of my throat and I shook my head, taking a step back. He thought they were love letters? Had he bothered to read all of them? I stared at the pieces of paper, feeling like a monster had just reared its ugly head. In a way, it had.

"His name is Lewis," I said, my voice barely audible. "He's a champion bull rider, and those aren't love letters."

"Then what the fuck are they?" he asked, throwing them into my open truck door.

"I'm not sure when or how I ended up getting noticed by him. I found the first note in my truck on my way home from a rodeo about six months ago. I'd locked the doors and gone inside to grab a burger to eat on the road. When I came back out, the note was on my seat."

His brow furrowed and he looked at the letters again. "He broke into your truck?"

"Yes, but it's worse. It means he was following me. Or had someone else do it. He's been leaving those in my truck ever since. I found another the day I left to come here. Someone put it on my seat while I was in the barn with my dad, or maybe when I'd gone into the house to get my bags."

"So he's stalking you. Why the hell didn't you say anything before now?" Ranger asked.

"I was going to, but I haven't really had a chance. I didn't even know I'd be staying at first. I didn't mean to hide it from you, Parks. I'd planned to talk to you about it."

He nodded and came closer, tugging me against his body. He gripped my hair with one hand and settled the other on my lower back. I snuggled into him. Now that he knew, he'd keep me safe. Lewis may have only been leaving letters, but I had no doubt things would be escalating soon enough. He wouldn't be happy leaving me notes.

I'd heard rumors from other women about Lewis. I'd been like everyone else and not believed them. Now that I'd been on the receiving end of his attentions, I knew I'd been wrong. He didn't just stalk the women he liked. Eventually, he assaulted them. If they didn't give him what he wanted freely, then he'd take it. And no one ever did a damn thing about it. Most of the women didn't come forward. The few who had tried to say anything were made into a laughingstock. No one believed them over the rodeo's golden boy.

"He can't get to you here," he said.

"Maybe not, but I can't stay inside the gates forever. It can't be only him. There are times when he's been at an event when a letter showed up, but I was miles from where he was riding. I'm not sure who's helping him, though."

"Could be he's paying people. They may not even realize the guy's a creep. The way those letters read, they could be love letters to a girlfriend."

He had a point. I hadn't really thought about it that way. What if Lewis had used innocent people to get the letters to me? I wouldn't want someone to get in trouble if they didn't realize what they'd done was wrong. While breaking into my truck wasn't legal by any means, if they'd thought it was to deliver a love letter, they may not have thought I'd mind.

"He's done this before," I said. "There are other women. He didn't stop at letters."

Ranger's body tensed and he glowered at me. "What the hell does that mean?"

"He assaulted them. Raped them if they wouldn't give in. The ones who weren't banged up weren't very believable. More of a he-said she-said type of thing. One girl had a black eye, but Lewis laughed it off as an accident, saying she was just making a fuss because he'd broken up with her."

"So this is only the beginning. You said it's been going on how long?"

"Six months," I said.

"He's probably not going to wait much longer. Was he scheduled for the rodeo you were going to before you stopped here?"

"I'm not sure. It's possible, but we don't attend all the same events."

"I know how much the rodeo means to you, Dani, but I don't want you going to any of the upcoming events if this guy has his sights on you. It's not forever. I promise I'm not trying to permanently ground you from doing what you love."

I leaned into him. "You're worried. Like, really worried."

"Yeah, I am. Guys like this one, who have never been stopped, will keep coming until someone puts them down. They don't change, Dani. He's not going to wake up one morning and be a decent guy."

I sighed and closed my eyes. I didn't like not being able to compete, but I understood. I hadn't been eager to run into Lewis again anyway.

"I'm going to ask Shield to look into this guy. What's his last name?"

"Stevens. Lewis Stevens," I said. "He can find out basic info on the PBR website since Lewis is one of the top contenders this year."

"You don't think he'd use your brother to get to you, do you?" Ranger asked.

I tensed, not having even thought of that. If anything happened to Jackson because I'd kept my family in the dark, I'd never forgive myself. I yanked my phone from my pocket and called Jackson. It went to voicemail. I knew he wouldn't bother listening to a message for days, so I decided to text him.

Call me. It's important.

The message showed delivered, but went unread. It was possible he was on the road, still asleep, or prepping for another event. I didn't think he was at home or Dad would have said something.

"I'm sure he's okay, Dani. Just keep trying to reach him. Once Shield has some information for me, I'll know better how to protect you. Your brother is an adult and can handle himself. I know he's your baby brother, but he's not a kid anymore."

He wasn't wrong. Jackson was well over six feet, and I knew he'd learned to fight from Tank. If Lewis tried anything, Jackson wouldn't be defenseless. I just hated that my brother would be blindsided because I'd kept my mouth shut. I knew better.

"Let me call Shield, and then I'll show you around town. I don't think anyone will try something while we're together," Ranger said.

He took out his phone, but stayed nearby. He clearly didn't care if I heard his conversation. I knew that wouldn't always be the case. Club business would remain club business. However, for now, this was personal.

"Shield, Dani has a man stalking her. Name of Lewis Stevens. He's with the PBR, so he's in the public. See what you can dig up." His eyes narrowed as he listened to whatever Shield had to say. "If you can't get to this now, hand it off to someone who can. But the Reapers don't know Dani is in trouble. Give her a chance to tell her family before Wire opens his big mouth."

Oh, shit. Just what I needed. I quickly shot off a text to my dad, just in case.

I lied about the letter you found six months ago.

It didn't take him long to answer.

Lied? Explain. Now.

Crap. Yeah, Dad was pissed, and rightly so. I had no doubt I'd get an earful the next time I saw him. And since he now knew I was in trouble, it wouldn't take him long to show up. Wouldn't surprise me if he brought along a few Dixie Reapers with him. One big happy reunion, and I'd only been gone a week.

Lewis Stevens left it in my truck. And he's left others. He's stalking me.

Within seconds of my message showing it had been read, my phone started ringing. I winced as I answered the call.

"Hi, Daddy."

"Don't you 'hi, Daddy' me, you little shit. Why the hell didn't you tell me some asshole bull rider was stalking you? Jesus, Danica! You know better."

Yep. He was pissed. Very pissed. He never cussed at me.

"I didn't want you to worry. I thought it would blow over, until I started listening to more of the rumors. I'm not the first one he's done this to. Ranger knows about it, and he's talking to Shield right now."

"Fuck, Shield! I'm getting Wire and Lavender on this. Your mom and I will see you tonight."

Tonight? I looked at Ranger, but he was still talking to Shield and not paying me much attention. I hoped he didn't really bring a bunch of people with him. If he did, I didn't know where everyone would stay. So far, Ranger and I had only had sex the one night, and I wasn't about to let my parents hear us. If they stayed in the house, I'd be back to being celibate.

"I'm sorry, Daddy," I said softly. "I didn't mean to keep it from you."

"Yes, you did."

I sighed. Yeah, I really had. "I didn't want you and the others to get in trouble. Lewis isn't exactly a nobody. If something happens to him, people will notice. He can't just vanish and everything will be all right. I don't want you or anyone else going to jail over this."

"Baby girl, it's my job to protect *you*. Not the other way around. We'll talk when I get there."

He hung up and I shoved my phone back in my pocket. I hoped Ranger was ready for my family to show up and be all kinds of mad when they got here. I only hoped my dad, and whoever came with him, kept things civil with Ranger. It wasn't his fault I hadn't said anything.

Ranger came closer and took my hand. I noticed he'd ended his call as well.

"How angry is he?" Ranger asked.

"Extremely, and he's apparently coming here. You may want to let Beast know. I have a feeling he won't be coming alone."

"Well, that's fucking fantastic." He rubbed the back of his neck. "I'm sure Torch will give the Pres a call. I'm staying out of it until they arrive."

I leaned my head against his shoulder. "Still want to go run around town? I have a feeling we won't have much alone time once my dad gets here. I don't think he'll leave until the problem with Lewis is settled."

"So, stay home?" he asked.

"Yeah, if you don't mind. I think I'd rather cuddle on the couch and spend some time with you before my family converges on us."

Ranger pressed a kiss to my forehead. "Honey, I will cuddle with you anytime you want. Especially if we're naked."

I laughed and led him back into the house. After I made sure the door was locked, I kicked off my boots and dragged him over to the couch. I collapsed onto the cushions and Ranger sat next to me. He reached for the remote and flicked on the TV but didn't take the time to pick a movie. Instead, he hauled me onto his lap and kissed me breathless.

Ranger had been right. Cuddling would be better if we were naked. I pulled back long enough to take off my shirt and toss it aside. Reaching behind me, I popped the clasp on my bra and let the straps slide down my arms. The moment my breasts were bared he cupped them in his hands, stroking his thumbs across my nipples.

"Fuck, Dani. You have no idea how much I want you naked right now."

I glanced down. "Looks to me like I am."

"Not entirely. Stand up and strip."

I got to my feet and unfastened my jeans. I slid them down my legs, along with my panties, then yanked off my socks. Shifting from foot to foot, I waited for him to stand and take off his clothes -- except he didn't. Ranger crooked a finger at me and patted his thigh. I swallowed hard as I crawled back onto his lap, straddling him.

"That's it. Open that pussy up for me." He reached between us, dragging his fingers along the inside of my thigh, just out of reach of where I wanted him to touch me. "How badly do you want my cock right now?"

"So bad, Parks. Please."

"Please what?"

"Make me come," I begged. My cheeks burned as I said the words. I didn't know if I'd ever get used to saying things like that.

He stroked his fingers over my clit before sliding two inside me. Not all the way. I whined and moved my hips, trying to take him in deeper.

"That's it, honey. Get yourself off. I want to watch you ride my hand."

His words shouldn't make me hot, but they did. I rocked my hips, fucking his fingers. Arching my back, I thrust my breasts up and reached behind me, bracing my hands on his knees.

"Fuck." His voice had thickened. Through slitted eyes, I watched him. His gaze had locked onto my breasts as they bounced with every thrust of my hips.

"I need you, Parks."

"Come for me, honey, then I'll give you whatever you want."

"Your cock." My cheeks burned hotter. "Your cum."

He growled and I felt his body tighten. I rode his fingers harder until I cried out his name. I felt the gush of my release. It wasn't enough. I wanted more. Wanted *him*.

"Take out my cock," he said.

My hands trembled as I obeyed. The rasp of his zipper seemed loud. I reached into his underwear and wrapped my fingers around his thick shaft. Dragging the waistband down with my other hand, I pulled him free.

"On your knees, Dani."

My heart pounded against my ribs as I got off his lap and sank to my knees between his splayed thighs. His cock jerked as I stared at it, pre-cum leaking from the tip. I licked my lips and he growled softly.

"Open up." I parted my lips and Ranger gripped my hair, dragging me closer. He forced his cock into my mouth and the salty taste of him coated my tongue. I gagged as he went deeper, only for him to pull back so I could take a breath. "That's it. So fucking good, Dani."

I flicked my tongue along the underside of his cock with every stroke. He groaned, making me take more of him each time. Ranger went to the back of my throat and lingered, making me panic a moment. He abruptly pulled free of my mouth and lifted me onto the couch, settling me over his thighs.

"As amazing as that was, I need to be inside you. I want to fill your pussy with my cum, not your mouth."

I sank onto his cock, digging my nails into his

shoulders as he filled me. I rode Ranger, my ass slapping against his thighs. "So close."

He rubbed my clit and I saw stars. I threw my head back and lost myself to the pleasure. As my movements slowed, he gripped my hips and thrust up into me. Ranger grunted as I felt the heat of his release. It felt like my heart was racing and every bone in my body had melted. I slumped against his chest, his cock twitching inside me.

"That didn't last nearly long enough," he said.

"We have enough time to go again. Maybe more than once." I lifted my head to look at him. "But I need to catch my breath first."

He grinned. "You saying I make you breathless?"

I laughed and rolled my eyes. "You and your cheesy lines."

"You enjoy them and you know it. Now, hold on tight."

I wrapped my arms around his neck right before he stood, taking me with him. I didn't know how he managed to get from the living room to the bedroom while his pants were around his knees, but amazingly enough he didn't drop me and didn't trip. I had a feeling I'd be sore as hell by the time my family arrived, but it was a small price to pay.

Chapter Eight

Ranger

"One of these days, I'm going to tie you to the bed. Spread-eagle. You'll be helpless." I kissed her belly. "Unable to break free. Screaming my name as I make you come again and again. I'll fuck you until neither of us can stay awake."

She tugged at the rope currently binding her hands. "We're already halfway there."

I leaned back on my heels, studying her face for any sign what I'd said had freaked her out. It hadn't. If anything, she seemed intrigued by the idea. I looked at the bedside clock. The last text she'd gotten from her family put them arriving around dinner. It was only four, which meant we had a little more time, but not as much as I'd have liked.

"Do it," she said.

I leaned over her, bracing my weight on my hands and knees. "You want me to tie your ankles? Force your legs to stay open?"

She shivered and I licked her nipple, making her moan. I knew she had to be sore. If she hadn't been a virgin, I wouldn't have hesitated. Knowing I'd been her first, and considering the number of times I'd already fucked her, I worried I'd end up hurting her.

"Do you want to be powerless to do anything but take my cock?" I gently bit her nipple. "Your body on display and mine for the taking? For me to use you. Take what I want."

"Oh, God." Her eyes went wide. "I trust you, Parks. I know you wouldn't hurt me, and all you're doing is turning me on even more. If it's too much, if I can't handle it, I'll let you know."

"Very well. But the second I go too far, or you

don't like what I'm doing, you tell me. Immediately."

She nodded. I got up and retrieved another two lengths of rope, along with a silk blindfold. I'd never used the items on anyone before, even though I'd always wanted to. It hadn't seemed right. Not to mention, I hadn't wanted the club whores in my house. No woman had ever been in this bed except Danica, and it would remain that way.

I secured her ankles with the rope by tying the ends around the bed legs. I crawled up the bed, straddling her body, and secured the blindfold over her eyes. She inhaled quickly but didn't tell me to stop. I waved my hand in front of her face. She didn't react, which told me it was thick enough to block out shadows and light.

"I'll be right back."

I went to the kitchen, stopping to make sure the doors were locked, and got a small bowl of ice. Carrying it back to the bedroom, I set it on the bedside table. I got onto the bed again and reached for an ice cube. I slipped it into my mouth, wetting it.

"You ready, honey?"

"Ready."

I circled her nipple with the ice cube, making her squeal from the cold. I smiled as her nipple tightened even more. Giving the other side the same attention, I sat back to admire her body. Her breasts weren't huge, but they were perfect. I trailed the ice down her belly, not stopping until I slowly dragged it over her clit.

"Parks!"

I chuckled and leaned down, licking her pussy. She shivered as I delved my tongue inside her. I popped the ice cube into my mouth before licking her again. As the cube started to melt, I used my cold tongue to circle and tease her clit. I flicked the hard bud before sucking on it. Easing a finger inside her, I pushed her closer and closer to orgasm, only to back off every time she nearly came.

"Not yet, Dani. You don't get to come until I say you can."

"Stop teasing me!"

I smacked my fingers against her pussy, making her yelp. "You don't give the orders. I do. Understand?"

"Y-yes. Please, Parks. I can't take much more."

Neither could I. We'd definitely do this again. Preferably when I could take my time with her. I braced my weight over her body and lined my cock up with her pussy before sinking inside her.

"You always feel like heaven," I murmured. "Fucking perfect."

I took her hard and fast, slamming into her. It only took four strokes before she was coming, screaming out my name as her pussy clenched down on me. I felt the tingle in my spine and my balls drew up. I didn't stop thrusting until I'd unloaded every drop of cum. It leaked out around my cock onto the sheets, but I didn't care. It was just another way to mark her as mine.

As I stared down at her, all flushed from her orgasm, and so trusting, I realized it would be easy to fall in love with her. Hell, I was already halfway there. Danica was amazing, and she was mine. And I'd do whatever the hell it took to keep her safe and in my arms. Even if it meant her dad would be sleeping in the room next to ours until Lewis had been handled.

"I think we need to shower again," I said. "And I need to talk to the Pres and find out where everyone will be staying. If your parents will be at our house, we may need more groceries."

"We'll need more anyway. Even if they don't sleep here, they'll be here during the day. I'm sure Langston will be with them, unless someone offers to keep him while they're gone. He's not quite ten yet."

"I don't think I've ever met him. You have two brothers, right?"

Yeah," she said. "Jackson is a little younger than me, but he's already graduated high school. Langston is the baby. He came along after Cowboy brought us to the Dixie Reapers."

"You make it sound like the stork dropped him off," I teased.

She huffed at me. "I'd just as soon not think about my parents having sex, thanks."

"Oh, so you think *you* were dropped off by the stork too. Just so you know, our kids aren't arriving by giant bird."

She smacked her hand against my arm. "Stop it! Let me get in the shower while you talk to Beast. If we get in together, neither one of us will actually manage to get clean. My parents should be here before too much longer. I'd prefer to be clothed when they arrive."

"Fine. Take away all my fun."

"Really? Fun? By all means. Greet my dad while you're stark naked. I'm sure it will go over famously. Maybe we should go another round, so I'll have memories to last me a lifetime."

I raised my eyebrows. "Why a lifetime?"

"Because my dad will geld you."

I winced and got off the bed, feeling the urge to cover my cock and balls. Damn. I knew she was right about getting cleaned up before her family arrived. I needed to change the sheets on our bed too and check the guest room. Danica hadn't actually slept in there, but it wouldn't hurt to make sure everything was in order.

She scurried into the bathroom, and I got my phone. I had five missed calls from the Pres and another three from Hawk. Great. I had a feeling they were going to chew my ass when I called back.

I dialed Beast first. He didn't even bother saying hello when he picked up.

"It's about fucking time."

"Sorry, Pres. We were, uh… I didn't hear the phone."

"Right. More than enough info. Cowboy is already here, along with his woman, their youngest, and they brought far too many Reapers with them. Grimm, Tempest, Warden, Wire and his woman, and Savior are here. I have no fucking clue where to put everyone."

Shit. Looked like her family would be staying here for sure. Unless Beast gave them the guest house. Although, seeing as how Wire brought his woman with him, they'd probably get the guest house.

"Wire also brought his oldest with him. Apparently the kid is friends with Cowboy's youngest. I'm going to put them and both kids in the guest house. There's enough bedrooms there for both families to stay at the house. I'll see if I can convince Cowboy and Jacey to give the two of you some space. No promises," Beast said.

"And the others?" I asked.

"I'm working on it. We definitely need more guest housing for the future. I'm thinking a set of apartments, similar to what the Devil's Fury put in. We could do four, all on one level, with at least two bedrooms in each."

"The club is growing," I said. "Before too long,

we'll have more in-laws visiting."

Beast sighed. "I know. I think Forge and Brick are at the top of the list of actually wanting a woman at home. Most of the others are content with things the way they are."

"They have no idea what they're missing," I said, glancing toward the bathroom. Dani had started humming in the shower and I smiled, thinking how much I loved having her here. We may have only been together such a short time, but already I knew this house hadn't been a home until she'd gotten here. She was my world.

"No, they don't," Beast agreed. "I'll get with Hawk and Forge, see what we can come up with for our guests. I can't hold off Cowboy much longer."

"Dani's in the shower, and I need to get cleaned up. She'd probably like a chance to change the bedding, even if they aren't staying here. I'm sure her mom will want a tour or something."

"Well, if Cowboy starts pounding on your front door, don't say I didn't warn you. He's pissed as fuck your woman didn't say shit about this Lewis guy. Can't say as I blame him. If it were my daughter getting those notes, I'd feel the same."

I heard the shower shut off and knew I'd have to tell Dani her family had already arrived. "Stall him another twenty minutes if you can. If not, at least hold him off long enough for me to shower."

I ended the call and went into the bathroom. Dani had her hair wrapped in a towel and another around her body. She wiped the condensation off the mirror before reaching for her moisturizer. Even though I knew I needed to rinse off, I couldn't help but lean against the wall and watch her. Everything she did fascinated me.

"You're starting to creep me out," she said.

"Your family is here. Along with a fuck ton of other Dixie Reapers. Beast is trying to figure out where to put everyone, but he's hoping your family can share the guest house with Wire, Lavender, and their kid."

Her shoulders drooped a little. "Who came with him?"

"I don't remember everyone mentioned. Except Grimm. He's here."

She nodded. "All right. I'll finish getting ready and make sure the house is picked up. So much for getting groceries."

"Make a list and call one of the Prospects. They can run and get whatever you need."

"I don't have their numbers," she said.

"Code for my phone is 7656. Look for Logan."

She blinked and turned to face me. "Did you just tell me how to unlock your phone?"

"Yeah. You're my woman, right?"

"Yes, but… I'm not sure my mom even knows how to get into my dad's phone. Why would you give me that information?"

I walked over and cupped her cheek. "Because I trust you. Just don't read my text messages or listen to my voicemails. If you did, I'll have to change the code and you'll have lost my trust."

She narrowed her eyes. "Better not be any women texting or leaving messages."

"You're cute when you're jealous. And no, it won't be. But I don't need you reading something that's club business. Understood?"

"Got it. Now shower and get dressed."

I swatted her ass, loving the way it made her cheeks flush. She bit down on her lip, her gaze dropping to my semi-hard cock. If her family wasn't here already, I'd bend her over the bathroom counter. Hell, if she hadn't already showered, I might have done it anyway. I didn't think she'd appreciate me getting her all dirty again.

While she finished getting ready, I washed off quickly and pulled on some clothes. I let Dani check the rest of the house and I changed the sheets on our bed, shoving the dirty ones into the washer. I'd just started the machine when it sounded like Cowboy was trying to knock the front door off the hinges. I knew it had to be him.

"I'll get it," I yelled out.

I heard Danica somewhere toward the back of the house. I didn't know what she was doing, but I hoped she was ready for her mom and dad. I wouldn't be able to hold them at bay. The second the door opened Cowboy pushed his way inside with Jacey on his heels.

"Come in," I said, shaking my head. "Dani should be out in a minute. She said something about straightening up."

"Is she okay?" Jacey asked.

I motioned for them to step into the living room and have a seat. "She's okay. A bit scared to leave the compound. She doesn't think Lewis is anywhere nearby, but it seems he's hiring people, or blackmailing them, into helping him."

"Wire and Lavender were going to head over to Shield's and see if the three of them could find some dirt on Lewis Stevens," Cowboy said.

"Uh, if they're going to Shield's, and you're here, where are the boys?"

"With Grimm." Jacey smiled. "He's rather good with kids. All the Dixie Reaper kids adore him."

I was thankful one of the kids in particular

hadn't liked the guy enough to hook up with him. I'd met him a few times. He seemed like a good enough sort, and he had the type of looks I knew women gravitated toward. Not to mention the slight Russian accent he let slip occasionally. I'd seen women lose their damn minds over a guy with a foreign accent.

Dani rushed into the room, her wet hair still up in a towel. Her dad gave me a glare, clearly knowing exactly why she'd need a shower this late in the day. I just shrugged a shoulder. He knew the score. I'd claimed his daughter. Hell, first chance I got, I was going to knock her up. Assuming I hadn't already.

"I can't offer you anything but coffee, which I haven't made yet," she said. "I was making a grocery list."

"Beer on there?" Cowboy asked.

"Uh..." Dani glanced at her phone, and I assumed she'd made the list on there. "Not yet, but it will be."

Her dad grunted and folded his arms over his chest, looking around the room. After heaving a sigh, he met my gaze. "Saw the fencing and lean-to for the horses."

"Once the issue with Lewis is settled, I'll be adding more fencing and a six-stall barn. Beast said I could have another three acres for the horses."

"How much is fenced now?" he asked.

"Little over an acre. I'll probably leave the small shelter up front and only take out a section at the back big enough for a gate. It will give her a way to pen them up near the house if she needs to."

"Know anything about horses? Or did you YouTube that shit?" Cowboy asked.

I took a seat in my favorite chair, figuring this conversation might take a while. If he wanted to grill me, I'd let him. He needed to know his daughter was safe with me, and that I'd see to her every need. Even the ones pertaining to her love of equines.

"My mom and stepdad have a farm a little northwest of here. I grew up around horses. I want to take Dani to meet them, but I was trying to give her time to settle in."

"They know you've claimed her?" he asked.

I shook my head. "I haven't told Mom about her at all. I knew if I did, she'd want to meet her right away. Figured I'd make the call and plan on visiting the next day. Otherwise, she'd nag me until I brought Dani to meet her."

I noticed the room had gone quiet. Danica and her mom had both vanished. I started to stand, until Cowboy held out a hand, stilling my movement.

"They're fine. She took her mom out to see the horses," Cowboy said.

"I didn't hear them leave."

He smiled. "Long as I've been with that woman -- and I wanted her long before I got to claim her -- I know when she leaves a room."

I wondered if the same would happen with me and Dani given enough time. I hoped so. I wanted what Cowboy and Jacey had.

Chapter Nine

Danica

Mom and I leaned against the fence as Pharoah and Sunny ran the length of the paddock and back. I couldn't wait for them to have more room, but I appreciated the effort Ranger had put into giving them a safe place to stay for now. At least I hadn't had to board them somewhere.

"Think you'll be happy here?" Mom asked, looking around.

I knew what she saw. Houses relatively close together. There wasn't anyone behind us, but one of Ranger's brothers lived about fifteen feet from the opposite fence line. Another lived on the other side of the house. Not close enough we could see into their windows. Still, it wasn't the same as living at my parents' place in the country. Everyone was nearby here. On the one hand, it could be a good thing if I needed someone quickly. On the other, I missed the wide-open spaces.

"I'm with Ranger and that's what matters. He's given me a way to keep the horses close, and he doesn't mind if I ride in the rodeo. Since we have a home and I don't need to save up to buy a house, there's no reason I need to go to as many of them. I can hit the ones within a day's drive."

"You've never really dated. Maybe a few here and there, but I don't remember you ever having a steady boyfriend."

"What's your point, Mom?" I asked.

"Are you rushing into this? Are you… settling?"

I blinked at her, not understanding why she'd ask such a thing. Ranger was all I'd thought about after he'd left. It had taken everything in me to pull up to the gates and ask to see him instead of driving straight through to the rodeo, but not because I didn't want him. I'd been terrified he'd changed his mind and wouldn't want me. It might be too soon to say I loved him, but I certainly cared about him. I wanted to spend my life with him.

"How long did it take you to fall for Dad?" I asked, trying to turn the tables on her.

"It's different. I'd been in a long relationship already."

"Right. You married a spawn of Satan and stayed faithful to him even when Dad was right there, wanting to take you away from the nightmare we'd been living. I love you, Mom. I really do. I just don't understand why you stayed with him so long. Why you didn't let Dad help before things became so dire."

She heaved out a sigh and looked out across the open land behind the house. "Because I was scared. For me. For you and your brother. I felt trapped and didn't want to risk your dad getting hurt. I didn't realize at the time he wasn't just a cowboy but was also a Dixie Reaper. If I'd known about his past, maybe I'd have opened up sooner."

"Do you regret how quickly things happened between the two of you once we left?"

"Of course not!" She glared at me. Then her face softened. "Oh. I see. You're falling for him, aren't you?"

"I care about him, and yes, I think I could love him. He accepts me as I am, Mom. And he knows about horses. He's the closest I've ever come to finding a guy like Dad."

She put her arm around me and squeezed. "Your dad is one in a million. If you think Ranger is even a little bit like him, then you've got a good one. I just didn't want you to wake up in a week, a month, or a year and decide you'd made a mistake."

"I didn't make a mistake. Ranger is good to me, Mom. He makes me happy. And he makes me feel safe. I'd planned to tell him about Lewis. He just happened to find the letters first. Except he thought they were love letters and got pissed."

"That's what happens when you keep secrets," Mom said.

I stared at her. "Really? You're going with that?"

She shrugged a shoulder. "Seems fitting. Look at the secret I kept from your dad. It nearly cost us our lives. Men like your dad and Ranger aren't afraid to face down danger, especially to protect those they love. If you're scared or feel threatened, let Ranger know. What if you hadn't said anything and Lewis cornered you somewhere?"

I knew she was right. I didn't like it, but I understood. I'd hoped it would all blow over. When I'd realized it wouldn't, I'd decided to confide in Ranger. "I said I'd planned to tell him."

"Just not your parents," she said.

"Give it a rest, Mom. You're beating a dead horse."

She gasped in outrage and glanced at Pharoah and Sunny. "They can *hear* you!"

I snickered and led her back toward the house. Whatever Dad had to say to Ranger, I hoped they'd gotten it out of the way. I should have known he'd give him the third degree. Even if Dad had been the one to push me to come, he'd had to beat on his chest and make sure Ranger knew not to hurt me. As if he would!

The house was quiet when we stepped inside, and I peered into the living room. Dad and Ranger were both drinking beer and watching TV. At least they hadn't tried to kill one another. Since they had cold drinks, I assumed it meant Logan had gotten my list and picked up everything I'd asked for. At least we would have snacks, drinks, and I could make something for dinner. My family might be here for a not-so-happy reason, but it didn't mean I couldn't enjoy my time with them. Soon enough, they'd go home, and I didn't know when I'd get a chance to visit again.

"Do the two of you want some pretzels or popcorn?" I asked.

Ranger looked at his watch. "No time, Dani girl. While you were outside, Beast sent out a message to everyone in the club. Church in twenty minutes. The Dixie Reapers will be going too, so you and your mom will be alone here. I already asked Logan to stay within shouting distance."

"Does that mean the hackers already found something?" I asked.

"Not sure, honey. Beast didn't say. I'll tell you what I can after Church, but you know how this works."

Yeah. Club business was off-limits. "I call bullshit."

My dad choked on his swallow of beer and Ranger just stared at me.

I folded my arms. "When your 'club business' pertains to me, then it damn well *is* my business. I want to know what's going on. Don't leave me in the dark! Information is power, Ranger. The more I know, the better I can protect myself. You can't be glued to me twenty-four seven."

"She's not entirely wrong," my dad said. "Protecting her is one thing. When your protection puts her in danger, that's something different. You can keep her in the loop with enough information she can keep herself safe. If you don't and something happens, you'll regret it the rest of your life. All two seconds of it."

Ranger set his beer aside. "Trust me. If I do anything to get Dani hurt or killed, you won't have to take me out. I'll do it myself."

"No, you won't!" I stalked over to him. "Take it back right now. You think I want that? For you to die and follow me to the grave? Because I don't. I want you to live your life. Find happiness."

"You want me to be with another woman?" he asked.

"Well. Not while I'm still breathing. But if you're asking do I want you to die alone? The answer is no. Everyone deserves to be loved, Ranger."

He reached out and took my hand, tugging me down onto his lap. "I will follow you to the ends of the earth. And yes, I would follow you into the next life. I will, however, make you this promise. If we have children, I will stay alive for them. I won't settle down with another woman. You'll always be a part of me, even if you stop breathing. But if I die before you, I want you to find someone who will keep you safe and treat you right. Someone to guide our kids, make all of you smile and laugh. And I'll be waiting for you on the other side."

I reached up to wipe the tears from my cheeks. What he'd said was both beautiful and heartbreaking. I didn't even want to think about having to ever live without him. It didn't matter how long we'd known each other. He was it for me.

"I can't make that promise," I said. "I won't. I guess you'll just have to live as long as I do. We'll grow old together. Raise a family. See our kids have children of their own. Maybe even our grandchildren will have families before we move on to whatever is beyond this world."

"You two are nauseatingly sweet," my dad said.

"Like I haven't had to watch you and Mom when you think no one is around?" I asked.

"Shut it," Dad muttered.

"Visit with your mom," Ranger said. "We'll be back as soon as we can. I don't know if Lavender is going to Church or not. If she's not, why don't you ask her to come over? The boys can play out back."

"I'll be glad when all this is over." I snuggled into him. "I don't want to feel like I need to hide or always be on guard."

"We'll take care of Lewis Stevens. One way or another," Ranger said.

"That's what worries me." I kissed him softly and stood. "I don't want anyone going to jail over this mess. Or worse, ending up dead. Promise me you'll be careful. I just found you. I can't lose you."

He got up from the chair and hugged me tight. "I will always come back to you, Dani. Always. Nothing will keep me from your side. As for Lewis, he'll get what's coming to him. Whether it's seeing the inside of a jail cell, or buried six feet under, I'll make sure he can't hurt you or anyone else ever again."

After Dad and Ranger left, I collapsed onto the couch. Mom sat next to me, texting on her phone. I figured she was checking on my brother, or asking Lavender to come over. I didn't know how she'd handled this all these years. The waiting and doing nothing part. Our men were off figuring out how to handle a rapist and stalker while we twiddled our thumbs. It didn't seem right.

"You get used to it," Mom said. "And as the Reckless Kings grow, you'll have more old ladies to befriend. Lyssa is coming over, along with Hayley. Lavender said she's bringing the boys. Why don't we see what's in your kitchen? We'll bake some goodies, maybe make a casserole or two, and carry it over to the clubhouse. When the men are finished talking, they'll need to refuel before they can carry out whatever plan they come up with."

I hoped the club whores weren't around. I wasn't sure I could handle some woman clinging to Ranger right about now. Well, not without wanting to seriously kick her ass. Since I hadn't been part of the Reckless Kings very long, I didn't know if I'd get into trouble for doing something like that. Lyssa could probably tell me. Or even Hayley.

"Is it always like this?" I asked.

"Pretty much. It's part of why your dad didn't want to live at the compound. He goes when they need his help, but for the most part, he's kept to himself. At least, until you and Jackson got a little older. When the two of you started traveling with the rodeo, he started attending more club events. Took me with him when he could. It's been good for Langston. He had the chance to grow up with Atlas and the other kids, and you made friends with a few of them too. It's like having a huge extended family."

"And after everything we went through, we needed a support system," I said. "You most of all."

Mom nodded. "I did, and your dad gave that to me."

"You don't ever worry about the women at the clubhouse, when he goes without you?" I asked.

She smiled. "No, baby girl. I don't. I trust your dad, and I know he loves me. He would never do anything to hurt me and cheating with one of those women would tear out my heart. You think Tank, Venom, or any of the others with wives or old ladies look twice at those women? They don't. They're faithful to those they love."

I looked down at the floor. "What if they don't love you? How do you trust them not to be tempted? What's stopping them from doing whatever they want?"

"From what I know of the Reckless Kings, they're a lot like the Dixie Reapers. At least as far as being faithful goes. Neither Beast nor Hawk would dare let those women touch them. I think Ranger is the same."

I wished I could be as certain. In a lot of ways, we were still strangers. We might have slept together, and he had claimed me, but we hadn't been together very long. There was so much I didn't know about him. What if I put my trust in him and he failed me? I didn't know if it was something we'd recover from.

There was a knock at the door a moment before it swung open. Lyssa stepped inside with her daughter, and Hayley followed with little Freya.

"Lavender was unloading the boys," Lyssa said. "We also have a few things in the back of my car. I didn't know what you had in your kitchen, so I packed what we'd need to make some brownies."

"And I brought a chicken casserole I made this morning," Hayley said. "All we'll need to do is warm it before we take it over to the clubhouse."

I glanced at my mom, and she just gave me a small smile. Looked like we were going to keep busy by feeding the men. I only hoped it didn't blow up in my face. If I walked in and found some club whore hanging on Ranger, and him letting her, it would gut me.

Langston burst into the house with Atlas on his heels. He beelined for me and flung his arms around my waist. "Missed you, Danica."

"I've missed you too, little brother." I hugged him tight. "Looks like us women will be cooking and baking. Why don't you and Atlas go out back to play?"

He nodded and took off, Atlas running right alongside him. They darted out the front door and I watched through the window as they ran around the side of the house. Langston knew his way around horses, so I didn't worry about them getting into trouble with Pharoah and Sunny.

"I'm sure you have a lot of questions," Lyssa said. "I'll answer them while we bake."

I eyed Madison and Freya. "And the girls?"

"I brought two options," Lyssa said. "I have a baby gate we can put across a doorway, if there's a room you think they can use without getting into mischief, or I have a playpen."

"There's a sunroom. It's completely empty right now," I said.

"Sounds perfect." Lyssa smiled. "I brought plenty of toys to keep the girls occupied. We'll get them settled, then get started on feeding the men."

"I'll show you where the sunroom is, and then I'll start unloading your car," I offered.

I led the way to the back of the house and my mother gasped as she saw the space. I knew exactly how she felt. I couldn't wait to decorate the room and be able to sit out here and enjoy the sunshine and quiet without having to sit in the heat. I didn't know if this part of Tennessee saw much snow, but if it did, I knew I'd enjoy the view in the winter too.

While we baked brownies, I peppered Lyssa with

questions about the Reckless Kings and what I should expect while living here. She eased some of my concerns. The rest I'd have to figure out as time passed.

"You'll like it here," Hayley said. "I was terrified when Hawk brought me to Tennessee. I'd spent time with Mariah, and I'd met some of the Dixie Reapers, but it wasn't the same as having grown up around them. I had a lot to learn, but I haven't regretted moving here."

"I'm sure I'll settle in soon," I said. "It's just all so new right now. I barely know Ranger, and I've met Beast, Hawk, and a few other Reckless Kings over the last year, but I don't really *know* them."

Lyssa hugged me, then Hayley wrapped her arms around both of us. Whatever the future brought, at least I knew these two would stand by me through it all. We'd stick together, just like the old ladies did at the Dixie Reapers. After all, they were our role models.

"Too bad Casper had Mariah sent to the Devil's Fury," Mom said. "Although, it might be a good thing. If the Reckless Kings start claiming all the Reaper girls, Torch and Venom might not want the club around as much."

"Farrah is with the Devil's Fury," I reminded her.

She nodded. "True. Janessa is with the Devil's Boneyard and Laken is with Ryker, even though he's no longer part of Hades Abyss."

I blinked at my mom. "Wait. He's a Reaper now? How did I not know that?"

"They didn't make a huge deal of it. He's been living there since he claimed Laken. We all knew it was bound to happen sooner or later." Mom reached over to squeeze my hand. "But with Ryker being Spider's son, we still have a family tie to the Hades Abyss."

"Wonder who Leigha will grow up and fall for,"

Lyssa said. "She's the next oldest, right?"

"Out of the girls? Yes," Mom said. "But Owen and Foster are both eighteen now. I know they want to prospect for the club. It's possible one of them will find their perfect match before Leigha is old enough to be claimed by anyone."

I cleared my throat and shifted on my feet. "Um, I don't know if anyone's noticed, but Foster has a tendency to flirt with Leigha. I have a feeling he's waiting for her to turn eighteen before he makes his move."

My mom groaned and smacked her hand over her eyes, shaking her head. "No. No, no, no. Preacher is never going to let Bull's son anywhere near his daughter. Not after last year."

"What happened last year?" Good grief. Had I been living under a rock? How did I miss all the stuff going on at home?

"There was a pregnancy scare," Lyssa said. "I heard all about it from Mariah. Some girl claimed Foster got her pregnant. She'd lied. The baby wasn't his, which we found out after it was born, and Bull demanded a paternity test. But the simple fact he'd slept with that girl, and the baby *could* have been his, pretty much put a nail in his coffin where any of the Reaper daddies are concerned. He won't be going near Leigha anytime soon. Not and live to see the next morning."

Damn. "New rule. Share the gossip as it's happening and not a year later."

Lyssa snickered. "Sure thing."

Chapter Ten

Ranger

The more I found out about Lewis Stevens, the more I hated the guy. How had a monster like him been allowed to roam free all these years? Not only had Wire, Shield, and Lavender found more than a dozen girls this asshole had beaten and raped, but it looked like he'd killed two girls when he'd been younger. The law hadn't been able to pin anything on him, and being under eighteen, his record had been sealed. Unless you had world-class hackers digging into the guy.

"From what we've been able to determine, he's getting close to his end goal," Wire said. "The letters are getting more frequent. With each girl he's assaulted previously, he made sure they disappeared from a rodeo he didn't attend. Our best guess is that he planned to have someone snatch Danica at the event she was heading to when she stopped here."

Jesus. I could have lost her, and I wouldn't have even known where to look. Bile rose in my throat as I studied the pictures Wire had found. They weren't from police records. The women hadn't gone forward. Probably too terrified. No, these were from Lewis' personal collection. One he'd kept backed up to a cloud storage of all places. Fucking idiot.

The images detailed not only the brutal way they'd been beaten to within an inch of their lives, but he'd also had someone take pictures of everything he did to them. Only a few women had gotten away with only a few bruises to outwardly show for what they'd suffered. Looked like he'd gotten slightly smarter over the years. Found ways to hide what he'd done to them.

"I want him dead," Cowboy said.

I glanced at Danica's dad and couldn't agree with him more. I wanted this asshole six feet under too, but he was in the spotlight. Dani had been right about one thing. Making him disappear wouldn't be easy.

"Any of these women willing to come forward?" I asked.

"A few," Wire said. "Most... aren't alive anymore to tell their story. Three committed suicide. Two have been committed to psychiatric facilities, too damaged from what happened to make it on their own. The others died in accidents. The ones who are willing to testify against him have changed their names and gone into hiding."

"There's more," Shield said, his gaze going around the table and stopping on Hatchet. "Brother, you remember knocking up some girl about twenty years ago?"

Hatchet leaned back in his seat and folded his arms. "I was sixteen. Just a dumbass kid. My girlfriend had an abortion, then moved out of state. What the fuck does that have to do with anything?"

"She didn't have an abortion," Wire said. He slid a photo across the table to Hatchet. "Your daughter is alive, and she's one of Lewis' victims. She's at Balmoral Psychiatric Hospital in Missouri. I've already asked Spider to have one of his crew go check on her."

Hatchet picked up the picture and studied it. He stood so abruptly, his chair fell over. The roar he released was a mix of rage and pain, the type of pain only a father can feel when his little girl has been brutalized by someone like Lewis. Hatchet put his fist through the wall -- twice -- before falling to his knees.

"Her name is Raven," Shield said. "If you want to head to Missouri to go meet your daughter, none of us will stand in your way."

Hatchet got to his feet, his hands fisted. "No. I'm staying. Before I meet her, I need to make this asshole pay. I want to look my daughter in the eye and tell her she's been avenged. That she no longer has to live in fear."

"Spider will take good care of her," Cowboy said. "She'll be in good hands until you get there."

Hatchet nodded and reclaimed his seat. I noticed Wire and Shield removed a handful of pictures from the ones they passed around the table. I knew they had to be of Hatchet's daughter. It was one thing knowing Lewis had assaulted her, and another to see it. At least they were sparing him that much.

"Lewis is competing in a rodeo in Wyoming right now," Cowboy said. "I checked his schedule. He has a fan site that lists all his upcoming appearances, and he's got a page on the PBR website. After Wyoming is Texas, Arizona, and Oklahoma. He's trying to rack up enough points to guarantee himself to be toward the top by the main PBR event."

"So how do we do this?" I asked. "Every town he stops in puts another woman in danger. If he can't get to Dani, he may grab someone else."

Wire tapped on his keyboard a moment before looking over at Hatchet. "According to Surge, Spider has sent Breaker after your daughter. He's a good kid. I remember him when he was a Prospect. Name's Teller, and he'll lay down his life to keep Raven safe."

Hatchet nodded. "Thanks. I hate not being the one to go get her, but I know this is where I need to be right now."

"How are we going to get him?" I asked, trying to keep everyone focused on Lewis. I needed this asshole off the streets. Not only for Danica, but for every woman who crossed his path. He didn't seem to have a type. The pictures showed women who were blonde, brunette, black-haired, purple-haired… he didn't seem to care. They were different races as well. Only thing they had in common were their ages. They seemed to range between sixteen and twenty.

Wait. I looked over all the information again. I wasn't wrong. Every last one of them was twenty or younger. Except Danica didn't fit the profile.

"Danica is older than all these women. Are we sure he's the one after her?" I asked.

"I thought of that," Wire said. "There's a chance it could be a copycat, someone who knows how Lewis operates, but has decided they don't want to work behind the scenes anymore. In which case, I've pulled up a list of men he's used to not only take pictures but also deliver the notes. Anyone tried to pull prints off the letters Danica has?"

"We don't have a way to run them," Beast said.

"I can do it," Wire said. "I brought everything I'd need. When we take a break, I'll check the letters for prints and run any I find."

"I handled some of them," I said. "So did Danica."

"I have hers already," Wire said.

I wasn't sure I wanted to know why he had her prints. Considering the trouble the Dixie Reapers had found over the years, it wouldn't surprise me if he had prints on everyone in the club, even the babies. Hell, they'd chipped Lyssa's vehicle, phone, and who knew what else. They'd probably done the same thing with Danica, and all the other girls. I couldn't blame them. In fact, I liked that they could find my woman at any given time.

"Let's figure out how we're grabbing Lewis, then

we'll focus on the men who have helped him. I think we need to take them all out," Beast said.

"I agree." Hawk leaned forward, bracing his arms on the table. "If we take out Lewis, there's no guarantee his little minions won't decide to take up where he left off. Anyone who would agree to watch any of that, much less take part in some way, is evil to their core."

"Or Lewis has something on them," I said.

"Shield and I will see what we can find," Wire said. "Right now, I think we have all the main players. We mostly focused on digging on Lewis. No reason we can't do the same for the other men. Might take a few hours."

"Until then, why don't we take a break?" Beast suggested.

I cocked my head, trying to figure out what I'd just heard from the other room. "Anyone else hear a scream?"

Everyone stood and rushed into the main part of the clubhouse, and then came to an abrupt stop. Holy. Shit. My eyes went wide as I stared at Dani, slamming Letty's head into the bar repeatedly. Lyssa was in the process of hauling another club whore out the door, by her hair. Or more accurately, dragging her since the woman was on the ground. Hayley kicked another in the stomach and followed it up with a punch to the woman's face.

"What the fuck?" I mumbled.

"I think our women have taken exception to the club whores being here in the middle of the day," Beast said. He didn't seem the least bit disturbed. In fact, he looked damn proud of his woman.

"Hayley, sweetheart, can we not teach Freya to beat on people?" Hawk asked, striding toward his woman. He hooked her around the waist and hauled her back against his chest.

Shit. Where were the kids? I looked around and saw Jacey in the corner with the two little girls, as well as Atlas and Langston. She didn't seem concerned by what was happening. If anything, she looked bored.

I made my way over to Danica and tried to pry her off Letty. "Dani!"

She stopped and glared at me. "Don't you 'Dani' me right now! I'm pissed at you. And this stupid slut."

She slammed Letty's head into the bar again, and the woman groaned before slumping to the floor. "What the hell is going on?"

Minnie scurried over from another corner of the room, her face pale as she stared at the other club whores. "It's not her fault."

Well, now, this was an unusual turn of events. Usually the club whores were catty and hated the old ladies. Not Minnie. She was defending Danica? "Come again?"

"Letty found out Danica is your old lady. She started mouthing off about..." Her cheeks flushed as she looked over at the kids and dropped her voice to a near whisper. "About how you like your cock sucked, among other things. Then the others chimed in about Beast and Hawk."

"But not you?" I asked.

She shook her head so hard I thought her neck might crack. "No! I respect your old ladies. I know I'm here to be of service to anyone who wants me, but I'd never try to go after anyone who has a woman at home."

"So these three were causing trouble?" Hawk asked, nodding to the club whores who'd taken a beating.

Minnie nodded. "I tried to tell them to stop."

"She stayed out of the way," Lyssa said. "Minnie can remain. These other three? I want them gone. I don't give a shit if you're pissed I'm talking to any of you like this right now. Either those three go, or the three of us do."

Beast yanked her against him and glowered down at her. "We've talked about this."

Lyssa sagged against him. "You don't understand. I can handle all this. Hayley is getting used to it too, but Danica hasn't had one of these bitches try to get between her and Ranger before. You didn't see the look on her face. I couldn't stand around and do nothing, then they started mouthing off about you and Hawk."

Beast tipped her chin up. "What did they say?"

"She said the next time you were here drinking with your brothers, she'd make sure she accidentally fell on your cock with her pussy. She said it would remind you I'm not the only woman in the world, and I'd be out on my ass before long." Lyssa sighed. "I know you'd never do that, but I couldn't let her get away with that shit."

Beast pressed his lips to hers. "They're gone. All but Minnie. We'll find new club whores, somewhere. Maybe some of the girls at the strip club would like to come party."

I pulled Danica into my arms and held her, pressing a kiss to the top of her head. "I'm not going anywhere near these women, Dani. Nothing they say or do could ever tempt me away from you."

She buried her face in my chest, and the tension in her body told me how hard she was fighting not to fall apart in front of everyone. I scooped her into my arms and carried her down the hallway. I kicked open the bathroom door, then shut it behind us, setting her on the counter.

"Dani girl, I know we're new, and I have no problem with you putting club whores in their place, but you have nothing to worry about." I caressed her cheek and wiped away her tears as they started to fall.

"I'm sorry. I should have more faith in you. In us."

"You're my girl. My old lady. And if you want to be, my wife. We can get married the old-fashioned way, or let Wire work his magic. I don't care. I want you to be mine in every way possible. No more doubts, Dani. You're it for me."

She nodded and snuggled into me. "I'd love to be your wife, and I don't care how it's done."

"I'll let Wire and Shield know. By tonight, you'll be Danica Saeed." I cupped her cheek, tipping her face up. "Just be prepared. Small towns and small minds. Some people will hear your new last name and give you shit about it."

"Did that happen to you? Before you only went by Ranger?" she asked.

"Yeah. A lot. Especially in school. Not too many kids in my county who had a parent from the Middle East. Most of the kids were white. A handful were African American or Hispanic, but not many. Where I lived, the population was about eighty-five percent white."

"It shouldn't matter," she said.

"No, it shouldn't, but it did. I was different. Not to mention, some had family members who fought in Operation Desert Storm. A few came back not quite whole, either physically or mentally. Didn't matter I wasn't from Iraq, or that my family had nothing to do with the war. They saw the color of my skin, heard my last name, and made me public enemy number one."

"I will be proud to be Danica Saeed. I don't care what anyone says." She pressed her lips to mine. "But just to be clear. If you're planning on buying a wedding ring, I don't want anything fancy or big. A plain band is more than enough. Anything else could get in the way when I'm with the horses."

"I can do that." I smiled. "As long as everyone knows you're mine, that's all that matters. I'd rather be at home with you than cooling my heels in the county jail for knocking a few heads together."

"Um, Parks. No one's ever really hit on me. Not in a way that would require you to start a fight. I think you're safe."

I kissed her again. Longer. Deeper. "Then they were idiots."

"As much as I'd love to continue down this path, we brought food. If you're hungry, you'd better go get something before your brothers eat it all. Or the Dixie Reapers. Grimm is known for eating his weight in brownies."

I helped her off the counter and walked back out to the main room with her hand in mine. I saw Cowboy and Jacey at a table, waving us over. Leading Danica over to them, I noticed there were extra drinks and plates. It seemed they'd made sure we were taken care of after we disappeared down the hall.

"Sit and eat," Jacey said. "Wire and Shield grabbed plates and went back into Church to keep working. Lavender went to get her laptop and said she'd stay and help for a little while."

"What about the kids?" I asked.

"Atlas can stay with us. He and Langston are joined at the hip anyway." Jacey took a sip of her soda. "I'm not sure how long Lyssa and Hayley will stay at the house, but their girls aren't any trouble. We put a gate across the sunroom doorway earlier and left them to play."

"Do what you need to," Danica said. "We'll be okay. Mom will stay with me even if Lyssa and Hayley need to go home."

"We found a lot on Lewis." I glanced at Cowboy, and he gave a slight nod. "One of the women he's hurt is Hatchet's daughter. He thought his girlfriend had an abortion. Turns out he has a twenty-year-old daughter. She's in a psychiatric hospital in Missouri, but Spider was sending someone to get her. They'll watch over her until Hatchet can get to her."

Danica leaned back in her chair and sighed. "You're going to kill him, aren't you? Lewis. Hatchet won't allow him to live after what he did to his daughter."

"Don't worry about it, Dani girl. Whatever happens, we won't get caught," I assured her. "You don't need to hear the details."

Cowboy snorted. "We don't even know the details yet. Just know that Wire and Lavender can cover up just about anything. None of us are going to jail, if that's your concern."

"Good to know," Danica muttered.

"Guess we need to hold off on asking Shield or Wire to help us out," I told her, taking her hand in mine.

"Help you?" Jacey asked. "With something other than Lewis Stevens?"

I nodded and looked at my soon-to-be wife. I didn't know if she wanted me to tell them now, or if she wanted to wait. Since it was her family, I'd let her take the lead.

"I want one of them to marry us," Danica said.

"The way Wire's done for a lot of others. I don't need a ceremony or anything."

Cowboy frowned as he stared at his daughter. "So I don't get to walk you down the aisle?"

Well, shit. I hadn't thought of that. Was it something Danica would want too? I tried to read her expression. I had no problem waiting and having a preacher or judge marry us. All right, maybe not a judge. Not sure I wanted to stand up in front of one of those anytime soon.

"You want to walk me down the aisle?" Danica asked her dad. "I didn't think you'd be into that sort of thing."

"Of course, I do!" He set his beer bottle down. "But what do you want?"

She chewed her bottom lip and looked at me. I knew right then what she wanted and needed. And I'd give it to her. Whatever it took. I looked around the room. Prospero would probably be up for what I had in mind. I caught his attention and waved him over.

"What's up, Ranger?" he asked.

"How do you feel about becoming an ordained minister? One of those online things that would allow you to marry someone in less than a week?" I asked.

"Uh." He looked from me to the others at the table and back again. "You want to get married?"

"Danica wants a real wedding where her dad can walk her down the aisle. We don't exactly have an aisle here, but we could fix up the clubhouse for the occasion. Push the tables aside. Hang some lanterns or something. Will you do it?" I asked.

"Absolutely. I'll use my phone to look it up now. I've heard there are online places where you can be ordained same day." Prospero winked at Danica. "Congrats, Danica. And welcome to the Reckless Kings family."

He walked off and I pulled up my phone, searching for a local bridal shop. Before I called, I needed some information from Danica.

"What size do you usually wear in dresses?" I asked her.

"A twelve," she said. "Why?"

"Preferred wedding dress style?" Her brow furrowed as she stared at me. I waited and she finally just shrugged. "All right. I'll ask for one of everything."

I called the shop and spoke to the manager. She promised to send someone by with six dresses for Danica to peruse and choose from. I offered to pay in cash for whatever she picked out, which thrilled the woman. She said someone would be by within the hour.

It occurred to me everyone would wonder why I was rushing to marry Danica. Knowing she could have been taken from me, that Lewis could have raped or killed her if she hadn't come here, made an icy chill skate down my spine. She'd already agreed to be my old lady. Now I wanted her to be mine in every way possible. I wanted my ring on her finger. More importantly, I needed the world to know she belonged to me and was under my protection, as my wife.

I stood and went to Jacey, quietly getting Danica's ring size, then went to find Logan. I'd send him for wedding bands, lanterns, and anything else we needed to give her a wedding she'd remember fondly. With some luck, we'd even get it done before anyone had to leave to handle Lewis and the others.

Chapter Eleven

Danica

I couldn't believe he was putting together a wedding. After taking a break for lunch, the men had gone back into Church and all the ladies had returned to my house. Prospero had sent a text to Lyssa letting her know he'd been ordained online and could perform the ceremony whenever we were ready. It seemed one of the Prospects was off buying supplies to transform the clubhouse. When Ranger had said he wanted to marry me right away, I hadn't realized he meant immediately. Minnie had offered to stay and help decorate, which I'd found sweet, if a bit strange. I didn't know why it had to be done right now. It would take time to find a dress and anything we needed before getting married.

"If it makes you feel better, Minnie and Ranger never hooked up," Lyssa said.

"How do you know?" I asked.

"Because she has a thing for Satyr, but he's never going to settle down. She always waits for him at the parties. Once he's had his fill, she usually clings to Brick." Lyssa shook her head. "Brick doesn't do anything but let her sit on his lap while he drinks and plays cards, or whatever else he gets into at the parties. She's a one-man woman, and Beast lets it slide."

"But he just booted the others. Won't she have to... you know?" I asked.

Lyssa smiled. "Whore herself out to anyone in the club who snaps their fingers at her? Typically, yes. With Minnie, I think Beast will make an exception. Everyone knows she has it bad for Satyr, except Satyr. He's fucking clueless."

"Have you ever heard of a brother keeping a club

whore as an old lady?" Hayley asked. "Hawk made it seem like something none of them would ever do."

"I haven't. Doesn't mean it never happens," Lyssa said. "For Minnie's sake, I hope Satyr gives her a chance. She's a sweetheart."

I twirled in front of my mom, Lyssa, and Hayley. "What about this one?"

They eyed the wedding dress I'd tried on. Dress number three. They were all beautiful, but none of them felt right. I was starting to think maybe I wasn't the type to wear a dress like these. I'd been comfortable in my boots and jeans all my life. Seldom did I ever put on a dress of any sort.

"Show us the other ones," Hayley said, eyeing me.

The woman from the bridal shop unzipped three other bags. None of those were any better than what I'd tried on already.

"I have one more in my trunk," she said. "It's not your traditional wedding dress. Not these days. I picked it up from an estate sale. The woman who'd worn it stayed with her husband for thirty years before he was taken from her. She lived the rest of her life alone, because he'd been her only love. It's been laundered and I was taking it back to the shop to put on the rack."

"I want to see it," I said.

My mom frowned. "Are you sure, Danica? You don't want a new dress? One no one's ever worn before?"

I shook my head. "These are all beautiful, but they aren't me. Maybe I'm looking at dresses from the wrong decade."

"I'll bring it in," the lady said, hurrying out to her car. She returned a moment later with a garment bag. When she unzipped it, I knew it was the dress I was meant to wear. I only hoped it fit.

"It's beautiful," I said. The material was an eggshell with tiny yellow roses stitched into the fabric. The neckline would rest along my collarbones, and it had capped sleeves. The skirt belled out and looked like it would stop just below my knees.

The lady handed the dress to me, and Mom followed me to the bedroom. She helped me out of the dress I had on currently, and into the new one. The moment I put it on, I knew it was the right one. It fit as if it were made for me.

"I don't have shoes for it," I told Mom.

"Let's see what she brought. She mentioned bringing a few pairs, just in case. Ranger didn't tell her you needed shoes, but she planned ahead."

Good thing too, or I'd be wearing this pretty dress with cowboy boots. I wore the dress into the living room to show Hayley and Lyssa. Their jaws dropped, and the bridal shop assistant clapped her hands.

"It's perfect," the woman gushed. "I think I have just the right shoes for it, too."

She rummaged through the shoe boxes she'd brought with her and handed me a pair of sling-back eggshell shoes with kitten heels. They were peep toes, which meant I'd need to give myself a pedicure. I hoped Mom had remembered to pack the few bottles of nail polish I owned. Or even better, her massive collection. Since she'd hooked up with Dad, she'd started doing manicures and pedicures with the other old ladies once a month.

"We'll take the dress and shoes," Mom said.

"Ranger said he'd be paying cash," the woman said. "For both the dress and shoes, it will be five hundred plus tax."

"I've got it," Lyssa said, pulling out an envelope. "He left this with me to cover whatever you bought."

While Lyssa took care of the bill, I changed out of the dress and shoes. Mom took the dress and put it back into the garment bag and the shoes back into the box. I didn't want Ranger to see them until the wedding. I hung the bag at the very back of the closet and hoped he wouldn't be nosy.

"I can't believe my baby is getting married," Mom said, tears gathering in her eyes.

"Just think. You have two more to marry off. Assuming Jackson stops chasing the next win long enough to actually find someone."

"I won't hold my breath. Langston will probably settle down before Jackson, and he's not even ten!" Mom smiled. "But Jackson's day will come. Some girl will come along and knock him on his ass when he least expects it."

"When do you think we'll have the ceremony?" I asked.

"As soon as possible. That boy wants you to be his in every way possible. I can tell by looking at him."

I rolled my eyes. "He's hardly a boy."

"Yeah, well, he's not much younger than me. The fact he's about to be my son-in-law means I get to call him a boy."

"Fine. You do that." I looked down at my feet. "I don't suppose you packed any pedicure stuff? Pumice stone? Polish? Anything to make my feet more presentable in those shoes?"

Mom laughed. "I did. Maybe not the right polish, though. We can see if Hayley or Lyssa has a color that would work. I think a pale pink would look nice."

"I have a feeling I'm about to have a spa day,

aren't I?" I asked. She knew I hated those. I'd let her do it when I was younger, knowing she needed the break from everything else going on.

"You have something better to do?" she asked.

"Nope." I sighed. "Let's see if the others want to join in. The more the merrier, right?"

I spent the next two hours letting my mom give me a mani-pedi, and thankfully Hayley had the perfect polish color. By the time we were finished, I'd started to feel antsy. No one had heard anything from Ranger or the others. As far as we knew, they were still in Church. Had they come up with a plan? Or were they still working on it?

The not knowing was going to drive me crazy.

"Now what?" I asked, looking around at everyone.

Lyssa checked the time. "The boys are probably getting hungry again. We can let them eat burgers at the clubhouse while we make something here, or we can cook something to take over there."

Hayley was shaking her head, her eyes wide. I didn't know what the hell was going on, but she apparently didn't want to go to the clubhouse. It made me wonder if maybe she'd heard from Hawk. I'd noticed she'd checked her phone several times, and I'd seen her texting.

"What's going on?" I asked, watching Hayley. She flushed and looked everywhere but at me. "Hayley, you know something."

"It's a surprise. Please don't ask me to ruin it."

I sighed. "Fine. Just tell me this… do we need to make dinner right now?"

"No, but, um. You need to put on your dress and shoes." She looked at my mom, then back to me. "And your mom needs to dress up too. We all do."

Huh. If I needed to put on my dress, it sounded like we were getting married right this minute. I wasn't complaining, but a little warning would have been nice.

"I'll stay while your mom gets whatever she needs. Then the two of you can get ready together. I think you need the time alone, so I'll head home. Hayley and I will meet you at the clubhouse. *Don't* go there before five." Lyssa narrowed her eyes at me. "In fact, wait here. I'll come back for you, and we'll ride over together."

"I'll be back shortly," Mom said, giving me a hug. Hayley went ahead and loaded Freya into her car seat and drove back to her place. I helped Lyssa pack up all the things she'd brought, and she was ready to go home by the time my mom got back.

"How did you know to bring a dress?" I asked, as Mom brought her stuff into the house.

"I didn't, but I've learned to always be prepared. Your dad likes springing things on me. So now when we leave town, I pack at least one dress. Sometimes two."

"Why don't you get ready first?" I suggested. "I need to feed the horses anyway."

"All right. Hurry back. You'll want to rinse off in the shower after going out there. You should probably wash your hair too. And shave!"

I eyed my legs and remembered they'd been a little prickly when I'd been trying on dresses. The clock on the bedside table said it was nearly four o'clock, which only gave me about an hour to get ready. I could make it. I hoped.

I rushed outside and made sure the horses were fed and had plenty of water. I checked their hay before heading back inside. As much as I'd have loved rushing through a shower, since it seemed to be my wedding day, I took my time. I washed and conditioned my hair, shaved, and when I got out, I slathered on a ton of moisturizer.

"Ready?" Mom asked as I stared into the mirror.

"As I'll ever be."

She helped me dry and curl my hair. I even let her do my makeup. By the time I'd dressed and slipped on my shoes, I hardly recognized myself. Mom had pinned up part of my hair. The rest hung in spirals down my back and over my shoulders. I looked... elegant.

"I brought something for you. I hadn't realized it would end up being for your wedding, but I think it's the perfect time to pass them on."

"Mom, what are you talking about?" I asked.

She took two velvet boxes out of her purse and handed them to me. "Your dad bought these for me the first year we were together. I'd always planned to give them to you at some point."

I opened them and saw the diamond studs and necklace she'd worn for special occasions. I reverently touched them, awed that she'd give me something that meant so much to her. She loved this set.

"Mom, I can't accept these."

"You can, and you will. I already told your dad what I wanted to do, and he agreed they should be yours. He's already bought me another set to wear when we celebrate special things like anniversaries or holidays." She hugged me. "And one day, you can pass these on to your daughter."

I placed a hand over my stomach. What if I was pregnant already?

The front door opened and shut, then I heard Lyssa calling out for us. "You two ready?"

"Let's go!" Mom smiled. "Time for you to get married."

We got into Lyssa's SUV and headed to the clubhouse. I saw Hayley's car already there, and the bikes that had been here earlier were still present. I got out and smoothed my hands over my dress.

Dad stepped off the porch and held out his hand to me. "You look beautiful."

"Am I really doing this right now?" I asked. "I thought he'd want to wait until after dealing with Lewis."

"That's for Ranger to tell you, when and if he decides to share his reasoning. Does it matter? He wants to be with you, and you clearly want to be with him. The timing isn't important. Let's get you down the aisle to your husband-to-be. He's been antsy as hell waiting for you to get here."

My throat felt tight as Mom and Lyssa hurried ahead of us. They went inside, without giving me so much as a glimpse of what they'd done to the clubhouse. I shifted on my feet as my heart pounded against my ribs.

Dad pulled me into his arms and hugged me. "Everything is going to be all right, Danica. That boy thinks the world of you. I have no doubt he'll move heaven and hell to keep you happy and by his side."

"I feel the same about him," I said.

He nodded and placed my hand in the crook of his arm. We walked up the steps, and he pushed open the clubhouse door. My breath caught when I looked inside. Chairs were on either side of a makeshift aisle. Decorative paper lanterns hung from the ceiling, and twinkle lights had been strung along the bar. Each chair had white and yellow ribbons tied to it in big, pretty bows.

"How?" I asked, taking it all in.

"Minnie did a lot of it. And the Prospects helped. One stayed on the gate. The other two worked on this. When Lavender took a break from helping Wire and Shield, she pitched in too." He tipped his head to a table on the back wall. "She called a few places to have food brought in, and Minnie tied the bows to the chairs. She didn't think you'd want her here for the event, so she took off when she finished."

I smiled up at him and the flash of a camera made me see spots. What the hell? I looked around and spotted Hayley with a camera in her hands. She waved and took another picture.

"And Hayley offered to make sure you had wedding photos," Dad said.

"It's perfect," I said.

Dad walked me down the aisle and I saw Ranger waiting. He'd changed into a white button-down but wore his cut over it with his jeans and motorcycle boots. I knew he hadn't been to the house to get anything, and it made me wonder if the shirt was new. It seemed he'd been busy.

Prospero winked when we reached him and Ranger. "Who gives this woman to this man?"

"Her mother and I do," Dad said. He kissed my cheek and gave my hand to Ranger.

Tears misted my eyes as I stared up at Ranger. I knew in that moment I wasn't falling for him. I'd already fallen. I only hoped one day he'd come to love me too. The ceremony passed in a blur and only lasted about ten minutes. Thankfully, Hayley seemed to be click happy, and the flash of her camera was constantly going off. I'd have plenty of pictures to remember this day.

I'd noticed Wire stood off to the side with his

phone. At first, I'd thought he was working still, or messaging everyone at home. Until I'd realized he was filming the wedding.

"I now pronounce you husband and wife." Prospero grinned. "You may kiss the bride."

Ranger tugged me up against him and slanted his mouth over mine. If I'd thought he'd give me a quick peck, I'd been wrong. His tongue slipped between my lips, and he kissed me until the room spun. Everyone hooted and stamped their feet, making him pull back.

"Mine," he said. "All mine."

I leaned into him farther. "I was already yours."

"Come on, honey. Time for our first dance." Someone started up music, and everyone pushed the chairs to the sides. Ranger held me close as we swayed to the music. "You look beautiful."

"You clean up nice too."

He pressed his lips to mine again as we danced. Soon, others joined us. My heart felt full to bursting. It was the most magical night I'd ever had. I was so thankful my dad had mentioned wanting to walk me down the aisle. This was so much better than letting Wire marry us in a not-so-legal way.

"Thank you," I murmured. "I don't know how you did it, but this is the perfect wedding."

He kissed the ring on my finger. "Only the best for my wife."

"Dad said Minnie did a lot of this," I said.

"She did." He tipped his head to the side a little. "That bother you?"

"No, I only wished she'd stayed to enjoy the wedding. I think we should give her a gift or something, I want her to know how much I appreciate all she did for us."

Ranger smiled and pressed our foreheads together. "You're one amazing lady. I don't know too many women who would want someone like Minnie at their wedding."

"Other than Satyr, is there anything she needs?" I asked.

Ranger threw back his head and laughed. "I'm sure she'd like anything you gave her. But if you find a way to give her Satyr, she'll love you forever. That girl's been chasing him for a while now. Idiot's too stupid to realize she doesn't touch anyone but him."

I had a feeling the same couldn't be said for Satyr. With a name like that, how many other women had he been with? I knew it had to hurt Minnie. She'd seemed nice.

Ranger stopped dancing and cupped my cheek, staring at me with such tenderness. "I love you, Dani. No matter what the future brings for us, I want you to remember that."

Tears misted my eyes again. I hadn't felt the need to cry so much since Champ died. "I love you too."

His words both warmed my heart and scared the crap out of me. What did he mean "no matter what the future brings"? Was he expecting things to go badly when they went after Lewis? If the cost of taking care of him, and whatever it entailed, was that I'd lose Ranger, it wasn't worth it. I didn't know why he had to be part of it. We'd just gotten married, and it scared me that I might lose him.

I hoped he knew what he was doing.

Chapter Twelve

Ranger

Marrying Danica made me so damn happy. I only wished my parents had been here. I'd called Mom and told her about Dani, and the wedding. After she'd yelled at me for keeping a fiancé a secret from her, she'd said making the trip was impossible. Both she and my stepdad were sick with the stomach flu. They'd even had to call in help for getting the animals fed and stalls cleaned. It smarted I'd been such a horrible son they hadn't thought to call me for help.

I assured her I'd bring Dani to visit once they were better. And I made a vow to myself to go visit more often. My mom had done a lot for me over the years. I'd make sure I did what I could to make her life easier. Plus I wanted her and Dani to have a good relationship.

"You sure you want to do this?" Beast asked.

"Yeah. I need to." At the very least, I wanted to see the fuckers who'd thought they could hurt Danica and get away with it. They'd been rounded up while I'd been getting everything ready for my wedding. Even if I hadn't had a hand in bringing them in, I needed to see them. Hurt them. They'd come after my woman. My wife. I knew Cowboy would want his daughter avenged. My guess was they had no idea who her dad was outside the rodeo. They only knew him as a rodeo champion, long retired.

He nodded. "All right. Well, Hatchet wants to finish it. I think he's earned the right since his daughter suffered at their hands. Not to downplay what Danica's been through, but they didn't go beyond stalking her. We know these men were the ones harassing Danica, and one of them slipped up and admitted to being part of the crew who hurt Raven."

I agreed. If anyone deserved to end their lives, it was Hatchet. I couldn't imagine not only discovering I had a child, but also hearing about all the horrible things these men had done to her. I was amazed Hatchet hadn't gone over the edge.

"These two the only ones who were watching Danica?" I asked.

"Yeah. Lewis harassed her at a few events, but these were the two leaving her letters and breaking into her truck. Lewis was the main instigator of everything, but these bottom feeders enjoyed hurting the women Lewis targeted."

I removed my cut and shirt before facing them. The two men hanging from the ceiling didn't look like much. Neither were in shape, and one was missing a few teeth already. The thought of either of them touching my wife sickened me. I thought of all the women they'd destroyed. The ones they'd terrorized, then stood back while Lewis beat the hell out of them and raped them. They were scum. The lowest of the low. If we didn't put them in the ground, they'd go after someone else.

"You boys fucked up," I said. "You should have never come after my wife."

Since they were both gagged, I couldn't understand anything they tried to say. I had a feeling it would be either a bunch of whining, or cussing. I didn't much care to listen to either. Instead, I got to work. Using my fists, I pummeled them both. I slammed my knuckles into first one and then the other, breaking as many ribs as I could. I wouldn't kill them. Hatchet would get that honor. I just wanted to make them suffer as much as possible.

I used them as punching bags until they were

choking on their own blood. As much as I wanted to toy with them for hours, making them wish they were dead, I saw Hatchet pacing, waiting for his turn. He needed this more than I did. If anything, I needed to be home with Dani. I didn't want her to look back on our wedding and remember I'd disappeared that night instead of spending it with her.

I'd planned to leave with Hatchet and go after the others. I knew that wouldn't be the right choice. Not now. Lewis was the only one left who'd been after Danica. As badly as I wanted to see the fucker bleed, I knew Hatchet would do his best to draw out the man's misery. He wouldn't let Lewis go easy.

"They're all yours," I said, going to the sink to wash my hands. I made sure I didn't have blood elsewhere before putting my shirt and cut back on.

"You sure?" Hatchet asked, eyeing the two men.

"Yeah. I need to get home to Dani. I won't be going with you." I saw the way his fingers twitched, and knew he wanted to get his hands on these men, and all the others. "Just make sure Lewis knows why you're torturing him. Not just for your daughter, but for all of them, including Dani."

He nodded. "Consider it done."

I walked out and got on my bike, heading home to my wife. She'd wonder about my bruised knuckles, but I hoped she didn't ask too many questions. I wouldn't be giving her answers, other than to tell her she was safe.

Cowboy and Jacey had retired to the guest house for the night, which meant Dani was alone at home. It ate at me, knowing I'd abandoned her tonight, even if only for a little while. If she forgave me, I'd count my blessings. Beating those men had been cathartic. I'd even go so far as to say I enjoyed it. Didn't mean it had been the right choice. Would I look back ten years from now and regret the decision I'd made?

I walked into the house and noticed the silence. All the lights were off as I made my way to the bedroom. I quietly opened the door and stepped inside. Even in the darkness, I could see the shape of her under the covers. I stripped off my clothes and decided to take a shower before getting into bed. Even though I hadn't noticed any blood on me before I'd come home, I didn't want to start our marriage feeling dirty. I might not have killed those men, but I would have.

I started the shower and climbed under the spray before it had a chance to heat. The cold made me shiver a moment. Reaching for the shampoo, I lathered my hair and rinsed before picking up the soap. I scrubbed at my skin, wanting to wash away any filth that might cling to me. Danica was sweet. Innocent. She deserved better than me. Too bad I'd never let her go.

When I'd finished, I got out and dried off. I tossed the towel over the rack before I went to the bedroom and slipped into bed next to my wife.

Dani turned toward me, seeking me out even in her sleep. I held her close and kissed the top of her head, breathing her in. My Dani girl. With her in my arms, I felt at peace. I'd leave Lewis and the others to Hatchet and whoever else wanted to chase after them. My club still had my loyalty, and I'd do whatever job Beast assigned me. But my priority would be Dani, now and always. Her and whatever children we had.

I held her closer, wondering if maybe she could be pregnant already. The thought of her growing round with our baby made me smile. The house wasn't overly large, but I hoped she wanted at least two or three kids. I'd grown up an only child and I had to wonder if I'd had a sibling would things have been easier.

Dani stirred and her eyes slowly opened. "Parks?"

"I'm here, honey."

"Everything go okay?" she asked, her voice still thick with sleep.

"Yeah. I decided Hatchet needed to handle this more than I did. I've handed it all over to him. I won't be going anywhere, unless Beast sends me on a different job." I ran my hand down her back. "Which means I'm yours. Whatever you want to do, we'll do it."

"I haven't met your family yet. Why weren't they here for the wedding?" she asked.

I'd wondered when she'd ask about them. I'd honestly thought she'd ask at the wedding. I hadn't kept it from her on purpose. There just hadn't been a good time to bring it up. Wire had already emailed a copy of the video to me, and I'd sent it to my mother. It wouldn't be the same as her having been there, but it would have to do.

"I called Mom. She and my stepdad are both sick. They want us to visit after they're better and know they aren't contagious. I gave them my word we would. Might be a few days, or more than a week. Hard to say for sure."

She trailed her finger down the center of my chest. "You know, it's our wedding night."

"Mm. So it is. Any particular way you'd like to celebrate?" I asked.

She smiled at me. "With orgasms?"

I laughed and rolled her under me, getting a good look at her. She'd put on some slinky pajama set that I couldn't wait to take off her. Her breasts nearly spilled from the top and I leaned down, rubbing my five-o'clock shadow over the swells before kissing them.

"Parks." She ran her fingers through my hair, holding me close. "I need you."

"You have me, honey. I'm yours, and you're mine. From now until eternity."

I peeled the sexy shorts down her legs and tossed them aside, groaning when I saw she hadn't worn panties under them. I shoved the top up over her breasts and leaned down to take her nipple into my mouth. She tasted so damn sweet. I tugged on the hard peak with my teeth. Danica shivered and arched up. I took my time, lavishing attention on both breasts.

I moved my hand down between her thighs and slid my fingers along her wet pussy. I'd barely gotten started and already she nearly dripped from how badly she wanted me. My cock throbbed as I worked a finger inside her, dragging it in and out. Slowly. She made the cutest sounds as she wiggled underneath me.

Stroking her clit with my thumb, I added a second finger, pumping them in and out of her. I wanted her to come multiple times before I got inside her. I had a feeling once I felt her pussy wrapped around my cock, I wouldn't be able to hold on long. Sex between us had been amazing so far, but knowing she was my wife now? It felt different. Better.

"Come for me, beautiful. Show me just how wet you can get," I murmured.

"Parks, it feels so good. *You* feel good."

"God, Dani. I've never wanted anyone as much as I want you. You turn me inside out."

I added a third finger, driving in deep. She cried out and I felt the walls of her pussy clench down. Another two strokes and she was coming. Her release soaked the bed as she squirted.

"Fuck! You're driving me crazy, honey. I need to taste you."

I pulled my fingers from her and slid down, shoving her thighs farther apart with my shoulders. I spread her pussy open and groaned at how pretty and pink she was. I lapped at her, flicking my tongue against her clit. I circled the bud before lashing it with my tongue.

"Parks! I… I… God, I think I'm coming again."

Fuck yes! I sucked her clit into my mouth, giving it a hard tug with my lips. She screamed and bucked. I heard her suck in a breath and felt her shudder. I licked her pussy until the last tremor had worked its way through her, then I crawled up her body, letting my cock brush against her.

"You ready for me, honey?" I asked.

She nodded. "More than."

I pushed inside her, my arms shaking as I fought for control. I wanted to drive into her, take her like a savage beast. But this was our wedding night. I needed to worship her. Show her how much I loved her. Adored her.

I looked down, watching as she stretched to take me. One of these days, I'd convince her to let me film us having sex. I'd make sure no one else ever saw it. Seeing her body take me, hearing her beg for me, had me so fucking hard.

"I love watching us together like this," I said, pulling back, then pushing inside her again.

"Parks, I… I want to try it a different way."

I stopped and looked at her. It was true I'd only taken her face-to-face so far. What exactly did she want? "How do you want me to fuck you?"

Her cheeks turned crimson. "From behind?"

I pulled out of her, then flipped her onto her stomach. Tugging her up onto her knees, I shoved her thighs apart. "Keep your cheek against the bed, Dani. Ass in the air. You want it hard? Deep?"

"Yes! Please, Parks!"

I lined up my cock and sank into her one inch at a time. Hottest fucking thing I'd ever seen. I took her slow, unable to look away from the sight of us joined together. When I knew I was getting close, I pressed my chest to her back, curving over her body. Bracing one hand on the bed and holding onto her hip with the other, I rode her, taking what I wanted and giving her exactly what she'd asked for.

"That's it, Dani. Take it." Her cheeks flushed and her lips parted. I felt her tightening around me. I drove into her harder. My hips slapped against her, the bed slamming into the wall with every stroke. Dani screamed out my name as she came, and the heat of her release triggered mine.

I filled her up, thrusting until every drop of cum had been wrung from me. I didn't want to pull out. I kissed her cheek. Her shoulder. I ran my nose along the length of her neck. When I started to soften, I knew I didn't have a choice anymore. I sighed as I sat back on my heels, my cock slipping from her body. She started to close her thighs. I reached out, holding them open, loving the sight of her pussy covered in my cum.

I'd never felt the need to mark anyone before. If I thought I had another orgasm in me, I'd jerk one out and spray cum all over her ass and back. I liked seeing my release on her. I ran my fingers over her pussy, rubbing my scent into her skin.

"Parks, I need to get cleaned up."

Not tonight she wasn't. I lay down next to her, drawing her back against my chest. I cupped her breast in my hand and held her close. "Just get some rest, Dani girl. No reason to get cleaned up. I plan to make you dirty again."

She sighed and her body relaxed. "All right. But if I'm glued to the sheets when I wake up, you better hope it doesn't rip out what little hair I have down there. I'll be pissed."

I chuckled and kissed the side of her neck. "No hair ripping. I'll make sure you're so wet, nothing will stick to you."

"Why do I get the feeling I won't be able to walk for a few days?" she asked, her voice getting softer as sleep pulled at her.

"Because I'm going to fuck you every chance I get. Not just tonight, but every night for the rest of our lives. I love you, Dani. I can't wait to start a family with you."

She hmm'd at me. "Maybe we already have."

I heard a soft snore escape her and knew she'd fallen asleep. And not too long after, so did I.

Chapter Thirteen

Two Weeks Later
Danica

I couldn't remember a time I'd felt so scared. Not this sort of fear. Having Lewis stalk me was one thing. Meeting my in-laws? What if they hated me? Parks' family had called, letting us know they were no longer sick. It had taken a few days for him to get someone to take care of my horses. I'd thought we'd make it a day trip, but since learning I was pregnant, he'd been overly cautious with me. Which meant he didn't want to drive a few hours from home only to turn around and drive back that same day. Instead, we were staying overnight and wouldn't return until tomorrow night.

He pulled into the driveway, and I checked out the house and barn. I'd thought we had a lot of horses, but his family looked like they had at least two dozen. Maybe more. They were beautiful. I could sit and watch them all day.

"I can't believe you got to grow up here," I said.

"It's beautiful, but a lot of work."

"I'm sure. Your mom and stepdad take care of all this on their own?"

"They have for a lot of years. When they got sick, they called in some help. I think they decided to keep them on. There's a small house out back. It was originally the foreman's house, except my stepdad didn't have one. It came with the property."

"My parents would love this place," I said.

"We'll bring them with us sometime. I'm sure Mom would love to meet them. Frank would too."

"Frank?" I asked.

"My mom is Rosalee, and Frank is my stepdad. Their last name is Rochester."

"And your father? Or sperm donor? I don't know how you think of him," she said.

"Sperm donor works. His name is Faizal Saeed. Since I turned eighteen, he's dropped all contact with us. Guess he figured his part in my life was finished since he hadn't wanted me."

"I'm sorry. Do you ever wonder about that part of your heritage? If your dad isn't around to tell you about your family, how will you ever learn about them?"

"I won't." He glanced at me. "Frank is my dad. Not by blood, but he raised me. He was there for me, every day of my life."

"I can't wait to meet him, and your mom." I twisted my hands in my lap. "What if they don't like me?"

"They're going to love you, Dani. Take a breath. Everything will be fine."

I hoped he was right.

We came to a stop near the house and Ranger got out. He walked around and opened my door, helping me down from the truck. He held my hand as we walked up to the porch. Before we had a chance to knock, the door opened and a couple who had to be Rosalee and Frank stood in front of us.

"'Bout time you came home, boy," Frank said, reaching out and pulling Ranger into a hug. He pounded on his back before turning to me. I squeaked as he yanked me into his arms and gave me a tight hug too. "Welcome to the family, Danica."

"Thank you."

He released me and Rosalee grabbed onto me. For a moment, I worried she wouldn't let go. When she did, she pulled her son to her. They looked nothing alike. It was clear he'd gotten his looks from the Saeed line.

"Come in! I'm sure you'd like a drink after that long drive," Rosalee said.

Their home was warm and inviting. The hardwood floors were a dark maple. They weren't perfect. I could see the scratches and scarring of a well-loved home. I wondered how many were from Ranger when he was little. The walls were a warm honey color.

"Have a seat," Frank said, waving toward two brown leather couches.

Rosalee hurried from the room only to return a few minutes later carrying a tray with a pitcher of tea and four glasses. I couldn't remember ever having someone serve drinks on a tray, except at restaurants. She'd also brought out crackers with some sort of spread.

"Thought you might be hungry," she said.

"Thank you. It looks great." Or it did until the smell hit me. My throat burned and my eyes went wide. I stared at Ranger, willing him to understand. He stood, dragging me down the hall and pointed to the bathroom.

I rushed inside and hit my knees, almost missing the toilet. I threw up until I was dry heaving.

"Oh, dear. Is she sick?" Rosalee asked from the hallway.

"No, Mom. I mean, yeah, but not like that. She's pregnant."

I heard Rosalee gasp, and I took a shuddering breath. "Sorry."

"Honey, you have nothing to apologize for. Come on. You can rinse out your mouth and we'll go sit again. Do you know what triggered it this time?" he asked.

"I think it's the spread. The smell hit me and suddenly my stomach revolted."

"I'll switch it for something else," Rosalee said. I heard her footsteps retreat and I slowly climbed to my feet.

Ranger handed me a mini bottle of mouthwash he found in the bathroom cabinet. I poured some into one of the disposable cups in a dispenser on the counter and swished. After I spit, I rinsed one more time before I tossed the cup into the trash.

"Feel better?" Ranger asked, rubbing my back.

"Yeah. I hope I didn't ruin anything."

He pulled me into his arms and hugged me. "No, honey. I'd planned to tell them about the baby. We just upped the timeline by a few minutes or so."

We went back to the living room, just in time to see Rosalee and Frank sharing a look. When they turned their gazes toward us, I couldn't tell if they were happy about the news or upset. Ranger sat and pulled me down onto his lap.

"Before you ask, no, we didn't get married because she's pregnant. We only found out about the baby last week when she kept throwing up. I made her see the doctor to make sure she hadn't picked up whatever bug the two of you had, or anything else going around right now."

"Then why the rushed wedding?" Frank asked.

Ranger laced our fingers together. "You know I'm part of the Reckless Kings. Danica is my old lady. I'd claimed her before I even thought to ask if she'd like to get married. We decided to get married when her family was visiting. Her dad wanted to walk her down the aisle. It's why we couldn't wait on the two of you to get better."

"Your family doesn't live nearby?" Rosalee

asked.

"No, ma'am. I'm from Alabama. My family still lives there. They came to visit and bring some of my things. My parents have horses, so they couldn't be away for too long."

Rosalee and Frank shared another look before she turned me with a big smile on her face. "Horses? You ride?"

"Danica is a barrel racer. She's won a lot of rodeos," Ranger said. "Her dad is a champion bronc rider."

"Who's your dad?" Frank asked.

"Ty Adler."

His eyebrows rose. "I've seen him ride. I've heard he has a son who rides bulls."

I nodded. "My little brother, Jackson. We have another brother, but Langston is still in elementary school. He already knows how to rope and ride. Wouldn't surprise me if he decides to ride in the rodeo too."

"Well." Frank smiled at Ranger. "I'm glad to see you found your way back to your roots, even if it was through your wife."

Ranger winced. "I'm sorry I haven't been around as much as I should have. And for not staying here at the house when I did come by. Living in this town wasn't easy. I ran first chance I had, by joining the Army."

Rosalee looked down at her hands, twisting them in her lap. "I'm sorry, Parks. We knew you were having trouble in school, even when you denied it. We should have stepped in. Done something to make it better."

"You did fine, Mom."

"Will you be coming around more often?" Frank

asked.

I looked at Ranger before answering. "Yes, we will. It won't be for long trips. I have two horses at the house, and there aren't a lot of people with the Reckless Kings who know how to take care of them. I won't trust my babies with just anyone."

Rosalee and Frank both seemed pleased by my answer, although I had a feeling it was more my comment on the horses than anything else.

"Danica, I remember being tired all the time during my pregnancy. Parks wasn't the easiest baby even before he was born. If you feel the need to rest, I've put you both in Parks' old room. He can show you where it is." Rosalee stood and gave me another hug. "I'm so glad he found you."

"Me too." I brushed a kiss against his cheek. "He's the best thing that ever happened to me."

"So, how did the two of you meet?" she asked.

I leaned against Ranger as he spent the next hour telling his parents about his first glimpse of me at a rodeo, and about meeting me at the Dixie Reapers. He told them about the wedding and gave them some of the pictures we'd had printed. Rosalee found a frame and immediately put one out on their mantle.

By lunch, I was fading fast. I took a nap and gave Ranger a chance to catch up with his family. It seemed like it had been a long time since he'd been home. Before I closed my eyes, I looked around his room. It didn't seem to have changed much since he'd been in high school. The posters of women in bikinis were still on the walls. It was the only personal touch in the space. The furniture and bedding were generic. But the mattress felt like a cloud.

My eyes started to close, and I knew I'd be out for a while. Every time I threw up, it seemed to drain me. I'd promised Ranger I'd go back to the doctor when we returned home. He worried something was wrong with me or the baby, even though I insisted I was all right.

I seriously hoped I wasn't lying to him -- or myself.

Epilogue

One Month Later
Ranger

It no longer surprised me when I found Danica asleep in our bed, even in the middle of the day. The doctor assured us she should feel less fatigued by the second trimester, which meant we had another five weeks to go, assuming he was correct on her date of conception.

I'd planned to tell her Lewis and all his minions were no longer an issue. Hatchet had tracked down the last of them and made sure they'd never harm another person. It would have to wait. She didn't live in fear. Even knowing those men were still out there, she trusted me and the Reckless Kings to take care of her. Sharing my news could be postponed until a better time.

I stripped out of my clothes and crawled into bed with her. Dani curled into me, and I hugged her to my chest. This was one of my favorite parts of the day. I loved holding my wife, even when she slept. We'd only been married a month and a half, but already I knew my life wouldn't be the same without her. If she were to die tomorrow, I'd follow her to the other side.

"What time is it?" she murmured.

"Little after lunch. Did you eat something?"

She nodded. "Lyssa brought over some homemade chicken pot pie. There's a plate for you too."

I rubbed her back. The Pres' wife had been feeding us several times a week. My sweet Dani tired easily, and I didn't like her expending so much energy in the kitchen. I'd gladly eat PB&J for every meal if it meant she got the rest she needed.

"Other than needing a nap, how do you feel today?" I asked.

"Better. Not as nauseated. I haven't thrown up since yesterday morning."

"Good. Maybe that part of the misery is finally over. Another four to six weeks and hopefully you won't be tired all the time either."

"Do we have to get up or can we stay in bed a bit longer?" she asked.

"I'll stay in bed with you as long as you want me to."

She snorted. "I hope you understand I meant just like this and not having sex. I'm not sure I'm up for that right now."

"No problem, Dani girl. I'll just wait. By dark, you'll be aching for me. You'll beg for my cock, and I'll get to make you come so much you won't be able to walk in the morning."

She lifted her head to glare at me. "That's not true. I'm not that horny *every* night."

"No, some nights you only want sex once."

She huffed at me, and I lightly smacked her ass. She knew I was telling the truth. If it weren't for the nausea and fatigue, she'd have been on my cock every second of the day, or at least she'd have tried. It was a perk I hoped would last until it was no longer safe for us to have sex. The doctor warned that by the third trimester we might have to hold off, depending how she carried and her overall health.

According to Beast, Lyssa hadn't had to abstain until the very end. I could only hope Danica had that same luck. Or rather, that I did. Not having sex with my beautiful wife for months would be the hardest damn thing I'd ever do. I seriously hoped it didn't come to that.

She wiggled against me, and I smiled, knowing what she needed. I slipped my hand between us and worked my fingers into her panties. She gasped as I brushed over her clit.

"Oh, God. Parks."

"You know you want to come, Dani girl. Let me make you feel good."

"Yes! Yes, make me come."

I nuzzled her. "You want my fingers or my mouth?"

"Both. And your cock. I want it all."

"Greedy girl," I murmured.

I rolled her to her back and stripped away her clothes. Spreading her thighs, I trailed my fingers over her slick pussy. I rubbed her clit, backing off each time she got close to coming. It didn't take much to get her off right now. I'd barely touched her the other night before she soaked the bed. Hottest thing ever.

I lay between her thighs and licked her pussy. I worked two fingers inside her as I flicked her clit with my tongue. I gave it quick, short strokes before circling the bud a few times. When I licked it again, I drove my fingers into her, curling them a little when I pulled back. Danica whimpered and her hips lifted.

"That's my girl," I murmured. "Come for me, honey."

"Parks."

I worked her pussy with my lips, tongue, and fingers, until she'd come twice. She lay panting, her legs open. I sat up, leaning back on my knees. Hooking her legs over my arms, I lowered her onto my cock. I held her ass off the bed, thrusting up into her.

"So hot. So wet." I fucked her harder, watching her breasts bounce with every stroke. "Do you have any idea how sexy you are?"

"Parks, please."

"Please what?"

"Make me come again. I need it. Need it so bad."

I managed to slide my hand over her belly and down to her pussy. I worked her clit with my thumb while I drove my cock into her again and again. She let out a loud, keening cry as her pussy clenched on me. The wet gush of her release was almost more than I could take. My balls drew up and before I could say another word, I was coming.

"Fuck!" I pounded into her. "So. Fucking. Good!"

When I had nothing left to give, I eased her down onto the bed. I curled myself around her, kissing every part of her I could reach. "I love you, Dani. More than words could ever say."

"Love you too, Parks."

"If I were to die with you in my arms, I'd be at peace. You're all I want or need, Danica Saeed. My old lady. My wife. My everything. You're my entire world."

She didn't say anything, and I looked down, smiling when I realized she'd fallen asleep again. I didn't need to hear her say it back. She showed me every day how much she loved me. It was in the way she made my favorite meals, when she felt up to cooking. The way she took care of our home. Took care of me.

I was the luckiest bastard ever, because I had the most amazing woman by my side. Together, we could overcome anything. I might be her king, but she was my queen. And for her, I'd move heaven and earth. Lay waste to anyone who dared keep us apart. She was the sun. The moon. She was my heart and the other half of my soul. Without her, I was nothing. With her, I knew I could conquer the world.

Fox (Hades Abyss MC 7)
Harley Wylde

Raven -- I learned the hard way not to trust anyone. First the men who'd hurt me, and then my mother when she turned her back on me. I had no one. Was it any wonder I didn't think I had a reason to keep living? A good Samaritan had other ideas, landing me in a psychiatric hospital. Too bad the guards were every bit as evil as those men I'd trusted.

I thought I'd die alone. Unwanted. Unloved. Forgotten. Until the Hades Abyss MC came to take me away. They claim my father sent them, except I've never met him. Don't even know his name. I'd try to run, but what's the point? Besides, there's one man who makes me feel safe. Fox. It doesn't matter that he's older than me. When he holds me, I know nothing will ever hurt me again. I just didn't count on losing my heart to him.

Fox -- Breaker brought Hatchet's daughter to the clubhouse, and the moment I looked into those vacant eyes, I knew she'd been badly broken. Some part of me wanted to fix her. Put the pieces back together. Watch her eyes light up and see her smile. She thinks she's dirty, that no one will ever want her. She's wrong. I want her. I even want the baby growing inside her.

Never thought I'd find the woman meant to be mine. Now that I've had Raven in my arms, chased away her nightmares, kissed her tears away, I know I can't let her go. I'll make her mine -- the baby too -- and I won't let anyone stand in my way.

Prologue

Raven

I hated the dark. I shuffled down the alley, heading for the back of the local diner. My skin prickled and it felt like ants crawled over me. My feet scraped along the pavement as I made my way closer to the dim light over the side entrance door. Not much farther.

The scratching of rats made me shiver. At least they wouldn't hurt me. I much preferred the furred type of vermin to the two-legged variety. I clawed at my arms, popping open scabs. Blood trickled from the wounds. I wiggled my fingers as the droplets fell to the ground below. Every sound made me twitch and jump. Shadows reached for me.

Nearly there. I paused just outside the spread of light and waited. I listened. Watched. When I didn't hear anyone coming, I hurried to see if I could find something to eat. I dug through and found half a sandwich. Pulling it out, I took a bite while I sifted through more of the garbage. I found a bruised apple, still whole. I slipped it into my pocket for later and snatched an open half-full bag of chips from the dumpster.

It wouldn't last long. It never did, but at least I wouldn't starve tonight or tomorrow. Finding shelter would be the biggest issue. At least a safe place to sleep. I didn't trust anyone. Not after what the cowboys did to me. I picked at the scabs on my arm again and rushed off, sticking to the shadows as I cleared the alley and nearly ran down the street.

An old parking garage loomed in the distance. I'd stayed there before. Most of the floors had been inhabited by others living on the streets. I avoided those people. Didn't know who to trust. Quiet as I could, I made my way to the structure, pausing when anyone got too close. Finally, I reached the parking structure and crept inside. I skirted around the people on each level until I found an empty one.

I took off my backpack and shoved it into the corner, using it to cushion me as I crammed myself into the tight spot, hoping to go unnoticed. Light didn't reach me, and I hoped its absence would keep me safe. I'd finished my sandwich and didn't dare eat the apple and chips, even if my stomach did still rumble.

Twisting, I unzipped the backpack and pulled out the small notebook and pen. I'd been scribbling in it the last few days. It kept me from losing myself completely. Although, the marks on my arms suggested otherwise. Even if I couldn't see the blood, I could feel it. The scabs would reform, but what was the point? I'd just open them again. Or make new cuts. It allowed me to bury the pain of what happened and take back a little control.

I didn't need the light to write. It didn't matter if it looked pretty. No one would read it. I only put the words on the page as a way to soothe the demons plaguing me. It never worked for long. No sooner would I purge the darkness inside me than more would seep in. I couldn't escape.

I pondered the bag at my back and stared blankly at the notebook in my hand. It wasn't entirely true, though. There would be *one* way to get away from it all. No more pain. No more nightmares. I wouldn't have to worry about anyone hurting me again. My fingers tightened on the pen.

Don't do it, Raven.

I wrote a little more, hoping it would be enough to dispel the ugliness brewing in my gut. I couldn't remember what it had felt like to be happy. Didn't think I'd ever feel it again. Mom hadn't wanted me back. Not after what happened. She'd called me a whore. Said I'd gotten what I deserved. That had been the first night I'd cut my arms. Not deep enough to bleed out, but the pain had helped a little. It had soothed the dark voices in my mind.

I poured everything out on the page in the little notebook. I felt the burn of tears as I remembered how I'd gotten here. Each and every filthy thing they'd done to me. The way it had felt when they touched me. The pain when they'd tried to tear me apart. It even eclipsed knowing my own mother hadn't wanted me.

Alone. Always alone.

Unwanted. Unloved.

The darkness calls to me.
Surrounds me.
It closes in from all sides.
Presses against me.
Fills me.
I welcome the nothingness.
A respite from the pain.
From the memories.
I'm dirty.
Tainted by their hands.
They ripped me from the light.
Now I dwell in the dark.
The shadows.
The emptiness.
Not even death can save me.

I shoved the pen and notebook back into my bag and stared at the glint of silver toward the bottom. The last phrase echoes in my mind. *Not even death can save me.* But what if it could? Reaching in, I gripped the handle of the knife I'd swiped from an outdoor dining area when no one had been looking. I'd cleaned the blade, but knew it now had the stain of my blood on it. I turned my arm over and took a breath before making the first cut.

The coppery scent hit my nose, and it felt like a dam inside me broke. Before I could second-guess myself, I cut again. And again. And again. Every slice of my skin brought relief. I couldn't seem to stop myself. The next cut went deeper, and I knew I couldn't turn back. I managed to cut the other side, feeling a strange sort of peace settle over me.

Dropping the knife beside me, I let my arms fall to my sides and stared into the nothingness. Waiting. Would I go to heaven? Or did the devil have a seat saved for me in hell? Anything would be better than the life I'd been living.

I felt my heart slowing as my blood pooled on the concrete. Everything went hazy and darkness crept into the edges of my vision. It wouldn't be long now. Soon, it would be over.

It never occurred to me someone would save me.

Too bad they didn't realize they were consigning me to a different sort of hell.

One I didn't think I'd ever escape from.

Chapter One

Raven
Six Months Later

Balmoral Psychiatric Hospital looked nice from the outside. Anyone visiting would think it peaceful. They didn't know the evil hidden in the night. Not even the doctors knew but trying to tell them never worked. They only upped my meds and muttered about hallucinations, delusions, and whatever else they decided to write in my file. They didn't realize I spoke the truth. Their precious staff became monsters once night fell. Or maybe they were always monstrous, but the masks slipped once the sun sank below the horizon.

It hadn't taken long before I stopped trying to talk to anyone. About anything. I'd remained mute for so long, I didn't know if my voice would even work anymore. Didn't matter. No one wanted to speak to me, except the doctor who only tried to shove more pills down my throat. Anything to make me better. Whatever that meant.

As long as I remained here, I'd never heal. The night guards would make sure of it. After the first time, I'd told the doctors. It hadn't gotten me anywhere, and next time, the guards were rougher with me. I tried to end it all. Hung myself with my sheets. It only landed me a spot on their suicide watch, and a room with nothing more than a pad on the floor and a toilet in the corner. It still hadn't saved me from the night guards. I'd been trapped, until I'd assured them I wouldn't try again, and managed to make them believe me.

During the day, I enjoyed a bit of freedom. Other than meeting with the doctor and going to a few group therapy sessions, I could roam the Rec room. We had puzzles, crayons and coloring books, a TV mounted high on the wall, and some magazines. Mostly, I chose to sit in a chair and stare out the barred windows. The world kept moving, people going about their day, while I'd been stuck in hell for far too long. Attempting to kill myself never seemed to work. I didn't know what else to do.

The sun sank beyond the horizon and my stomach knotted. I knew what would happen next. A chime sounded, letting everyone know we needed to move to the cafeteria for dinner. I followed the group from the Rec room, my skin crawling as I passed Guard Simmons. He winked at me, letting me know he'd be by later. As if I wanted him to touch me.

I went through the line and accepted my tray with bites of grilled chicken, rice, and carrots. Nothing I'd need to cut. None of us were allowed to use knives of any sort. Not even plastic ones. Even forks were forbidden. I picked up a napkin, spoon, and juice before heading to the nearest table. We didn't have assigned seating, but since I hadn't made friends, it didn't matter whose table I joined. None of them would speak to me. I'd made sure of it by keeping to myself.

The food tasted bland. The chicken and carrots had been overcooked. When I'd first arrived, I'd inhaled my food, so thankful to have regular meals. The guards had left me alone the first two days. It had almost seemed a bit like paradise here. Roof over my head. Full belly. Afterward, I'd have starved myself to death if I could. I forced myself to eat every bite, knowing if I didn't, I'd get a lecture tomorrow about needing to eat nutritious meals. They didn't realize anything would be a step up from eating out of dumpsters, but no amount of food would change what happened to me after lights out. How could I enjoy anything knowing I'd have nightly visitors?

Dinner only meant one thing to me these days. It was nearly time for my nightly torment to begin. I couldn't look forward to a meal when I knew about the monsters waiting for me when I had to return to my room.

By the time I'd finished, the next chime sounded. I carried my tray to the stack by the door and headed down the hallway. Each patient went into their room. I kept walking until I reached the end of the hall and stopped to stare at my door. I didn't want to go inside.

"Raven!"

I flinched as Guard Larson barked my name. I glanced in his direction. His eyebrows were raised as he looked from me to the door. Steeling myself, I went into my room, waiting for him to come by and lock me in. Crawling across my bed, I didn't bother yanking the covers over my head. It wouldn't help. I took deep breaths, trying to remain calm.

Minutes ticked by and the hospital began to quiet. The woman in the room next to mine started snoring, and I knew the guards would be by any minute. Once the nurse decided everyone would be quiet for a bit, she'd slip outside to smoke, and the guards would take advantage. She took three breaks every shift, and the guards came to my room one at a time after she'd left her post. Sadly, they tormented more than me, but the others kept their mouths shut. I often wondered if they'd learned to keep quiet the hard way, like I had.

My heart pounded in my chest at the squeak of shoes outside my door. I heard the lock twist before the door opened and then shut softly.

"How's my girl doing?" Guard Simmons asked. "Been eager and waiting?"

I didn't answer. I never did. I heard him move closer and saw his shadowy outline. He ran his fingers through my hair, and I forced myself to hold still. I heard the clink of his belt buckle and the rasp of his zipper. At first, I'd cried. I'd begged and pleaded. It hadn't gotten me anywhere. Now I knew to endure it, keep my mouth shut, and wait for it to be over.

His fingers closed around my ankles, and he yanked me to the edge of the bed. He never got it over with quickly. No, Simmons like to draw things out the full fifteen minutes of the nurse's smoke break. Felt like longer. He petted me, murmured disgusting things in my ear. When he reached for the waistband of my pants, I retreated into my mind, hiding from reality.

I usually came back to the present and found myself tucked into bed, a wet stickiness and pain between my legs. This time I heard shouts and what sounded like someone hitting another person. I blinked and tried to focus. Looking over my shoulder, I saw the nurse fluttering in the doorway, her eyes wide and hands dancing as she murmured, "I didn't know," over and over.

I stood on shaky legs, pulled up my pants, and turned to watch a younger, less bulky man trying to beat Guard Simmons into unconsciousness. The man wore jeans, a dark tee, and a black leather vest with writing and a flaming skull on the back. No, a skull with horns and flames. *Hades Abyss MC.*

"Please, Mr. Breaker. You need to stop!" The nurse shifted foot to foot, looking like she wanted to physically pull them apart.

The man she'd called Breaker landed another blow against Guard Simmons' jaw. I realized the man hadn't had time to zip his pants. As he lay on the ground, pleading for Breaker to stop, he suddenly had a knife up against his flaccid cock.

"I should cut this off, since you don't know the proper way to use it," Breaker said. "You think it's okay to rape women?"

"Sh-she likes it," Guard Simmons said.

"No, she fucking doesn't!" Breaker jammed the knife into the guard's thigh. Guard Simmons screamed like a girl and thrashed on the floor. "She'd checked the fuck out in order to put up with your filthy hands on her. That girl has been through hell. You were supposed to keep her safe. Help her. I should gut you right here and now."

The nurse wailed and rushed off, most likely to get help. Breaker stumbled back, his chest heaving with every breath. Fury etched his features, until he turned and saw me watching. The change happened so suddenly. Instead of being angry, I could only see sorrow in his gaze. Breaker held out a hand to me, blood splattered across his fingers. He moved slowly, as if trying to coax a feral animal closer.

"I'm here to help you, Raven. Your dad sent me."

I blinked and shook my head. My dad? I had never met him, nor did I even know his name. Mom hadn't shared it with me. Whenever I'd asked, she'd become tight-lipped and looked like she'd been sucking on lemons. My dad couldn't have sent this man. *Wouldn't* have. Had he known about me, surely he'd have been here sooner. Unless he hadn't cared.

Breaker stopped and dropped his hand. "I know I'm a stranger. Your dad is with another club. The Reckless Kings MC. He goes by Hatchet. He didn't know about you until today. The second he found out where you were and that your mom hadn't aborted you like she claimed, he asked my club to come get you. Will you please come with me?"

I glanced at the guard and saw the hatred in his eyes when he looked at me. If I stayed, things would get worse. Even if I didn't know Breaker, he couldn't hurt me more. Unless he killed me, but death would only be a relief at this point. The way he'd attacked the guard led me to believe he wouldn't force himself on me.

I reached out and took his hand, letting him pull me from the room. The nurse came running down the hall, Guard Larson on her heels. Whatever he saw in Breaker's face made him pause.

"You can't just leave with a patient," Guard Larson said.

"The one your buddy was raping?"

Guard Larson audibly swallowed and glanced at me. I tightened my hold on Breaker's hand, drawing his attention. I looked from him to the guard and back, hoping he'd understand. He seemed to, since his lips thinned, and he growled as he faced Guard Larson again.

"Or maybe I should say the patient you've both been raping?" Breaker asked.

The nurse gasped and stepped away from the guard. At least I knew for certain she hadn't been in on it. She seemed too horrified for her reaction to be faked.

"Here's what's going to happen. I'm walking out of here with Raven, and no one from this hospital and certainly not the law, will come looking for her. If they do, I'll make sure any guards she fingers as her rapists will get the same treatment in the worst prison possible. Are we fucking clear?" Breaker asked.

The nurse nodded. "I'll speak with her doctor

tomorrow. She'll need her medication. I swear I didn't know what was going on."

"Doesn't matter. You aren't exactly helping her out of the goodness of your heart now that you do know. Your ass is on the line, right? Since it happened right under your nose. I have a doctor who will see her. I don't trust any of you fuckers." Breaker led me past them, pausing to look back at Larson. "I find out either of you hurt the nurse to keep her quiet, and things won't go well for you."

He turned and kept going, out the secured door at the end of the hall. We made our way downstairs and into the night. I breathed deep. It had been so long since I'd been in the fresh air.

He led me over to a truck parked at the curb and opened the passenger door. Breaker took a step back, giving me space, and I hauled myself onto the seat. He reached in and buckled me before shutting the door and walking around to the driver's side. When he turned the key, the engine rumbled to life and cool air blasted me from the vents.

"I'm taking you to the clubhouse. It may be loud and rowdy, and I have no idea what we'll walk in on. I need you to know the women there aren't forced to do anything. They come to the clubhouse to party, and they can leave whenever they want." He gazed at me as he put the truck into gear. "No one will hurt you, Raven. Not on my watch."

I trusted him. Or rather, I trusted him more than I had anyone in a long time. No one had ever stood up for me. Not after the incident with the cowboys. Once my mother called me trash and a whore, I lost the last bit of confidence I'd had. The few friends I'd had turned away from me, and it felt like everyone stared when I left the house. I could almost hear them whispering about me. I sat quietly as we drove. The clock on the dash showed the trip had taken nearly an hour when we pulled up to a gate.

Breaker rolled down the window and waved at someone. The gate opened and he eased the truck through, pulling up to a building I assumed was the clubhouse he'd mentioned. Music blasted from inside and trepidation built inside me. He'd warned me women weren't abused here, which made me wonder what I'd see inside that might make me feel otherwise. I unbuckled and opened the door. Before I could get out, Breaker lifted me into his arms.

I tensed but clung to him, not wanting to be dropped to the hard ground.

"Easy," he said. "I don't want you to hurt your feet. And the inside isn't all that clean. Probably best you sit on a stool or chair, but don't put your feet down."

I tried to relax against him as he carried me inside. Smoke filled the air, and I coughed a little. It seemed rude to wave a hand in front of my face. My eyes and throat burned. As I scanned the room, I saw no small number of men wearing leather vests like Breaker. Some had their pants open and women on their knees, sucking them off. I inhaled sharply and tried not to freak the hell out.

They won't hurt you. Maybe if I told myself that enough times I'd believe it.

Breaker walked up to the bar and set me down on an empty stool. The man next to me turned and I froze. His hair was going a little gray. Same for his neatly trimmed beard. He looked me over before focusing on Breaker.

"You really think bringing her here was the best idea?" the man asked.

"Sorry, Fox. If I took her to my place, she might have flipped out. I thought being around other people might be better. Plus, I thought Spider might be here. I have no idea where she's staying."

Fox. The name suited him. The man oozed sex appeal. In his younger days, he'd probably had to beat the women off. For that matter, he could very well have to beat them off now. They all had strange names. Who called their kid Breaker? Or Spider?

"You thought taking her somewhere quiet, and away from all this, would freak her out? But taking a rape victim to a clubhouse where people are openly having sex shouldn't be a problem?" Fox narrowed his eyes. "Were you dropped on your head?"

Breaker tensed. "No."

Fox switched his gaze to me. "Sorry, Raven. You shouldn't have to deal with all this."

"Want me to take her to Church?" Breaker asked.

Fox nodded. "I'll call Spider and gather the other officers. We'll be there in a few minutes. I'll send a Prospect with a bottle of water for her."

Breaker lifted me into his arms again and carried me through the room and down a long hall. He shoved open two doors and cursed as we entered the dark room.

"Shit. I can't find the light switch while I'm holding you. Can you feel along the wall for it?"

I slid my hand from the doorframe outward, then up and down, until I felt the plastic plate. I flipped the switch and blinked at the bright light. Breaker carried me to the long table and pulled out one of the chairs with his booted foot. He set me down, then moved to lean against the wall within view.

"Only patched members are allowed in here," Breaker said. "But I think it's better to discuss your situation in here than out there. You okay with that?"

I nodded and folded my fingers together. So far, the men here hadn't hurt me. If anything, the two I'd met seemed concerned about me. A knock sounded at the doors and Breaker cracked them open, reached out, and pulled a water bottle through the gap before closing it. He handed the drink to me, and I screwed off the top, taking a sip. He probably thought me rude for not saying thank you. It had been so long since I'd spoken, I wasn't sure my voice even worked anymore. My last few months with the doctor had consisted of me nodding or shaking my head to answer questions. Anything more complex he'd had me write out, once he'd realized nothing would make me talk. Even when I wrote my answers, I didn't tell him anything. What would have been the point?

The doors opened and Fox came in, with several other men in his wake. They took a seat, each eyeing me in curiosity, except Fox. I couldn't read his expression. The man with *Spider* on his vest claimed the spot at the head of the table.

"Raven, welcome to the Hades Abyss," Spider said. "I'm the President of this club, for now."

Fox growled and shot a glare at the man. Spider cleared his throat and flipped off Fox before focusing on me again. I didn't know what to make of their interaction. What did he mean by "for now" and why did it seem to upset Fox?

"Hatchet asked us to get you from Balmoral," Spider said. "You'll be safe here until he comes for you. I'm sure you're confused and have questions."

I stared at him. Yes, I had some questions. No, I wouldn't be asking them. I glanced at Breaker and found him watching me, his brow furrowed. He'd likely figured out by now I didn't speak.

"Pres, there's something you should know," Breaker said. "They abused her at Balmoral. The guards raped her. Caught one of them in the act when I got there."

I shifted on my chair and looked down at my lap. And now they all knew. I'd be labeled a whore. Dirty. Just like before. They wouldn't want me here now. Or maybe they'd expect me to join the women in the other room. Breaker had said those women were here voluntarily, but what if he was wrong? What if the women felt they had to do those things?

I heard a roar and jerked my head up in time to see Fox standing and throwing his chair against the wall. I felt my eyes go wide as I watched him proceed to pound his fist into the wall. I saw his knuckles split open and a small sound escaped my throat as I lurched to my feet. He turned, his gaze landing on me. Before I could second-guess myself, I rushed to his side and took his hand in mine, checking on the damage he'd done to himself.

"Sorry, pretty girl." His voice sounded scratchier than before. "Didn't mean to scare you. It pisses me off those men abused their power and did that to you. I want to string them up, torture them, and kill them slowly for daring to touch you."

I lifted my gaze to his and saw the sincerity there. He meant every word. First Breaker had defended me, and now Fox wanted to rip the guards apart? Their quick leap to violence should have scared me. If it had been aimed at me, it certainly would have. Knowing they wanted to hurt the men who'd touched me? It made all the difference. I hadn't realized men like them existed. They might look rough, and liked sex as much as other men, but I had to wonder if maybe deep down they were honest, decent men.

They'd rescued me. Had they done the same for others?

"She hasn't spoken," Breaker said softly. "Not once. Not even when…"

I watched Fox and understanding lit his eyes.

"They told you to be quiet, didn't they?" he asked.

I nodded.

"And if you talked, they'd hurt you." He reached out and cupped my cheek. "You're safe, Raven. Those men won't hurt you ever again. You can scream, cuss. Do whatever you want. You don't have to stay silent anymore."

I felt the burn of a tear slip down my cheek and before I knew it, I was in Fox's arms and sobbing. I hadn't cried in so long. It felt satisfying and horrible at the same time.

"Surge, I need you and any other hackers to look into Balmoral. See what you can find so we can bury those fuckers," Spider said. "Raven, I don't have a place for you to live on your own. Breaker brought you here. Do you want to stay with him?"

I sniffled and looked up at Fox. A slight smile kicked up the corner of his lips and he ran his hand over my hair. "She can stay with me. I have an extra room."

"That what you want, Raven?" Spider asked. "To stay with Fox?"

I nodded, not looking away from the first man to ever make me feel seen. Understood. My heart raced and I trembled, but it wasn't from fear. Not this time. For once, I felt like things might be okay. I didn't know the man they claimed was my father, but if they trusted him, I'd at least meet with him. Until then, I'd stay with Fox. I could feel it deep in my gut that he'd keep me safe. Possibly even from myself. I couldn't promise the dark thoughts wouldn't return. I might always have days where I wanted to end it all.

The thought of staying with Fox made me feel warmer inside. The shadows were still there, pressing in, but they were held at bay. If latching onto Fox would make things better, even a little, then I knew I needed to hold onto him.

Chapter Two

Fox

I didn't know why Raven came to me. If anything, my display of anger should have scared her. Instead, it seemed to have made her feel safe. I couldn't tell if Breaker had wanted her to go with him. He'd blanked his face when Raven rushed over to me. The speculative gleam in Spider's eye didn't bode well. Ever since he'd settled down, he seemed to think all of us needed old ladies.

Raven had been so badly abused I didn't think she'd ever want to belong to someone. She could prove me wrong, but for now, I'd treat her gently and try not to scare her. With some luck, her dad would arrive before too long and take her home with him. I couldn't imagine having a fully grown daughter and not knowing. Then to find out she'd been left to die by men who'd used her? Hatchet had to be losing his mind.

"She doesn't have shoes," Breaker said. "She shouldn't be on this floor."

I looked down and saw her bare feet. Shifting my hold on her, I lifted her into my arms and cradled her against my chest. Raven settled against me, tucking her head under my chin. Breaker's eyebrows shot up and his jaw dropped a little. It seemed she hadn't reacted this way when he'd picked her up to bring her into the clubhouse. I didn't know what to make of it.

"She's going to need clothes and other essentials," I said.

"Luciana has more than she needs. I'll gather a bag of toiletries and bring them over. Don't think her clothes will fit Raven, though. She's a tiny thing," Spider said.

Surge snorted. "Don't let your woman hear that. She'll think you're implying she's fat."

"She knows I love her," Spider said. "No one I'd rather be with."

"I need to make a run to the store," Knox said. "I'll grab a few things just to buy a little time before taking her shopping or ordering shit online. Raven, if you don't want to talk that's fine, but could you write down your sizes?"

She buried her face against me and held on tighter. I gave her a slight squeeze, hoping to reassure her. I didn't understand why she wouldn't write down her sizes. We'd just have to guess and hope we got close enough that whatever Knox brought home would be comfortable for her.

"Get some women's size small pajamas, two shirts, and find some shorts with elastic waist." As much as I hated thinking about someone else buying her under garments, I knew she'd need at least some panties. "Get a package of underwear. Just guess the size best you can. Anything else we can get later."

"Raven, can I hold up your foot to guess your shoe size?" Knox asked, standing and coming close.

If anything, she tried to burrow into me, getting as far from my brother as she could. She hadn't seemed scared when she'd been sitting at the table. What changed?

"Pretty girl, can you hold out a foot for Knox? He won't touch you if you don't want him to, but he needs to use his hand for a rough measurement."

She stuck out her foot, and Knox held his hand up next to it. He gave a brisk nod and walked to the doors. "I'll leave the stuff on your porch and knock. Think it's best I don't come inside until she settles in more."

He left and Spider cracked his neck. "I'll go home and get some soap, shampoo, razors, and that sort of thing bagged up. I'll get a Prospect to drop it by your house. He can leave it on the porch like Knox plans to do, but I'd rather get home and send the stuff over now. She might like a shower."

"I'll take her home and show her where she'll be staying," I said. "If anyone needs me…"

Spider waved me off. "Take the next few days to get her situated. I want her to feel safe while she's here. Don't worry about the rest. I know I've been dumping a lot on you lately, but I'll handle things."

Honestly, as much as he'd been offloading, I'd started to wonder if he planned to step down. He'd already told me a while back when the time came, he'd be handing over the President patch to me. His comment earlier, about being President for now, made me think he was ready to hand the reins over. Technically, the club needed to vote, but I didn't see any of them having a problem with the decision. Far as I knew, no one else wanted the job. Finding a new VP, however, would be interesting.

When I got to the parking lot, I realized I'd ridden my bike. I eyed the machine and wondered if Raven would be willing to ride behind me. She lifted her head and tilted it sideways, as if asking why I'd stopped.

"I rode my motorcycle to the clubhouse. I live just down the road, but I wasn't sure if you'd want to ride behind me or not."

She patted me and I assumed it meant she would be fine. Walking over to the Harley Davidson, I set her on the seat before getting on the bike. I started it and walked it back away from the clubhouse. Once I made sure Raven held on tight enough, I eased down the road toward home, keeping the bike under twenty miles per hour since I didn't know if she'd ever been on one before. Last thing I needed would be her toppling off and ripping her skin open.

At the house, I turned off the bike, swung my leg over the seat, and led Raven into the house. She looked around, taking everything in. I didn't rush her. This would be her home until her dad arrived, and I needed her to feel comfortable. I gave her a brief tour and stopped at the guest room. I never really had company stay over, but I kept a bedroom with a queen-sized bed and dresser just in case. I'd even mounted a small TV on the wall across from the bed.

"This will be your room while you're here," I told her. "You can help yourself to whatever you want in the kitchen, although it's a bit bare at the moment. I'll order some groceries in the morning. I showed you the bathroom a minute ago. Spider will get some girly soaps and stuff to us tonight. I just keep generic shit in there."

She stayed close. I could feel the heat of her body. It bothered me she wouldn't speak. Hearing what she'd been through tonight, and possibly every day since she'd entered Balmoral, I could understand her not wanting to talk. I wondered how long it had been since she last heard her own voice. Or did she talk to herself and just not others?

The doorbell sounded, making her jump a little. I reached out to give her hand a reassuring squeeze. "It's probably the stuff Spider said he'd send. I'll be right back."

I left her to explore on her own while I retrieved whatever the Pres had sent over. I found a plastic bag with bottles of shampoo, conditioner, and shower gel. I also saw a tube of scented lotion, a pack of pink disposable razors, generic shaving gel, and a brand-new lip balm and brush. Even though I never allowed women into my home, I kept a few toothbrushes and extra tubes of toothpaste stocked. I'd make sure she had one of each.

I carried everything to the guest bathroom and set it out on the counter. I placed a razor and shaving cream on the edge of the tub. I heard soft steps behind me and turned to face Raven. She came closer, reaching out and lightly touching each item on the counter.

"They're for you. Do you want to shower?"

She cast a longing look at the shower and nodded. I winced, thinking about why exactly she'd want one tonight. If I'd been the one to pick her up and had witnessed the man hurting her, he'd likely be dead right now. I had a feeling Breaker left him alive, but I hoped like hell Surge found some shit to make the guard's life miserable. Anyone who had hurt Raven had better watch their back. I wouldn't rest until she'd been avenged. The thought of anyone hurting someone so fragile, so sweet, made my stomach sour.

"Um." I rubbed the back of my neck. "Knox hasn't gotten back with your clothes yet. I could loan you a shirt if that's okay?"

She nodded, her gaze still fastened on the shower. I reached over to start the water, placed the shower gel, shampoo, and conditioner on the edge of the tub, and left to get her something to sleep in. When I returned, she'd left the shower curtain open, but had stripped out of her clothes and gotten under the spray. I dropped the shirt and stared, unable to look away.

Why the hell was the curtain open? I opened and shut my mouth a few times, my brain seeming to have short-circuited. I'd ask her about it later. Right now, I needed to get my shit together.

My cock started to harden, and I felt like the worst sort of man for noticing her curves. Her breasts weren't overly large, but the perfect handful, tipped with pretty pink nipples. I swallowed hard. My fingers twitched with the need to touch her. *Fuck.* She deserved better than having me stare at her like this. I needed to get my shit together before I scared her off.

"What happened to you, pretty girl?" I murmured, taking in the scars along her arms and bruises on her hips. I had a feeling the guard had left the marks on her hips, but the others? Had someone done that to her, or had she hurt herself as a way to escape? My gaze shot over to the razor, and I questioned if I should have left it in here. Would she use it to try and end her life? Hopefully the damn things weren't sharp enough to more than nick her. I refused to stare at her while she showered and make her feel like a prisoner.

I picked up the shirt and set it on the counter. Averting my gaze, I backed out of the bathroom and collided with the opposite wall. Leaning against it, I tried to shake the images loose from my mind. The more I learned about Raven, the more I wanted those men to suffer. All of them. The cowboys and the guards at the hospital.

The water shut off and I realized I'd not given her a towel. Cursing under my breath, I closed my eyes and felt my way into the bathroom. I knelt at the sink and opened the cabinet underneath, pulling out a towel. I held it up and felt her take it before I stood and backed away again. I collided with the doorframe and grunted before managing to get out of the room. I waited in the hall and gave her a smile when she stepped out wearing my shirt. It fell to her knees, covering most of her.

"Ready to get some sleep?" I asked.

She appeared hesitant, creeping toward me, but not looking too eager to go to her room. Did she have nightmares from everything she'd endured? I reached out and took her hand, leading her down the hall. When we got to her room, I pulled down the covers and motioned for her to crawl into bed. She slipped under the covers. I started to pull them, but she reached out to stop me. I didn't know what she wanted, until she patted the bed next to her.

"You want me to stay until you fall asleep?" She shook her head and patted the bed again. Did she… "Are you wanting me to stay all night?"

I got a nod and a slight smile. Well, shit. I ran a hand through my hair and wondered if I should do what she wanted or talk her out of it. I wouldn't hurt her. Not intentionally. But I didn't want her to freak out when I got morning wood. I didn't know if she'd understand it was something common and happened every damn day, or if she'd think I wanted her to take care of the problem.

"Raven, earlier… in the bathroom… You didn't shut the curtain." I needed to know what she'd had going through her head. Had she thought she wasn't allowed to shut it? Did she not understand I didn't expect anything of her? Her brow furrowed, and I realized she had no idea why the curtain had been an issue.

"Raven, you can shut the shower curtain. You have a right to your privacy. I don't expect you to…" I gestured with my hand. "You know. Do anything sexual with me."

She tipped her head to the side and frowned at me. Her lips parted like she wanted to speak, but nothing came out. If anything, she seemed frustrated.

"You knew you could shut the curtain, right? That I wouldn't get mad if you did?" I asked.

She nodded. All right. She'd understood. So why… and then it hit me.

"You didn't have a shower curtain at Balmoral, did you?"

She shook her head. Right. No shower curtains, because the patients could use them to hang themselves.

"It didn't occur to you to shut it, did it?"

She shook her head again, her brow smoothing and a slight smile on her lips. Well, at least we had that sorted. She hadn't left it open because she felt she had no choice. She just hadn't thought anything of it after not having a shower curtain for a bit.

"It's okay to shut the shower curtain next time you take a shower."

I heard a fist pounding on the front door and nearly breathed a sigh of relief. I rushed off to answer it, needing to put some space between myself and the sweet woman in my guest room. I found three sacks on the porch and carried them inside. Since I knew they were for Raven, I took them to her room so she could see what Knox had found for her.

"Looks like you have some new clothes," I said, giving her a smile as I set the bags on the bed. "Want to take a peek?"

She reached out to take a sack, then jerked her hand back. I opened the one closest to her and took out three plain shirts. One in blue, another in pink, and a gray one. Knox had picked up three pairs of black knit shorts with an elastic waist so I set those out for her to see as well. She touched the material, rubbing it between her fingers, before craning her neck to see inside the other bags.

"Let's check out bag number two." I pulled out a package of cotton panties and two nightgowns. One had short sleeves and looked like it would fall nearly to her ankles. The soft material had pink and blue flowers all over it. The second… it made me want to knock Knox the fuck out. The silky garment had thin straps and didn't seem very long. I didn't know what the asshole had been thinking when he'd bought it.

Raven touched the silky nightgown, a frown tugging at her lips. Great. Now she'd think I'd planned this shit. I held back a growl, knowing I'd need to confront Knox later.

"Sorry about that, pretty girl. I guess Knox thinks he's funny. You don't have to wear that one."

She wrapped her arms around her middle, eyeing the stuff strewn across the bed. I opened the third bag, hoping there weren't more surprises Raven wouldn't like. I pulled out a pair of flip flops and some black canvas tennis shoes, as well as a small package of no-show socks. Whatever the fuck those were. I also found a package of hair ties in the bottom of the bag.

"Do you want me to wash all this before you wear it?" I asked. "Or do you want a pair of the panties and a nightgown tonight?"

She pushed everything toward me. I took that to mean she wanted it washed.

"I'll take care of it, and I'll need to shower before I come back. Get some rest, okay?"

I set the shoes on the floor by the dresser and picked up everything else. I dropped the hair ties on the bathroom counter before making my way to the laundry room. I set the black shorts aside, not knowing if I should wash them with the other stuff. I'd found some of the clothes I bought from that store had a tendency to bleed the first time I washed it. I tossed everything else into the machine, added detergent, and started the cycle. I'd try to get the shorts cleaned before she needed them tomorrow.

Hurrying past her room, I went to the master bedroom and shut the door. I stripped out of my clothes and went to run the shower. Staring down at my dick, I felt like a sick bastard. Raven had been to hell and back, and the last thing she needed was me getting hard. But fuck! Even with the scars, she'd been beautiful. Closing my eyes, I could see her soft curves. Her perfect breasts and pretty nipples. Her pussy had a fine layer of hair, and I'd seen her clit peeking through the lips.

I groaned and got under the water, knowing I'd need to get myself under control before I went to check on her. I grabbed the soap and slicked my palm before wrapping my fingers around my cock and giving it a stroke. Bracing my other hand on the wall, I bowed my head and shut my eyes again. My heart thundered in my chest as I pictured Raven, lying back with her legs splayed. A slight smile on her lips, and trust in her eyes as she beckoned to me.

I stroked faster, gripping my dick harder. I'd lick her pussy, make her come so she'd be all hot and wet when I slid inside her. Imagining her tight pussy wrapped around my cock, I quickened my strokes. In my mind, I pounded into her sweet pussy, making her cry out and beg for more.

I came so hard my knees nearly buckled, my cum splattering the wall. I let go of my cock and leaned my head against the wall, shame washing over me. The last thing I should have done was picture her like that. She needed my protection.

"You're an asshole," I muttered to myself. "A right fucking bastard."

I rinsed my cum off the wall and quickly washed. I'd go to the clubhouse and get some relief from the girls there, but the mere thought of touching them left me feeling hollow. What the hell was wrong with me?

Looked like I'd be getting a lot better acquainted with my hand until Raven's dad came to get her. I could last that long without sex. Wouldn't be the first time. But staying in the bedroom with her? Shit. I knew without a doubt I'd be hard as fuck, and she didn't need that shit right now. Or ever.

I took my time going back to the guest room, hoping she'd have fallen asleep. After I pulled on fresh boxers and another tee, I checked all the windows and doors, making sure to lock them. With Raven under my roof, I didn't want to take chances. Even if one of my brothers came in, they could startle her. Not everyone knew she was staying with me. Not yet anyway.

My phone started buzzing in my hand. I didn't recognize the number but answered. "Fox."

"I hear you have my daughter." Hatchet. Of course, he'd want to check on Raven.

"Yeah. She just got into bed. In the guest room," I clarified so he wouldn't think I had ulterior motives. "Our Treasurer picked up a few things for her. Depending how long it will take you to get here, I'll need to get more stuff. She came here only wearing the shitty hospital pajamas Balmoral had given her."

"This might take me a while. I'm not going to face her for the first time unless I can tell her the men who'd hurt her are no longer a problem," Hatchet said.

"Then you'll need to add more to your list. The guards at Balmoral..." I trailed off not sure how to tell a father his baby girl had been repeatedly raped in a place that should have kept her safe.

The sounds of something being smashed made me wince. Seemed he'd gotten the gist of what I had left unsaid. I let Hatchet rage as I stood in the hall, waiting on him to finish. I wasn't about to go back into Raven's room while her dad was losing his shit over the phone.

"You keep her safe, Fox. Whatever it takes," he said.

"You have my word, Hatchet. No one will hurt Raven. I'll kill anyone who tries."

He let out a ragged breath. "I'll stay in touch. How… how is she?"

"She won't speak. For whatever reason, she clings to me. I guess I make her feel safe. There are scars on her arms from wrist to elbow. Some worse than others." I cleared my throat. "She's beautiful, Hatchet. And sweet. You'd be proud of how strong she is. She learned to survive, even though she had no one to support her."

"Thanks, Fox. Just… tell her I'm thinking about her, and I'll see her soon. I can't believe her mother kept her from me. If I find that bitch, she's dead."

Couldn't blame him for feeling that way. "Take care of business and don't worry about Raven. She can stay here as long as she needs to."

Hatchet ended the call, and I decided to check on Raven's clothes before I did anything else. The washer had finished, so I tossed her things into the dryer. Then I loaded her shorts into the washer. It wouldn't take them long to dry when I got up in the morning.

I walked softly down the hall. When I got to Raven's room, I'd hoped to find her asleep. Instead, she watched the doorway. If she wanted me to stay in the same bed with her, I needed to make her understand how a man's body worked, without freaking her the fuck out. I had no idea what sort of experience, if any, she'd had before the cowboys raped her. Clearly her luck with men had been utter shit since meeting those fuckers.

She patted the bed again and I went to stand beside it. "Before I agree to stay in here with you tonight, there's something we need to discuss. Or rather, something I need to say, and you'll have to let me know if it's a deal breaker."

Raven tipped her head sideways and waited for me to continue. Too fucking cute. I rubbed at my chest, where an odd ache had started to build. I'd never met someone like her, and I worried I'd get attached while she stayed with me. Maybe Hatchet wouldn't take as long as he'd thought.

"I know men have been hurting you for a long while." She slightly tensed but didn't bolt. I considered that a small win. "Um, I'm guessing you don't know much about men other than the bad parts."

She lifted a shoulder in a shrug. Well, that was clear as mud.

"In the mornings, I...ah..." I cleared my throat. "My dick gets hard in the morning. Doesn't matter if I'm alone or with a woman. For that matter, sometimes my dreams are so real I'll get hard in the middle of the night. If I share the bed with you, I can't stop it from happening, and I'm worried it will freak you out."

She pressed her lips together and her gaze dropped to my crotch. Did she worry I'd be hard right now? I couldn't read her expression at the moment, but the longer she stared at my dick, the more I wanted to run from the damn room.

"It doesn't mean I expect anything from you. Do you understand? It's not something I can control. It will go down on its own, or I can take care of it in the shower."

She still hadn't looked up. I shifted, ready to bolt from the room, when she shocked the shit out of me by reaching out and placing her hand over the front of my boxers. My cock started to get hard, and I tried like hell to make it soften. Thinking of rotting flesh, maggots, or seriously fucked-up porn I'd stumbled across by accident. None of it seemed to help. Fuck my life.

"Raven, if you keep touching me, my dick is going to get harder." She lifted her gaze to mine, a hint of challenge in her eyes. She pressed her hand to me a little tighter. What. The. Fuck? "Pretty girl, you don't want this. You've been hurt. Badly. If you want me to hold you until you fall asleep, I can do that. I won't touch you anywhere you don't want me to. Ever."

Her brow creased and she removed her hand, patting the bed again. I shook my head, telling myself what a rotten idea it was. Still, if she felt safer with me in here, I'd give her that. Might fucking kill me, but I'd do it. I got into bed next to her, keeping as close to the edge as I could. Raven inched closer and I lifted my arm. She snuggled against me and placed her head on my chest. The moment her body relaxed, I felt my own tension drift away. I had no idea where this was going, or what she was thinking, but if she needed me close I could give her that much.

Chapter Three

Raven

Waking up next to a man should have terrified me. Except I knew it was Fox. With my recent experience with men, I ought to have been running. I didn't know why he made me feel safe. Something about being in his presence calmed me, made me feel as if nothing and no one would ever hurt me again. I knew it was illogical, but it didn't change how I felt.

Even when he'd seen me in the shower, before he averted his gaze, I hadn't felt as if he were a threat to me. He handled me gently. The way he'd tried so hard to not share a bed with me, because he'd known he'd wake up hard, had been sweet. If he'd planned to hurt me, he'd have done it already. The others hadn't hesitated. The moment they'd had me alone, they'd struck.

I wondered if he knew I'd heard him on the phone last night. He'd been speaking to the man who claimed to be my father. Fox had not only called me beautiful and a survivor, but he'd promised to kill anyone who dared harm me. I hadn't thought of myself as anything other than broken. I held up an arm, looking at the scars he'd mentioned. I'd done them to myself. How could anyone see them and think me beautiful, or strong? I certainly didn't *feel* either of those.

He shifted in his sleep, drawing my gaze. The blankets had gathered near his waist during the night. I couldn't help but look where his cock tented the covers. Part of me wanted to recoil and get as far away as possible. That particular part of a man had hurt me too many times already. But the side who knew Fox wouldn't touch me wanted to take a closer look. I knew women enjoyed being with a man. I just hadn't understood it. Still didn't.

I looked up at his face, checking to see if he still slept. His eyes remained shut and his chest rose and fell in deep, even breaths. Slowly, I reached for the blankets and lifted them a little. I couldn't hold back my gasp as I stared. His cock had worked free of his boxers and rose in the air. The shaft looked smooth and incredibly hard. The head had turned almost a purple color.

I checked again, making sure he hadn't woken, before I reached out and brushed my fingertip along the length of his cock. It jerked and I yelped, yanking my hand back. Fox groaned and shifted, his hips lifting a little. Had he… liked it? The men who'd used me had gotten off on causing me pain and said how good I felt. None had asked me to touch them with my hand.

I reached out again, trailing my finger from just under the head down the shaft. When Fox groaned again, I swallowed hard and wrapped my shaky fingers around him, giving his cock a stroke.

"Raven." His voice seemed hoarse and strained. When I met his gaze, I saw heat blazing in his eyes, and something else… remorse. "I'm so fucking sorry. Did I… Did I make you touch me while I was sleeping?"

Oh. Oh… He'd thought he'd made me do this? I shook my head, watching him. I hadn't released his cock and felt it twitch against my fingers.

Fox licked his lips. "Raven, sweetheart, why are you touching my cock?"

I stared, not willing to speak. I waited, hoping he'd let the matter drop. Giving his shaft another stroke, I couldn't help but watch as my hand slid up and down. The skin felt silky smooth, and I didn't understand how something could feel pleasant in my hand but cause so much pain when a man put it inside me.

"Raven." My name was a near whisper on his lips. "Please. If you keep that up, I'm going to come. I don't want to freak you out, and you really don't have to do this. I told you I'd be hard this morning, but I didn't expect anything from you. You don't have to touch me."

I held his gaze as I worked my hand up and down a few more times, needing him to understand I didn't feel coerced. I'd never touched a man willingly before. I couldn't explain why I felt like I needed to do this. Perhaps it was the thought of him believing I was brave. Or maybe I needed to prove to myself this particular part of a man wasn't scary. It was the man attached to the appendage who could make it terrifying or intriguing, and the fact the others had *wanted* to hurt me.

"Raven." His gaze held a hint of warning and a moment later, his cock gave a jerk and hot sticky fluid erupted from the head and slid down my hand. The scent made my nose wrinkle. It had a musky odor. Not necessarily unpleasant. Just different. I didn't stop stroking until he shuddered and reached out to grip my hand.

He released me the moment I tried to pull free, and I stared at my fingers. Fox shoved his cock back into his boxers and bolted from the room. He returned a moment later with a wet cloth and cleaned my hand. I saw a hint of pink tinging his cheeks and I wondered if I'd embarrassed him by doing such a thing.

Fox left with the rag. When he returned, he folded his arms and stood by the bed, staring at the floor. He cleared his throat a few times, opened his mouth, then seemed to change his mind. I crawled a little closer and sat on my knees in front him. He still refused to look at me. Tugging on his shirt, I finally snagged his attention.

"I'm sorry. I should have insisted on staying in my room. After everything..." He audibly swallowed. "I'm an asshole, Raven. I don't know how you can ever forgive me."

My brow furrowed as I tried to puzzle out his words. It sounded like he blamed himself for what I'd just done. He hadn't had any part in it. If anything, I should apologize for touching him while he slept. My breath caught and I scrambled back. Oh, no. No, no, no. I'd done to him what those men had done to me. I'd touched him without his permission. He'd offered me sanctuary, a safe home, and I'd done the unthinkable.

A keening sound escaped me, and I rocked myself, fear crawling up my throat. Panic surged in my veins. What if he sent me away? He'd told Hatchet I could stay as long as I needed, but now that I'd touched him without permission... Dots swam in front of my vision, and I felt myself listing to the side.

"Raven!" The mattress dipped and I felt Fox's arms go around me. He held me close, running his hand over my hair. "Forgive me. Please."

Tears burned my eyes and slipped down my cheeks. The panic receded and I clung to him. How did I make him understand? There was nothing to forgive. Not on my part. I did, however, need *him* to forgive *me*. I'd done something horrible. I'd despised those men touching me when I hadn't wanted them to, and I hadn't even given Fox a chance. No, that wasn't right. He'd told me to stop, and I'd kept going.

I struggled free of his embrace and ran for the

bathroom, falling to my knees in front of the toilet seconds before I threw up. I purged everything in my stomach until all I could do was dry heave. Sobs wracked me as I collapsed to the floor.

"Raven, I'm calling the doctor. I'll make this right. Somehow."

I heard his footsteps fade. How could I have done something so horrible to him? He'd been kind. Let me stay in his home. He'd comforted me when I'd been upset and scared. How had I repaid him? By forcing my attention on him.

The mere thought made me dry heave several more times. I hated myself. Scooting back from the toilet, I bumped the side of the bathtub. The razor he'd given me fell onto the floor and I stared at it. My fingers twitched as I fought the urge to pick it up and start cutting. But I didn't deserve relief from the pain. Not this time.

Whatever Fox wanted to do to me, I'd let him. My behavior merited nothing less. I curled into a ball, shoving myself into the corner. He'd said he would call the doctor. Would they take me back to Balmoral now? He wouldn't want me in his home anymore. I couldn't blame him.

I didn't know how much time passed before Fox returned with a woman on his heels. I turned my face away, too ashamed to look at either of them. Had he told her what I'd done? Would she yell at me? Call me names?

"Raven, my name is Luciana." The woman knelt within arm's reach but didn't come any closer. "You met Spider yesterday. The grumbly older man? He saved me once, the way the club is trying to save you."

She had my attention. I turned my head to face her. She lifted her shirt and showed me scars along her stomach and lower belly. I held out an arm so she could see mine as well. A faint smile curved her lips.

"Yes, we both have battle scars from what we endured. Like you, men hurt me. I came here thinking the Hades Abyss would do the same. Until I saw the horrified look in Spider's eyes when I started stripping out of my clothes."

I tipped my head to the side and listened. I could have told her these men were honorable. Breaker hadn't touched me more than necessary to save me from Balmoral. And Fox… Shame made a fire build inside me, like my own body wanted to incinerate itself.

"Fox told me what happened," she said.

I swallowed hard and looked away. I didn't want to hear what she had to say. Not anymore. I'd done something repulsive. I knew it. Whatever punishment they gave me, I'd take it. Even if it meant going back to Balmoral and the guards.

Luciana's touch was light as she pressed her fingers to the back of my hand. "Raven, he said he's sorry. He didn't mean to scare you, or make you feel like you had to… um…"

"I tried to be clear last night," Fox mumbled. "I'd warned her I'd get hard and knew I should have stayed in my own room. I've made a mess of everything."

I looked up at him. Wait. *He'd* made a mess of everything? Did he still think he'd made me touch him? How was this his fault? I didn't understand. I glanced at Luciana, hoping she'd be able to help. The way she watched me made it clear she didn't understand either. They both thought Fox had done something wrong.

I opened my mouth and placed my fingers

against my throat. Could I even speak? Only one way to find out. I couldn't let Fox think he'd been the one to hurt me. It had been the other way around. Even if it hurt to speak, even if my voice sounded horrible, I needed to try. I had to apologize to him.

"My… fault…" My throat felt like I'd swallowed razorblades as the words barely escaped my lips.

I heard Fox inhale sharply, and soon he'd shoved Luciana out of the way and dropped to his knees next to me. His hands shook as he reached out, pulling me against his chest.

"Jesus, Raven. You think it was your fault?" he asked.

I nodded. "Touched… without… permission."

He rocked me, pressing kisses to the top of my head. "Sweet girl, you didn't do anything wrong. Is that why you freaked out? You thought I didn't want your hands on me?"

I nodded. "Like…them…"

"Like?" He stopped and held me away from his body, forcing my chin up so he could look into my eyes. "Like them? The guards? You think what you did makes you the same as those monsters?"

I nodded again, tears burning my eyes.

"No! Fucking hell. No, Raven! You're nothing like them!"

"Thought you said she didn't speak," Luciana said.

"She hasn't until now. The way she rubbed at her throat, I'm guessing it hurts to speak." He cupped my cheek. "But you did speak before, didn't you? You tried to tell someone you were being hurt, and you paid the price. Is that what happened?"

"Yes." My voice was getting softer. Weaker. I didn't think I could say much more. At least, not without having something to drink first. I didn't know how long it had been since I last spoke to anyone. Weeks? Months?

Luciana placed her hand on Fox's shoulder. "Seems you don't need me after all. I'll call the doc and let him know he doesn't have to rush over."

I tightened my hold on Fox. They'd already called the doctor? The same one who'd been treating me at Balmoral? I didn't want to go back, especially knowing Fox wasn't angry with me. He didn't blame me for what happened. Unless he was lying?

"Tell him not to come at all," Fox said. "I'd worried I'd hurt her in some way. Seems we just had a misunderstanding."

"He needs to see her, Fox. You know she needs a full health check-up, especially after what she went through at the hospital." Luciana leaned down to hold my gaze. "The doctor the club uses is really nice. He won't hurt you, and if you want, Fox can stay in the room with you. Since this is your sanctuary, I'd recommend going to the doctor's office. Fox won't let anyone take you away. Understand?"

I nodded and curled tighter against Fox.

"Thanks, Luciana. I'll get some breakfast made, and we'll head over to the doc's office first chance we get. Make sure he knows she's terrified of medical personnel."

"Will do. Welcome to the Hades Abyss, Raven. You're in good hands with our VP."

I didn't understand what she meant, but it didn't matter. As long as I had Fox by my side, I would be safe. I'd never met anyone like him before. Maybe if I had, I wouldn't have been chasing cowboys at rodeos. Then none of this would have ever happened. But if being hurt by those men meant I got to meet Fox, I'd try to be okay with what had happened to me. Was it possible for something good to come from something so awful?

Chapter Four

Fox

I'd been terrified I'd hurt Raven, if not physically at least emotionally, and instead, she'd been worried *she'd* hurt *me*. After everything she'd been through, I could see how she might think I hadn't wanted her to touch me. Nothing could be further from the truth, although, I felt like a monster since I'd enjoyed it. Hell, I'd be reliving that moment for a while. Next time I yanked one out, I'd be thinking about her small hand wrapped around my dick.

Yep, the devil definitely had a spot reserved for me in hell. No doubt in my mind. And if Hatchet ever found out his daughter had gotten me off, on her first night here no less, he'd be sending me there immediately. Even knowing I should keep my distance, I didn't think I could. She sat at the kitchen table while I made eggs, toast, and bacon. I found myself glancing over my shoulder every few minutes, just so I could look at her.

Raven had changed into a pair of the black knit shorts and one of the tees Knox had picked up last night. I'd managed to toss the shorts into the dryer while I'd waited on Luciana to arrive. I hadn't wanted to face Raven, worried I'd only fuck shit up even more. She remained barefoot, and God help me, she was also braless, and I couldn't help but admire the way the shirt hugged her breasts. Her nipples weren't hard, but I could still see the faint outline of them.

"Hope scrambled eggs are all right. I always break the yolk if I try to make them over easy," I said.

She didn't make a sound. Knowing she could speak, I'd hoped to talk to her a bit more. I wondered if her throat still ached. I didn't have any hot tea. Last time I'd been sick, Vasha had brought some over. I pulled out my phone and opened the grocery app. Ever since Luciana had shown it to me, I'd been addicted to buying my groceries that way. It made it easy for a Prospect to pick up the order and I didn't have to worry about them fucking it up.

My phone chimed and I yanked it off the counter. Surge. I clicked on the message to see what he had to say.

Three guards fired from Balmoral this morning. Doctor noticed Raven missing. Think the nurse came clean.

Shit. *Are they looking for her?*

I saw dots appear and waited for him to finish typing. *Doesn't look like it. Think they want it to stay quiet. But that could be a problem later.*

Right. How far would they go to make sure no one knew what happened? *Keep me posted.*

If these fuckers were coming for her, I needed to know. I'd promised to keep her safe, and I'd do just that, no matter the cost. Not only because I'd told her dad she'd be protected here, but because I wanted to chase the shadows from her eyes. Raven deserved to find happiness.

I added two types of hot tea to the list, and some honey. I didn't have any idea what Raven liked to eat, and since she wasn't currently talking, I couldn't very well ask her. I added chicken breasts, steaks, and pork chops to the list. I tried to keep a decent selection of canned vegetables stocked so I wasn't worried about side dishes. I did wonder when Raven had last been able to eat something sweet like cake or pie. I couldn't bake for shit, but I accessed the bakery section and added an apple pie and a chocolate cake to the list. Hopefully she'd like at least one of them. Whatever we didn't eat, I'd take to the clubhouse. Someone there would demolish the leftovers.

My phone went off again. This time I had a message from Shield with the Reckless Kings.

You seen Hatchet?

Had they lost him? Or had he gone off the grid after speaking to me last night? *Talked to him. Seen him? No.*

I waited a minute to see if he'd say anything else. Another text came through.

He's not answering calls. Sent back the brothers he took with him.

Well, fuck. Whatever he was doing, he didn't want his club to know. I hoped like hell he didn't get caught. If the cops picked him up while he was off avenging his daughter, it wouldn't end well. She only just now discovered she had a dad who gave a shit. I didn't want her to lose him already.

I finished cooking breakfast and plated it. I carried both dishes to the table before getting out forks and cups. While I typically had coffee in the morning, I did enjoy a glass of juice a few times a week. The jug in the fridge had only been opened yesterday so I knew it hadn't gone bad yet. I poured us each some and quickly added another jug to the groceries I needed.

"You don't have to talk since I'm sure it's painful, but could you shake your head yes or no if I ask some questions about food and drinks you like?" I asked.

She nodded and took a bite of her eggs.

"Do you have any food allergies?" I asked.

She shook her head. One less thing to worry about. I didn't want to accidentally make her sick. I went through a list of breakfast and lunch items, adding anything she liked to the list, and making notes in another app of anything she disliked so I wouldn't buy it next time. Assuming she remained here longer than a few days or even a week. The way Hatchet talked, he could be gone a while.

"I'll have someone pick up and deliver the groceries while we're gone. We should probably buy you a few more clothes too." I tried damn hard not to let my gaze drop to her breasts. "And a bra. You need at least one of those. Maybe more."

She blinked at me before looking down at her breasts. I shut my eyes and sucked in a breath. *Don't be a dick.* I wouldn't look. I absolutely wouldn't… I opened my eyes and looked. Dammit. I slammed them shut again and shook my head. I needed to do better. For her.

"Sorry. I didn't mean to…" I cleared my throat and opened my eyes again. "I'll get dressed after we eat, and we can head over to the doctor's office. If you're up for shopping after, we'll get you more clothes. If not, it can wait a day or two."

No idea how I'd cope with her being braless for days, but that was my issue to deal with and not hers. I'd just do my best not to draw attention to the fact I found her body fascinating. Harder to do after she'd gotten me off this morning, but I'd manage. Somehow.

"So you met Luciana. Like she said, she's with Spider, our club President. Her sister, Violeta, is with Rocket. They don't live too far down the road. There's a third woman who lives here. Vasha. She's from Russia, and she's with Slider." I took a bite of my toast before addressing the club whores. "The women at the clubhouse, the ones… having sex with my brothers, they aren't forced to be here. Some come in from town when they want a wild night of fun. Others are regulars and show up nearly every night."

The way her nose wrinkled told me she didn't

understand why they'd want to do that. Honestly, I didn't know either. I'd heard more than one over the years talk about landing one of us, but it wouldn't happen. Those women were here to party, and that's all we wanted from them. I'd definitely been with more than my fair share over the years, but lately it hadn't been as exciting as it once had. Maybe I was getting too damn old for this shit. At fifty, I didn't feel decrepit, but I wasn't exactly eighteen anymore either.

Shit. How old was Raven? My stomach turned when I realized she could be far from legal. She'd looked young, but I'd assumed…

"Uh, how old are you?" I asked her.

"Twenty," she said in a soft rasp.

Thank-fucking-Christ. I felt the tension ease from my neck and shoulders. Crisis averted. Sort of. It still made her too fucking young for me, but if being around Spider and Luciana had taught me anything, it was that age was just a number. There was still the issue of her having gotten me off earlier. It had left me unsettled, even if I'd certainly enjoyed it. I shouldn't have. I felt both eager to do more with her and disgusted with myself for wanting her to touch me. She should be coddled. Protected at all costs. And what was I doing? Wondering what it would feel like to have more than her hands on me.

I finished my food and stood with my plate, taking it over to the sink. I rinsed the dish and set it aside. I'd load the dishwasher later. After I moved the two skillets I'd used over to the sink as well, I wiped my hands off on a towel and decided I needed a little space from Raven.

"I'm going to get dressed. Take your time eating." Before she could stop me, I bolted from the room like a chickenshit.

Badass biker. I snorted. Yeah, right. More like coward. How the hell could one tiny woman scare the hell out of me? No, not her. Raven made me feel a lot of things, but not any of those were fear. How I felt about her? The intense desire to touch her? Yeah, *that* scared me shitless. I reached my room and pushed the door mostly shut before hurrying over to my dresser and grabbing clean clothes.

I stared at the jeans in my hand a moment. Luciana and Violeta had been badly broken and abused when they'd arrived. Yet they'd fallen for Spider and Rocket. Vasha hadn't had an easy life either, but she adored Slider. Would it be possible for Raven to ever have a semi-normal life? Maybe have a family? I tightened my hold on the denim, feeling the sudden urge to beat someone into the ground. I didn't like the idea of her being with anyone other than me.

I was fucked. Like, well and truly fucked -- without lube.

"Shit," I muttered. "Hatchet is going to kill me. Then resurrect me so he can do it again."

I heard a noise behind me and spun, finding Raven in the doorway, her eyes wide. Why the hell did I keep saying the wrong things around her? I needed to keep my mouth shut until she went home with her dad. Otherwise, Hatchet wouldn't have to murder me. I'd take my own self out if I did anything to hurt Raven.

"Sorry, sweetheart. Just mumbling to myself. Did you need something?"

She took one hesitant step after another until she stopped right in front of me. "He'd… kill… you? For… what?"

I sighed, not wanting to lie to her, yet not wanting to tell her the truth either. I didn't see any way around it. If I kept silent, she'd likely come up with something even worse. If there *was* anything worse in her eyes. Having me want her all to myself, to make her mine in all ways, would probably be the stuff of nightmares for Raven.

"It's kind of complicated." She stared at me, and I knew I'd have to say something more. I ran a hand through my hair. "I was thinking about the way Luciana, Violeta, and Vasha all had horrible things happen to them. They were scared of men when they came here, but now they love the men they're with. And it made me wonder if you'd want that. A family. Someone to love, or if you'd even be able to after everything you went through."

She silently watched me. Yeah, she was going to make me completely spill my guts like a high school girl. Great. If this backfired and she hightailed it out of here, I'd never forgive myself.

"I got angry, thinking about you with another man. Made me realize I didn't want you to be with anyone other than me. Your dad would string me up from the nearest tree. He just found you, and now I'm trying to keep you. Not to mention, he'll think I took advantage, and let's be honest, I kind of did. I could have made you stop earlier. I just… didn't really want you to. It felt too damn good."

I winced, thinking I'd really gone too far with that last bit. Instead of running from the room, and from me, she leaned in closer and pressed her cheek to my chest. I let my clothes fall to the floor as I put my arms around her. It felt right -- holding her. Like whatever had been missing in my life had suddenly been found.

"I thought my confession would make you want to leave," I said.

She drew up and reached toward my face, her fingers lightly touching my beard. "Want… to… stay."

My lips kicked up on one corner. "I'd like that. A lot."

I held her another minute before I felt myself getting hard again and stepped away from Raven. She might want to remain here with me, but I didn't want to push my luck. Yes, she'd gotten me off this morning, but after speaking with her, I had to wonder if she'd done it more out of curiosity than anything else.

"Let me get ready, Raven. We'll go when I'm done."

She patted my chest and waved at the bed. I furrowed my brow, trying to figure out what she wanted. She sighed, tapped me again, and motioned to the bed.

"Am I going back to bed?" I asked.

She pressed her lips together and shook her head. With a huff, she walked across the room, pulled back the covers and got into my bed. She snuggled into the pillow and held out a hand to me.

"You want both of us to lie down… in my bed." I didn't know where she was going with this. Did she want to sleep some more? Cuddle? I knew talking had made her throat hurt, but I wished she'd speak to me again.

She eyed my boxers before flicking her gaze up to mine, still waiting on me to join her. Hell, did she plan on touching me again? Because I wasn't a fucking saint. There was only so much I could take before I'd likely do something stupid. Like try to fuck her. Shit. Goddamnit. It just hit me I'd been dressed, or mostly undressed, when Luciana had stopped by. Spider would have my balls. I'd been too worried about Raven to think about it.

"Not sure that's the best idea, Raven." Her eyes narrowed and she waggled her hand in the air, insistent. "All right. You win."

Jesus. I didn't know if I'd survive her being in my house. It was both heaven and hell all at the same time.

Chapter Five

Raven

He'd run from me again. Frowning, I stared at the empty doorway. Fox claimed he'd liked what I'd done to him earlier. So why had he run when I'd asked him to join me in bed? He said he wanted me to stay. He didn't like the idea of me with another man. It meant he wanted me, didn't it? The way Spider wanted Luciana, and the other two couples he'd mentioned. We'd have the same thing they had, wouldn't we?

Logically, I knew he'd never be satisfied with me using my hand on him. He hadn't pushed for more, and I didn't think he ever would. It didn't mean he wouldn't find what he needed elsewhere. As much as he didn't like the thought of me with other men, I didn't want to think about him with another woman. If Fox found someone else, they wouldn't want me here. I knew I wasn't ready to have the sort of relationship he would need, but I suddenly felt selfish and wanted to hold onto him.

My reasons for asking him to come to bed weren't unselfish. I'd liked touching him, proving to myself that part of a man didn't always cause pain. I'd given him pleasure without the humiliation and suffering it caused when the guards had taken what they wanted. Perhaps I needed to prove something to myself. It was wrong to use Fox, and I needed to explain.

The minutes ticked by and he finally returned, tension radiating off him. I patted the bed and waited, hoping he'd join me. When he did, I snuggled closer and realized I'd need to use my voice. It didn't matter if my throat hurt. He needed the words, to know exactly why I wanted him in this bed, and what I wanted from him.

"When I… touched… you earlier… you liked… it."

He nodded. "I did. It was wrong of me to enjoy it. You were simply curious, weren't you?"

"Yes and… no." I swallowed, wishing it hadn't been so long since I'd spoken. How long would it hurt to use my voice? "It made me… realize that part… of a man… doesn't cause pain… on its own. It's the men… who hurt me."

Fox wrapped his arm around me and tugged me against his side. "Right. Those men were assholes, and they will pay for what they've done. Not all men are like that, Raven. Your dad isn't. I'm not. Hell, every man in this club would lay down their lives to protect you."

"I'm sorry I didn't ask." I'd finished a sentence without needing to pause. I smiled, feeling proud of myself, even if my voice had been nearly a whisper.

"What do you need from me, Raven?" Fox asked. "Want me to strip off my clothes and let you see that it's just a body? The limbs themselves can't do anything unless I make them. Well, my cock gets hard without my permission, but it's not going to do anything to hurt you. Tell me what I can do to help you."

I lifted up on my elbow and looked down at him. "You'd get naked?"

He nodded and cleared his throat. "Yeah, but I can't promise I won't be hard. Lying here with you… I want you, Raven. The way a man wants a woman, but I won't act on it. You're safe with me."

I smiled. "I know."

His brow furrowed. "Why did you rush to me

yesterday? At the clubhouse."

"You'd hurt yourself. You were angry over what they did to me. I needed to make sure you were okay. No one has ever cared before. You didn't see me as a whore."

His jaw went tight and his nostrils flared. "You. Are. Not. A. Whore!"

His harsh words would have made me flinch, had it been anyone other than Fox. I could tell he wasn't angry with me, but over the fact someone had clearly called me that word before.

I shrugged a shoulder. "To some, I am. I'm not a virgin. Those men took my innocence, and so much more. I'd flirted with them, not realizing the consequences of my actions."

Fox jolted to an upright position and nearly dragged me onto his lap. His arms felt like steel around me. "No! You are not to blame for any of it. A woman should be able to flirt with someone she admires without worrying the asshole is going to rape her. The actions of those cowboys, of the guards, aren't the deeds of decent men. They're monsters. Predators. And one way or another, they're going to be stopped."

I nodded, believing him. Part of me knew I wasn't to blame for what they'd done to me. I hadn't forced them to touch me. To hurt me. They'd enjoyed every second of it, liked hearing me scream and plead for them to stop. I'd seen the evil in their eyes before they'd left me for dead. With Fox, all I saw and felt was kindness. He had a gentle touch, soft words, and a noble heart.

He audibly swallowed and something shifted in his eyes. I wondered about it but didn't ask. The longer he watched me, the more I felt he held something back. What did he know?

"You're a good man," I said.

"I try to be. Most of the time. I'm not a saint, Raven. I've done bad things, and I've hurt people. But I would never harm an innocent woman or child. It takes a sick person to do something like that." He sighed. "There's something you need to know. The guards at Balmoral were all fired today. Surge dug into their systems and said no one seems to be looking for you. I asked him to keep an eye on things and let me know if you might be in danger. I'll protect you with my life, Raven."

His words sent a frisson of fear through me. The guards had to be angry they'd lost their jobs. Would they take it out on me? Breaker had taken me from Balmoral, and he'd been wearing his cut. They knew the Hades Abyss had come for me. What if they came here?

Fox seemed to sense my inner turmoil and ran his hand down my arm. The gesture soothed me. I wished I'd met someone like Fox long before now. Would he have been interested in me before those men had destroyed me? I knew he was quite a bit older than me. If I hadn't been hurt, been locked away, would I be with him? I couldn't help but feel meeting him on the street would have had a different ending. He'd have seen a silly young girl and kept walking. We wouldn't have talked, and I certainly wouldn't be in his bedroom.

"Will you hold me?" I asked.

Fox leaned back against the pillows, dragging me down against his chest. He kept his arms around me, and I felt the thump of his heartbeat. "You're not hard anymore."

He snorted. "No. Talking about what happened to you seems to deflate my cock faster than ice water.

What they did to you wasn't sex, Raven. You know that, right? If you're ever ready and find someone you trust enough, what happens between a man and woman can be beautiful."

I had a hard time believing I'd ever enjoy sex. The movies and books had all lied to me. It wasn't wonderful. It didn't make me want to beg for more. It had been messy, painful, and degrading.

"Won't it hurt?" I asked. "It's always hurt."

His hold tightened on me. "No, sweetheart. It won't hurt. The man you choose will want nothing more than to make you happy, to bring you pleasure. He'll make you feel things you've never experienced before, and you'll only want more."

"Is that why women giggle and laugh when they talk about sex? Because it's supposed to feel good and be fun?" I asked.

"Yeah. That's why."

I wondered if I'd ever be brave enough to find out firsthand what it would be like. If I did, I knew I wanted it to be with Fox. I couldn't imagine anyone else being as nice to me as he was. Every moment spent with him healed a small part of me. I'd not trusted anyone in a long time. Until him.

If I felt confident he wouldn't hurt me in other ways, it stood to reason I could rely on him to only bring me pleasure -- assuming I was bold enough to ask for it.

"Have you ever been kissed?" he asked.

I didn't know what made him ask. I thought back to the only boy who'd ever kissed me. It had been my senior year of high school. I'd been so excited, only to be sorely disappointed afterward.

"Once. I didn't care much for it. He slobbered a lot, and I felt like I needed a towel when he'd finished."

Fox chuckled. "Sorry about that, sweetheart. Sounds like he didn't know what the hell he was doing."

"I've seen kisses in the movies. It always seemed romantic. I'd hoped my first kiss would be like that. Instead, I'd wanted it over with quickly." I curled my fingers, pressing my hands against his chest, my heart hammering against my ribs. "Would you… would you kiss me?"

He tensed and I wished I could recall the words. Clearly, I'd misjudged the situation. The man might find me attractive, but I'd made him uncomfortable. I tried to ease away from him. Fox held me tighter, taking a deep breath and letting it out before sitting up.

"I'm sorry," I said.

"Why do you want me to kiss you?" he asked.

There were several reasons I could give, and each would be true. I didn't think he'd like me thinking of him as being gentle. Or safe. But…

"I trust you," I said.

He groaned and closed his eyes. "You probably shouldn't. I'm just a man, Raven."

"You don't have to kiss me if you don't want to."

He gave a sharp bark of laughter. "Sweetheart, trust me when I say I very much want to kiss you. I'm just worried I'll get carried away and scare you."

"Will you stop if I want you to?" I asked.

He narrowed his eyes. "Of course."

I stared at him, waiting. He nodded, understanding what I meant. He might think he'd lose control, but the moment I tried to back off, he'd let me go. Fox wasn't like the other men I'd known. He was… honorable.

His hold on me relaxed a bit and he urged me to

move in closer of my own accord. I cuddled against him, trying not to flinch as he reached up to lightly touch my cheek. Before I could change my mind, I leaned closer and let my lips touch his.

Fox took control, his mouth coaxing mine into a sensual kiss that made my toes curl. I'd never known being in a man's arms could be anything like this. My nipples tightened and I felt a tingling start in my belly and spread lower. I gasped and he took the opportunity to flick his tongue into my mouth.

As Fox tasted me, showed me passion for the first time in my life, it felt like the world spun around us. My heart raced and my hands shook where I'd placed them on his chest. He broke the kiss suddenly, panting for breath as he pressed his forehead to mine. It felt like little bees were buzzing under my lips. I reached up and lightly touched them.

"That's what a kiss is like?" I asked.

He huffed and leaned back, his eyes flashing with amusement. "No, sweetheart. That was something else entirely. I'm fifty years old and not once have I ever experienced anything like that before."

His words sent a rush of warmth through me, and I felt my cheeks heat. I brushed my fingers over my lips and wondered if he'd kiss me again sometime. It hadn't been scary like I'd thought it might be. In fact, I almost wanted to ask for another one now. I felt the hard ridge of his cock pressing against me and I hesitated. Fox hadn't done anything to make me think he'd go further than I wanted. Still, would I be asking for too much to request another kiss and not let him do more?

Fox reached up and ran his finger down the bridge of my nose. "You're thinking too hard. Was it too much?"

I shook my head.

"Talk to me, Raven. I need to know you're okay and not retreating into your head. Did our kiss have a negative impact on you… in *any* way?"

"No. Except…"

"Except what?" he asked.

"I wanted another kiss." My cheeks burned hotter. "But I didn't want to ask for one and upset you when I didn't want to do more than that."

"Ah, sweet girl." He sighed. "Never hesitate to ask me for whatever you want. I'll kiss you as much as you'd like, and I won't expect anything more from you. And if you decide you never want to kiss me again, that's all right too. Might break my heart a little, but I'll live."

When he kissed me this time, I melted against him. I let Fox lead the way, and I savored every second of his lips against mine. If anyone had told me I'd enjoy kissing a man, I'd have thought they were crazy. But Fox wasn't just any man. I didn't think there was another like him in all the world. And for now, I'd pretend he was mine.

Chapter Six

Fox

Every time I looked at Raven and saw her kiss-swollen lips, I smiled. She'd surprised me by asking for a kiss the first time. The second time she'd about knocked me on my ass. I hadn't lied when I said kissing her had been unlike anything I'd ever experienced before. If she remained in my home for much longer, I knew I'd end up falling for her. I loved her strength, her softness, her smile… just… everything.

Her hands twisted in her lap as we waited to see the doctor. She'd balked at putting on a hospital gown and the nurse hadn't pushed the issue. I stood beside the padded table, close enough to offer protection yet keeping enough distance Raven didn't feel crowded. I knew she didn't want to be here, but it would be another step toward healing. She needed to see not all doctors were like the ones at Balmoral.

A brisk knock at the door had Raven tensing. Dr. Briar came in, giving her a reassuring smile.

"Hello, Raven. I'm Dr. James Briar." He held out his hand, but she refused to take it. He shoved his hands into his pockets and leaned against the cabinet opposite Raven. "I understand you've been through a lot and don't trust doctors. And that's all right. I'll just have to prove you can trust me."

"She's only been out of Balmoral one night," I said.

"I'm aware. Surge managed to get her records and sent them over to me this morning. If Raven is all right with it, I'd like to run some blood work, listen to her heart, and do a general checkup for today. We need to make sure she's healthy and get a decent baseline so we'll know if something out of the ordinary pops up in the future."

He made it sound like Raven would be here forever. Little did he know her dad would be coming for her, and Hatchet didn't live anywhere near the Hades Abyss. My heart constricted at the thought of losing her. Not that she was really mine. I'd offered her a safe place until her father arrived and nothing more. It was on me if I ended up wanting her to stay. I'd never force her to remain with me.

"Raven, will you let him take some blood to run a few tests?" I asked.

She reached out and I took her hand. It trembled in mine, and I moved closer. She leaned toward me a bit and held out her other arm.

Dr. Briar gathered what he needed from the cabinet behind him, then slowly approached Raven. He prepped her arm and stuck the needle into her arm. He filled several vials of blood, and I wondered if he was searching for something in particular.

"All done," Dr. Briar said, sliding the needle out and putting a bandage over the puncture site. "If I give you a cup and show you where the bathroom is located, could you give us a urine sample?"

Raven looked up at me, her lips pinched together. The crease above her nose had me pressing a kiss to her forehead. "It's all right. I'll stand outside the door the entire time you're in there. I'll even open the bathroom first to make sure it's empty."

I helped Raven off the table while Dr. Briar got the specimen cup. I carried it down the hall and peered into the bathroom. Raven went inside, took the cup from me, and shut the door. I heard the lock click. While I waited on her to give the doc a sample, I scrolled through the notifications on my phone, making sure I hadn't missed anything important.

The door behind me opened and Raven came out. She held the cup in her hand, and I pointed to the little window cut into the wall. "Place it inside that tiny door, sweetheart. The nurses will get it and the lab will run whatever tests Dr. Briar requests."

She deposited the cup, washed her hands, and joined me in the hallway. It seemed she was back to not speaking. Since I knew she could talk, even if she spoke at a softer level than most, I had a feeling the anxiety she felt over being at the doctor's office kept her silent.

I led her back to the room and helped her onto the table. Dr. Briar had stepped out. While we waited, I held Raven's hand. She leaned against me, and I put my arm around her shoulders. The slight tremor running through her body made me wish I could carry her out of here. I knew the doctor wouldn't hurt her, and he needed to run the tests to make sure everything was all right. It didn't stop me from wanting to shield her from any pain, even the anxiety from being at the doctor's office.

"Not much longer," I murmured, hoping I wasn't lying.

Dr. Briar came back, a slight scowl on his face. He blanked his expression when he saw me watching and I knew whatever he'd discovered while he'd been gone wouldn't be welcome news. If those fuckers had given Raven an STD, I'd track them down and rip off their dicks. She'd suffered enough at their hands already.

"Raven, I need you to think really hard for me," Dr. Briar said. "When was the last time you had a menstrual cycle?"

Raven blinked at him before lifting her gaze to

mine. My heart slammed against my ribs, his words ricocheting around my brain. Shit. He'd only be asking that question for one reason.

"Sweetheart, do you remember the last time you had your period?" Her face turned scarlet, and she glared at me. I leaned down closer, realizing she didn't understand why he needed to know. I dropped my voice to a whisper. "Raven, is it possible you could be pregnant?"

The color drained from her cheeks, and she swayed, panic flaring in her eyes. I hated to be the one to cause such a reaction in her. The last thing she needed was a baby in her belly, especially since it would be a constant reminder of what she'd suffered. Since I hadn't noticed a baby bump, it was safe to assume she'd gotten knocked up by one of the asshole guards at Balmoral.

"Raven, look at me."

She shook her head, refusing to lift her gaze from the floor, or wherever she'd decided to stare. Could have been my boots for all I knew. I tipped her chin up and didn't relent until she looked me in the eye.

"Sweetheart, do you think you might be pregnant?" I asked, trying to keep my tone soft and even.

Tears pooled in her eyes, and I had my answer. I gathered her against my chest and stroked my hand down her hair. Christ. Just when I thought things couldn't get more fucked up, the universe had to go and prove me wrong.

"She'll need to see an OB/GYN, and she'll need prenatal vitamins. Her blood work seems fine, so over the counter ones should work for now. But her doctor may prescribe some if they feel she needs a stronger dose. I can make a few recommendations if you'd like."

"If you already ran the tests, you knew she was pregnant," I said.

He nodded. "I'd hoped the test was wrong or maybe the sample got mixed up in the lab. I know this is the last thing she needed. If Raven decides she doesn't want to keep the baby, there are alternatives her OB/GYN can discuss with her."

My stomach knotted just thinking about his implication. If she didn't want the baby, she'd be facing either an abortion or giving birth, then letting the baby be adopted by someone. No matter what she chose, she wouldn't have an easy road to travel. People wouldn't understand her decision for either option, but I didn't know if she could mentally and emotionally handle keeping a reminder of the guards who'd abused her daily.

"Thanks, Dr. Briar. Can you call with the information later? I think I need to get her back home."

He nodded. "Absolutely. If you have any questions in the meantime, don't hesitate to call."

I gathered Raven in my arms and carried her out of the office, not even bothering to sign anything at the front desk or pay for the visit. Dr. Briar knew where to find us. He could send a bill. I knew the club would handle any expenses, and if they didn't, I damn sure would.

Hell. Someone needed to tell Hatchet. I had a feeling it would fall to me, since I'd had the most contact with him. With his daughter staying at my house, the news should come from me.

I placed Raven on the seat of the truck I'd borrowed, then buckled her in. She seemed shaken, and I worried what the news would do to her. It had only been twenty-four hours since I'd met her, but I'd seen an improvement already. Would finding out she was pregnant end up setting her back?

I cupped her cheek, drawing her attention to me. My sweet girl looked so damn lost. I wished I could take away all her pain. If anyone deserved a shot at happiness, it was Raven. The world had knocked her down again and again, until I worried the next time she might not get back up.

"You hungry?" I asked. "The diner isn't far. They have the best pie in town. I don't know about you, but I could use a slice about now."

Raven stared but didn't answer. I sighed, wishing I knew what thoughts were whirling through her mind. I caressed her cheek and pressed a kiss to her forehead. I nearly missed it, but there was a hitch in her breathing and then a soft sob.

Drawing back, I saw the tears spilling down her cheeks. I unbuckled her and pulled her into my arms, twisting us so I could sit on the seat and hold her on my lap. Raven curled into me, gripping my cut like she might never let me go. I ran my hand up and down her back, and murmured nonsense to her, knowing she needed to get it all out.

"Why?" she asked in a near whisper.

My heart broke. I didn't have the words to magically make it all better. I couldn't wish away her past, or even the last half hour. Reality was a bitch that way. All I could do was hold her and give her whatever comfort I could. I'd help her in any way possible.

"I don't know, sweetheart. I don't have any answers for you. But this isn't something we can wish away. You don't have to make any decisions right now, or even think about it. Let's get something to eat, find something fun to do, and then we'll go home. Sound okay?"

She took a deep breath and nodded. "All right."

I wiped the tears off her face and gave her a soft, brief kiss. A bit of the despair faded from her eyes, and I hoped I could take her mind off things for a bit. Once I had her buckled up again and I'd gotten behind the wheel, I drove straight to the diner. With some luck, we'd miss the lunch crowd. I didn't know how Raven would react to a bunch of people.

I found a spot to park not too far from the door and led her inside. Cool air greeted us, and the bell over the door jingled. My favorite waitress, Nan, looked like she'd been run off her feet. She cast me a quick glance, then did a doubletake, her lips spreading in a smile.

"Well, look what the cat dragged in. Pick a spot. I'll be there in a minute."

I led Raven to a booth in the back corner. I took the side that kept my back to the wall and gave me a clear view of the diner, letting Raven sit across from me. Not only would it give me the best advantage for keeping her safe, but it would also keep her from noticing the stares we'd garnered. I'd come here rather frequently over the years, and not once had I ever walked in with a woman.

Nan looked a little too gleeful about it, and even some of the regulars gave me smiles. Shit. I hoped no one said anything that would spook Raven. Maybe the diner hadn't been my best idea yet. It hadn't occurred to me everyone would be so damn nosy, but it should have. They loved to gossip.

Nan approached with two menus and some silverware. She placed them on the table and folded her hands over her belly. "So. Fox, you want your usual coffee and water?"

I nodded. "Sounds good. Raven, what would

you like to drink?"

Her gaze held mine and her lips trembled. She still hadn't spoken to anyone other than me. I reached over to place my hand on hers. It seemed to help settle her a bit. She skimmed the menu and pointed to the tea.

"Sweet tea?" I asked, not knowing a single southern person who'd dare order unsweetened. Not unless they wanted to be run out of town. Raven gave a quick nod.

I could see the speculative gleam in Nan's eyes and narrowed mine in response. She seemed to take the hint and rocked back on her heels.

"All right. Coffee, water, and a sweet tea coming right up." Nan rushed off and Raven relaxed almost instantly. I didn't miss the furtive glances she gave the woman.

"That's Nan," I said. "She's worked here a while. Always makes sure the orders are right. She's a good sort."

Raven stared at me, and I realized what she wanted to know, even if she hadn't said anything. It seemed my sweet girl worried I had something going with Nan. I didn't. Except great service at my favorite place to eat.

"I've never dated Nan," I said. "Or slept with her. She's a… friend. I come here a lot, so I've gotten to know her and the other staff, as well as the regulars. The two men to your right who are trying to look like they aren't watching us? That's Bert and Oscar. Nosy bastards, but they're good men. Both served in the military and are widowers. They go fishing twice a week when the weather permits and take any extra to the church in case any families need some food."

Raven gave me a smile. "That's nice of them."

Ah. There she was. I bit the inside of my lip so I wouldn't grin like an idiot. I'd hoped she wouldn't remain silent forever.

"It is. Nan has a bin she keeps in the back. People bring her a few pieces of clothing here and there, things they don't want anymore, and she makes sure they go to people who need them. The woman at the counter with the poofy red hair is Sandra. She owns a salon in town. Once a month, she sets up a workspace in the church parking lot, and those who are down on their luck can sign up for a spot to have their hair trimmed."

I saw the way she looked at everyone in a new light. Maybe knowing the good things these people did had set her at ease, made them a little less scary. In recent years, the club had started becoming more active in the community. We ran a toy drive in October and November for families who couldn't afford to give their kids a Christmas. In the summer, we gathered school supplies and dropped a few boxes at each of the local schools. It had gone a long way in making the community more accepting of us. A few still gave us a side-eye, convinced we would murder them in their sleep, but for the most part, we'd showed the town we were just average guys.

They didn't need to know exactly how dirty our hands were. And neither did Raven. At least, not at the moment. I'd kill to protect her, or the other women at the Hades Abyss. I'd done a lot of things that weren't exactly legal, and a hell of lot that would push the boundaries of even what other clubs would accept. At the end of the day, I didn't lose sleep over any of it. In my own way, I'd made the world a better place.

"You want a meal or just dessert?" I asked. "Order whatever you want, as long as you don't give me shit if I order two pieces of pie."

She rolled her lips into her mouth, and I saw the laughter in her eyes. Good. It was a start. Sooner or later, I'd get her to actually laugh, and I'd consider it a huge win. I didn't know what Raven liked to do, or if she even knew. We'd try a few things today, as long as she didn't get overwhelmed, and see if I could take her mind off her troubles for a bit.

Chapter Seven

Raven

I'd thought he was joking when he said he planned to order two slices of pie. The way he scraped up every last bit, I half expected him to pick the plate up and lick it clean. It seemed he had a sweet tooth. I didn't know how he could eat like that and not gain weight. It had been so long since I cared how I looked. I hadn't even looked in a mirror in a long while. The ones at the hospital had been metal and blurred my image anyway. Caring how I looked felt odd, but not unwelcome. I wanted Fox to find me attractive, to be proud to be seen with me. As long as no one knew about my past, they wouldn't have a reason to look down their noses at me.

My burger lay half-eaten on my plate, and I'd only managed to eat a handful of fries. It had been entirely too much food, no matter how delicious it had been. Between being on the streets and nearly starving, then landing in Balmoral where the food didn't have much taste, the grease on the burger and fries had almost been too much for my stomach to handle. I'd also gotten used to much smaller portions.

"What?" Fox asked, catching me in the act of staring.

"I didn't think you were serious about two slices of pie." I looked at his plate. "Think you missed a smear of cherry."

He scowled at me, reached down and swiped his finger through the cherry filling he'd missed, then stuck it in his mouth. It started as a snort, but soon I couldn't stop the laughter that bubbled up inside me. I held my stomach, the muscles aching, as I laughed so hard, I cried.

"You actually did it. I'd wondered if you would but..." I said trying to catch my breath. He seemed a little poleaxed and I smoothed my hair, fighting the urge to see if I had food on my face or something. "Um, something wrong?"

"You should laugh more often," he said, his voice low and rough. "Your face lights up, and you go from being beautiful to stunning."

My cheeks burned. After the cowboys had their fun with me, hearing anyone call me beautiful had been a nightmare. With Fox, it made me feel special. Laughing had felt wonderful. Freeing. For the first time in so long, I'd been happy. Now other thoughts crept back in, about the baby I hadn't asked for, how I'd become pregnant, and everything else... the darkness wanted to reclaim me.

"You ready to go find something to do?" Fox asked. "We can go home if you prefer, or we can... go bowling? Walk through the park? I could take you to the ice-skating rink, and you could laugh every time I fall on my ass."

"You'd go ice-skating even knowing you'll fall?" I asked.

He nodded. "Yep. If that's what you want to do, and if it makes you smile, I'll gladly fall a million times. Just don't take any video of me landing on my ass. My brothers would have a field day with it."

Brothers? I hadn't thought about him having a family. It had just been us in the house, and I hadn't noticed pictures of him with anyone. Were his parents alive? Did he get to see them? Had he ever been married? Have kids? I realized I didn't know anything about Fox, except that he treated me well.

"I've never been bowling, or ice-skating," I said.

"Which do you want to try first? Although, you

might get cold in what you have on. Maybe we should save ice-skating for after we get you some more clothes."

Clothes. I glanced down, remembering what he'd said about needing bras. As much as I didn't want to go shopping, I knew he'd been right. I did need more things. "Could we get a few things now?"

He leaned back in the booth and folded his arms. "Why? Eager to see me bust my ass?"

I smiled a little. "No, I just..."

How did I tell him, without *telling* him I wanted to buy bras? I hadn't thought much about running around without one, until now. I hunched my shoulders, wondering how I could explain why I wanted to go buy stuff. The motion drew his gaze down and his eyebrows rose.

"Ah. Right. Yeah, we definitely need to, um..." He cleared his throat. "Any preference? Where did you used to shop?"

"One of those shops in the mall that only carried that type of stuff. But it was a long time ago. Or so it seems. Considering I was homeless before going to the hospital, it doesn't much matter where you take me. I'm not picky."

Fox leaned forward and reached for my hand. "That will never happen to you again. Any of it."

"You can't promise nothing bad will ever happen to me," I said.

"Sure, I can. Anyone so much as thinks about hurting you, I'll make sure they're buried in a shallow grave. As to the homeless part, you can live with me for as long as you want, but I think your dad may want you to go with him."

What if I didn't want to go with him? The fact he hadn't known about me soothed a bit of the hurt I'd always felt. I'd thought he'd abandoned me. Turned out my mom hadn't just screwed me over. She'd done the same to him. Not surprising when I thought about it. But the thought of running off to live with a man I'd never met…

All right, so I was doing that already by staying with Fox. Maybe when I met my dad, everything would click, and the piece of me I'd felt had been missing all this time would feel whole for the first time. Or he could take one look at me and bolt.

"The mall might be a bit too crowded for your comfort," Fox said. "Why don't we start a little smaller?"

I nodded, trusting him to make the right decision. He paid for our meal, or rather my meal and his dessert, and then led me out to the truck. I watched the scenery pass as we drove through town, trying to take in everything. The town seemed quaint. The quintessential small American town. Mixed in with the bigger chain stores were mom-and-pop type shops.

Living in a place like this wouldn't be bad. Fewer people meant fewer chances for me to panic. When Fox parked outside a large store, I scanned the lot and realized it wasn't even half full. *I can do this.* I unbuckled my seat belt and got out of the truck.

Fox took my hand and we walked inside together. He grabbed a shopping cart and led the way to the women's clothes. Shopping for bras and panties should have been awkward since a man I'd just met stood next to me. Since we'd kissed earlier, I'd been thinking about Fox quite a bit, and what it would be like to have a relationship with him. I could tell he was the sort who'd be patient. Even though he'd been hard earlier, he'd stopped. We'd only kissed, and he hadn't tried to coax more from me.

I tried to check the price tags, not wanting to spend too much. Since I wasn't paying for any of it, I didn't want to get carried away. Except Fox kept glaring at me. Once he saw the size I kept picking up, he started grabbing handfuls and tossing them into the cart. I eyed the small mountain and wondered how many bras he thought I needed.

"There are only seven days in the week," I said.

"And?"

"You put about twenty bras in the cart. You have a washing machine. Why do I need nearly enough for a new bra every day of the month?"

"Nothing wrong with having a bit of variety. Don't be afraid to spend money, Raven. This trip to the store isn't going to break me."

His words made me pause. I'd realized I didn't have money, and someone would be paying for everything I picked out today, but it never occurred to me Fox would foot the bill himself. If my dad was coming for me, wouldn't he reimburse the club for helping me? If he didn't plan to, I'd make sure he gave them something, especially Fox.

He lightly gripped my chin, making me focus on him. "It's just money, Raven. I can always get more, but there's only one of you. If buying some clothes or pretty things makes you happy, then it's worth every penny."

I stopped arguing and finished picking out the things I'd need. By the time we checked out, the basket had been more than half filled and I refused to look at the total, not wanting to see exactly how much I'd cost him. I helped carry the bags to the truck. As we loaded everything into the backseat, I dug through one of the bra sacks and grabbed a cotton one. Slipping into the backseat, I shut the door and removed the tags from the garment.

I fastened the band before pulling my arms from my sleeves. It took a bit of maneuvering, but I managed to get the bra into place and my arms through the straps without flashing anyone. After I'd finished, I opened the door, whacking Fox in the back. He let out an *oomph* and staggered forward, making me wince.

"Sorry. I didn't realize you were right outside the door."

"Making sure no one was watching you," he said.

"I don't think I showed anything but maybe a bit of my stomach. Thank you, though. For both the clothes and for standing guard."

He helped me into the front seat, taking a moment to buckle me in again. Before he closed the door, he brushed a kiss against my cheek. I didn't know what to make of the little bits of affection he'd shown me today. I couldn't exactly say I disliked it. Every time he gave me a quick kiss, my skin tingled, and it felt like butterflies were swooping around in my stomach.

I glanced out my window and the breath stalled in my lungs. It had to be a trick. I was only seeing things. Guard Simmons, with his bruised face, stood five spaces down, his gaze narrowed as he stared at me. I swallowed the ball that had lodged in my throat and turned to say something to Fox. The way he smiled at me, the warmth in his eyes… I didn't want to see it go away. If I told him about Simmons, he'd go after him.

"Now where to?" he asked.

"Would you mind if we went home?" I asked. As much as I'd looked forward to doing more things with him, I felt a bit overwhelmed. Between the doctor's office and the news about the baby, to eating at the diner, and now shopping… I felt mentally and emotionally exhausted. I'd have pushed through it, but… Seeing Guard Simmons had shaken me. I didn't want to risk the man approaching, or worse try to get me alone. I'd tell Fox later.

"Not at all." He reached over and took my hand, lifting it to his lips. I hadn't ever had someone kiss my hand before Fox.

Something told me if I stayed with Fox too much longer, I might never want to leave. How much of what he'd shared with me was true, and how much was meant to set me at ease? If my dad showed up and I didn't want to leave with him, would Fox really let me stay? And as what? His roommate? A… girlfriend? I'd never dated anyone before.

As we pulled away, I looked for the guard, but didn't see him anywhere. Had I only imagined he'd been there? I scanned the lot. If the man had really been there, he'd vanished. *Get it together, Raven. You can't fall apart now.*

It took the entire drive back to convince myself Guard Simmons hadn't really been there. No one could disappear that fast. I had to be on edge after hearing Fox say the men had been fired. It was only that. Right?

At the house, Fox unloaded all my bags and carried them to the guest room. Instead of going inside, he hesitated in the doorway. Indecision crossed his face and he seemed to be warring with himself over something.

"Fox?" I touched his shoulder. "What's wrong?"

"Can we talk for a minute? Before we put your stuff away?"

A pain hit me straight in the center of my chest, and I wondered if he was about to ask me to leave. Had I done something? Said something I shouldn't have? Why else would he not put my bags into the guest room? I swallowed hard and gave him a nod.

Fox carried my things into the living room and set them on the floor. My hands trembled and I fisted them, hoping he hadn't noticed. I took a seat on the couch, wondering where I'd go if he asked me to leave. Maybe the man who'd taken me from Balmoral would have a room I could use, but did I want to stay there? No one made me feel as comfortable as Fox did.

He took a seat next to me, his body tense and his knee bouncing up and down. If he were nervous, whatever he had to say must be bad.

"Fox, whatever it is…"

He held up a hand. "That's part one. When we're alone, you don't have to call me Fox. It's my road name, and it would be disrespectful to call me anything else when my brothers, the other men who are part of this club, are around or we're out in public, but in the house is different. My name is Josh."

I blinked. "Uh. No offense, but you don't look like a Josh."

He smiled and shook his head. "Fair enough, but it's what my parents decided to name me. My dad was friends with Spider. When I was four, I became an orphan. Spider helped take care of me, and when I was old enough, I decided to prospect for the club."

"When is the last time someone called you Josh?" I asked.

"Not since I earned the name Fox." He reached over and took my hand. "So, if you want to use my real name, you're more than welcome to."

I realized he'd shared a part of himself with me

not many people would know about. Not just his name, but possibly about his parents as well. I didn't understand where this was going. It didn't sound like he'd want me to leave, so why hadn't he taken the bags to the guest room? If anything, his actions and words were only confusing me more.

"I know you may never be ready for a relationship that involves more than kissing. I'd never push for more than you were willing to give. You know that, right?" he asked.

I nodded.

"Thing is… I'm not getting any younger, and until meeting you, I've never wanted a woman in my house before. The thought of you leaving makes me want to grab on to every second we have together, even if it's just sharing a meal or watching a movie. And it made me realize how much I'd miss you when you're gone."

I squeezed his hand. "I'll miss you too."

"Raven, I…" He stopped and cleared his throat. The uncertainty in his eyes, the nervous way he shifted his weight, made me lean a little closer to him. "I want you to stay. Not as a guest, but as… as… mine."

My heart skipped a beat. "Yours?"

I didn't know what being his would entail. He said he'd never ask for more than I could give. What if one day he woke up and it was no longer good enough? What if *I* wasn't good enough anymore?

"You saw Luciana was wearing a cut like me. Hers says *Property of Spider* on the back. She's his old lady, and no, it doesn't have anything to do with her age. It's kind of the biker equivalent of a wife." His brow furrowed. "That's the best way I can describe it. If you stayed, I'd want you to be my old lady."

It felt like time stood still as I processed his

words. I pressed a hand to my stomach, wondering if he'd forgotten about the baby. Or was he asking me to stay with him *because* of the baby?

He noticed where I'd placed my hand and put his other hand over the top of mine. "I won't force you to keep the baby if you don't want to. You have my support whatever you decide. But if you do want to keep the baby, I'll raise him or her as my own. They never have to know we didn't create them together. Unless you want to tell them. At some point, they may have questions if they don't look like either of us."

"You want to marry me?" I asked.

"If you're asking do I really want you to be my old lady, the answer is yes. If you're asking if I'm willing to legally marry you in the eyes of the law and everyone else, the answer is also yes."

"Why?"

He huffed a little. "I guess I'm not explaining things very well."

Not really. He claimed he'd miss me if I left, and I knew I'd miss him too, but that wasn't a reason to make me his wife, or whatever he'd called it. That seemed a bit extreme. There had to be more to it. Did he worry my dad would get here and force me to leave? Could he do such a thing? I'd never met the man. It didn't matter if we shared the same DNA. I wasn't a child and could live wherever I wanted. Right?

Then again, I seemed to be in a world I didn't quite understand. These bikers didn't play by the same rules as everyone else. Breaker had nearly beaten a guard to death, threatened another, and walked out of Balmoral with me. No one had come after us. Fox said he'd kill anyone who hurt me, and I didn't think he was just spouting off. Something told me he'd literally murder someone if it meant I'd be safe.

"There's never been a woman I thought I could spend the rest of my life with, someone I wanted to fall asleep next to every night or wake up to in the mornings. I want that with you, Raven, but I don't want you to feel like you have to accept. You can tell me no and still stay here as long as you want. I'm not going to throw you out of the house if you don't think you want a relationship with me."

I liked it when he kissed me. And I loved spending time with him. I'd had fun today, even if it had been a bit much for my first outing. If I decided to keep the baby, I wouldn't want to raise him or her alone. To me, those weren't good enough reasons to tie my life to his forever. It wouldn't be fair to him.

"Can I think on it a little?" I asked.

His shoulders seemed to sag a bit and I saw a flash of disappointment in his eyes. "Yeah. Take all the time you need. I shouldn't have even brought it up. We're still strangers, and you have so much going on. I'm sorry if you feel like I put you on the spot."

I released his hand and turned so I faced him, getting on my knees. A tremor shook me as I slowly eased a leg across his lap and settled my ass against his thighs. Fox didn't move. I wasn't even sure he'd drawn a breath. Placing my hands on his chest, I felt his heart pounding against my palms.

"I don't want to accept your offer only to have you regret it later. I'm not sure I'll ever want to be touched. In another year, or three years, ten years… however long we're together, will you still be satisfied if all I can give you are kisses? Because you say yes right now and I'm not sure you'll feel the same later. Unless you plan on using those other women for your… needs."

He reached up, threading his fingers through my hair. "I will never, *never* cheat on you. It doesn't matter if you get me off or not. I don't care if we don't ever have sex. All right. That part's a lie. I do care, but it's not a deal breaker. I'm capable of using my hand if I need some relief. Sex is fun, and I admit I enjoy it, but having you in my life is more important. Do you understand?"

His heart thumped harder against my hands, and I felt him shift under me. His hold on my hair loosened, even though he didn't completely release me. How was it possible such a wonderful man existed? He almost seemed *too* perfect. There had to be a downside to all this.

"When something sounds too good to be true..."

He smiled a little. "It usually is. So, the disadvantage of being with me? It's forever. There's no divorce. No changing your mind in six months. Once you're mine, I'm not letting you leave. I'm a possessive asshole. Someone looks at you too long, I may have to put my fist through their face. I'm also bossy, and if I tell you to do something, I expect it to be done. Not in a house-cleaning sort of way, but in a this-may-save-your-life way."

"So... you want me forever. You won't sleep with other women. And you'll keep me safe. That's what I got from all that," I said.

His brows lowered. "What are you saying, Raven?"

I licked my lips and took a breath to steady my nerves. Part of me worried I might be making a mistake, but I wanted to be happy, and the closest I'd come was right here with Fox.

"I'm far from perfect. I may always be broken. I'll always be scarred, both inside and out. I can't help but worry if we keep the baby, we'll always look at them and remember what happened to me. The other side is that if we give the baby away, we could regret it forever."

He cupped my cheek. "We?"

I nodded. "We. If you're serious, and you really want me, then I'm yours. It may never be in the capacity you hope for, but being with you makes me happy, and I want to try… try to be normal again."

"Normal is overrated." He winked before tugging me closer. When his lips touched mine, every reservation I felt melted away. The worries might come back later, but for now, I'd enjoy the possibility of a bright future. With Fox by my side.

Chapter Eight

Fox

She'd agreed to be mine. I needed to call Church and take it to the table. I had a feeling Spider would chew me the fuck out. I'd not only told her she was as good as mine if that's what she wanted, but Hatchet would probably lose his shit when he found out. He'd discovered he had a daughter less than a week ago, and now I'd gone and claimed her. If our roles were reversed, I'd be ready to rip the fucker's head off.

Raven had insisted on her putting her things in my room. *Our* room. She'd fallen asleep pressed against me and seeing the peaceful look on her face gave me hope one day she'd find a way to move past the trauma she'd suffered. I knew it would always be there, lurking in the back of her mind, and something would inevitably set her off, but I'd help her through it. I placed my hand on her belly. I wanted her to keep the baby, even though it made me a selfish asshole. On the off chance she never let me touch her that way, it would be our only opportunity to have a child.

I reached for my phone on the bedside table and realized I had some missed calls and texts. I scrolled through the messages, then listened to the voicemail from the doctor's office. I should have thought to check in with the clinic sooner. I'd known they'd run tests but hadn't realized we'd have the results so fast. The clinic had run a rapid test to check for STDs and she was in the clear. Thank fuck! Poor girl had enough to deal with already.

Deleting the message, I opened my texts and pulled up Spider's name. *Need to call Church.*

I hit SEND and hadn't expected a response until the morning. The fact he answered almost right away meant Marianna wasn't having a good night. Something must have happened. Their precious girl had Asperger's and sometimes what the rest of us took in stride would be just the thing to send her spiraling.

Something wrong with Raven?

Did I really want to tell him I wanted to claim Raven? He had enough to deal with tonight.

She's fine. Sleeping next to me.

Shit. Probably should have left off that last part.

Call me. NOW.

Fuck. Fuck, fuck, fuck. I dialed Spider and eased out of bed, not wanting to wake Raven. I walked down the hall and to the living room, sitting down on the couch. When he picked up, I could hear Marianna in the background and winced.

"This could have waited," I said. "You have your hands full."

"That little shit Luka set her off." He sighed. "It's not his fault. Kid doesn't understand. He knows Marianna is different, but…"

"Knowing and understanding are two different things," I said.

"Right. Now, tell me why the fuck Raven was in bed with you. She's been through hell, and you couldn't keep your hands to yourself?"

I tried to bite my tongue. I really did. And I failed. "You mean the way you fucked Luciana the first day she was in your house?

Had I been sitting in the kitchen, I'd have smacked my head on the table in an effort to knock some sense into myself. Shit. The Pres was going to be pissed as fuck, and I had it coming.

"You trying to tell me Raven asked you to fuck her?" I wasn't fooled. His voice might sound calm, but had Spider been in front of me, he'd likely have thrown me into the wall. "Because that girl doesn't speak and looks scared of her own shadow."

"Actually, she does speak. We've talked quite a bit. In fact, she's the one who decided she wanted to be mine. I may have offered, but she let me know it's what she wants. And I haven't touched her. Not in the way you think. I've kissed her, which she allowed and even instigated, but that's it."

Spider groaned. "Hatchet is going to have your balls."

"Then it's a good thing Raven is pregnant, or I'd never have a chance to have a kid."

I squeezed my eyes shut. I either needed sleep, or alcohol. Possibly both. Where the fuck was the filter on my mouth? Or my brain for that matter. I needed to shut the hell up.

"She's pregnant?" he asked softly. "Shit. How'd she take the news? Or did she know already?"

"She wasn't aware until we saw the doctor today. I have no idea what she wants to do. I told her if she'd like to keep the baby, I'll raise it as my own. And if she decides not to keep the baby, I'll support her decision."

"That girl has traveled a long, hard road and can't seem to catch a break," he said. "I have no issue with you claiming her, but since Breaker is the one who pulled her out of that shithole, he should have a chance to vote. I'll call Church after everyone has had a chance to get some sleep. For your sake, and hers, I hope everyone is in agreement with Raven being yours."

"Same here, Pres."

"How's she doing?" Spider asked.

"Other than the misunderstanding Luciana helped solve?"

I heard a soft growl. "What misunderstanding?"

Goddamnit! I closed my eyes and slammed my head against the back of the couch. "Her first night here, she didn't want to sleep alone. I didn't sleep naked or anything, and explained I had a tendency to get hard overnight and thought it would be best if I didn't share the bed with her. She insisted. I woke up with her jerking me off, and then she panicked."

"Motherfucker! You didn't think I needed to know about that?"

"I didn't realize Luciana had come over without telling you. I thought what happened freaked out Raven. Turns out, she thought touching me in my sleep was the same as what the guards had done to her. She'd horrified herself, believing she was no better than them. We got it sorted once I realized *why* she'd curled up to make herself small."

Spider made a humming sound. "So, she decided to play with your dick while you slept. Sounds like she needed to prove something to herself."

"She did. We talked about it after Luciana left. I told her my dick wasn't going to get hard and I'd turn into some sort of beast who'd pinned her down and hurt her. She realized it had nothing to do with anatomy and more with the person, or in the case of the guards and those asshole cowboys, the monsters."

"It sounds like you've been good for her."

"I'd like to think so. We went to the doctor, then ate at the diner. Afterward, I took her shopping for more clothes and shoes. She didn't want to spend my money, but I didn't give her a choice. It wore her out, though, so we can home after."

I heard Marianna get louder and winced. I felt sorry for Spider and Luciana on nights like this one. Usually, one or both of them could calm her, but sometimes it lasted for hours until the poor girl wore herself out. I knew they adored her and took it all in stride, but it had to be exhausting after a while.

It made me wonder what our baby would be like, if Raven decided to keep it. I'd need to fix a nursery for him or her. We'd still need a guest room, in case Hatchet came to visit, and the house only had one other room. At the moment, I'd been using it for storage.

"Spider, I don't want to necessarily move, but I may need more space."

"Let's see how Church goes tomorrow, then we'll talk. Are you thinking about adding on? Or do you want to take Raven to see the two new homes?"

"You don't think anyone will be pissed if I claim one of them?" I asked.

"Son, you're the VP and one day, you'll be stepping up to take over my position. No one is going to say shit about you taking one of the new homes. And if they do, just knock their damn teeth down their throats and remind them where they stand."

I snorted. "All right. After Church, I'll ask Raven if she'd like to look at a different house. If she wants to keep this one, maybe I can add on or something. You know Hatchet will want to visit, and I'd like to have a few kids, if Raven is up for it."

"Go snuggle with your woman. I think my little hellion is calming down so I'm about to do the same. I'll put out the call sometime after ten. You know damn well the boys partying at the clubhouse tonight won't fall into bed until after four in the morning."

"In that case, maybe we need to have Church at four-thirty just to fuck with them."

Spider laughed. "If I thought I could get my ass out of bed that early, I would. I'm getting lazy in my old age."

I heard Luciana in the background going off in Spanish and smiled. Every time Spider said something about being old, she went off on him. Far as she was concerned, he was perfect. I'd always liked seeing the two of them together. Luciana smoothed Spider's rough edges, and he gave her the kindness and gentle touch she'd never experienced before coming here. Despite the fact he was roughly forty years older than her, they made it work.

"Uh, Pres. Any idea how old Hatchet is?" I asked.

He chuckled. "Younger than you."

Fuck. My. Life. He was going to kill me when he found out I'd claimed Raven. The good shit in life never came without a cost, and I'd pay any price to have her in my life. At least I could prepare myself for whenever Hatchet graced us with his presence.

"Better call Hatchet. Give him a heads-up," Spider said. "Don't want him hearing anything secondhand."

"Yeah, I know. I'm on it."

I disconnected the call and scrolled through my call history. I found the number Hatchet had called from and saved it to my phone. Before I changed my mind, I hit SEND and put the phone to my ear, listening to it ring. I didn't know where he was right now, or what time it would be at his location.

He didn't even bother with a hello when he picked up.

"What's wrong with my daughter?" Hatchet asked.

"Why does something have to be wrong?"

"You're calling in the middle of the night. If there's nothing wrong, why didn't you wait until morning?"

I tipped my head back and shut my eyes, fighting off the headache building between my eyes. "Because there are some things we need to discuss, and I'd rather do it when Raven isn't listening. She heard part of my conversation with you before. Sneaky little thing is so quiet I didn't realize she was eavesdropping."

He chuckled. "Gets her stealth from her dad."

"She's talking now. To me anyway. I've gotten to know quite a bit about her since she decided to move into my house the other night."

"What's my girl talking about?" he asked, sounding genuinely curious.

"A little about what she's afraid of, but mostly we've just talked about normal shit. What she likes to eat, that sort of thing. Went to the doctor today." I went silent for a minute, debating if I should tell him. "I don't know what she's going to decide, and I told her she has my support either way, but… she's pregnant, Hatchet. Had to be one of the guards at Balmoral."

If I hadn't heard him breathing, I'd have checked to see if the call dropped. I didn't know how long it would take him to gather his thoughts, or for his anger to fade, so I filled the void.

"Took her to the diner today. She made fun of me for ordering two pieces of pie." I smiled. "She laughed at me. Like full-on laughed until she cried."

Hatchet huffed, but I could hear the emotion behind it. "I'm glad she found something to smile about. Fuck knows she hasn't much of a reason to."

"Took her shopping for more clothes. She didn't want to spend my money, so I dumped about twenty bras into the cart. Everything she picked up, I added ten more. She has a decent wardrobe now, and several pair of shoes. Need to get her some decent motorcycle boots, though."

"Did you just say you bought her bras? As in you picked them out?" Hatchet asked, his voice going soft.

"About that..." Moment of truth. Just how pissed would he be over my news? "Spider is calling Church in the morning. I'm asking the club to vote. Raven agreed to be mine."

"Are you fucking shitting me? I just found out I have a daughter and you're already taking her from me before I even get a chance to meet her?" he asked.

"I didn't plan it. Hatchet, she's amazing. So strong. Beautiful. She's the sweetest woman I've ever met, and the only one who's ever made me want to hold on tight and never let go. I understand if you want to kick my ass whenever you get here, but I won't let her go."

"Sounds to me like you love her," he said after a moment of silence. "Do you?"

I hadn't really thought about it. Did I? Sure, I felt more for her than I ever had for someone before. Was it love?

"Do you know what love feels like?" he asked.

"No. At least, not that sort of love."

He grunted. "You'll figure it out. I took care of those cowboys and tracked down a few others with a bit of help. I'm not too far from you right now. As much as I'd rather see my little girl after I've taken out all the men who hurt her, I don't think I can wait anymore."

"We have a guest room. It's all yours whenever you want to stop by."

"Fox, I know you're the VP of your club, but if you hurt my little girl, I'll make sure they never find your body."

"Wouldn't expect anything less. But for the record, I'd sooner die than hurt her. She's my everything. Might seem fast, and I guess we really don't know much about each other, but I will treat her like a fucking queen."

"All I needed to hear. Don't tell her I'm coming. Not sure she'll be too excited to see me. No telling what her mom has said about me over the years. Poisonous bitch!"

We talked another few minutes before I hung up and went back to bed. Raven had rolled to her other side and curled into a ball. A slight tremor raked her small frame and I slid into bed next to her, pulling her back against my chest. I held her close.

I didn't know what nightmare had her in its grip, but it clearly wasn't good. I wished I had a way to ensure she only had happy dreams. Bad enough she suffered during the day. At night, she should get a reprieve.

"I've got you, sweetheart. You're safe," I whispered. "No one will hurt you again."

She started to calm, and the tension eased from her body. I placed my hand on her belly, holding her still. She whimpered and wiggled a bit. It had the unfortunate effect of making my dick hard, and I tried to pull my hips away from the curve of her ass. Raven cried out, bolting upright, her chest heaving and her eyes wide with fright.

"Hey!" I ran my hand down her hair. "It's okay. I'm right here."

She turned to me, tears shimmering in her eyes. "I'm tired of being afraid. I hate that other than a few kisses with you, I don't have anything pleasant to associate with sex. When I close my eyes, the darkness creeps in and I don't have anything to use against it. I can't think of a single happy memory that's big enough to win over the despair."

My heart broke at her words and the anguish on her face. I'd do anything for her, give her anything. I hadn't lied to Hatchet. Raven was my entire world. I might not know what love felt like, but she'd had me wrapped around her finger since the moment I met her. She'd wormed her way past my defenses.

"What do you need from me? Whatever it is, just ask."

She reached down and took my hand, then yanked it toward her, placing it over her breast. I tensed and stopped breathing. I stared at my fingers curving over the soft mound under her nightgown and couldn't figure out if I should pull away or let her do what she wanted.

"Um, Raven."

"Please, Josh."

It was the use of my name that made my resolve crumble. I pulled her down, lying her on her back, and leaned up on my elbow. I slid my hand down her belly, then up again, letting my fingers lightly trace the underside of her breast. She trembled but looked up at me with complete trust. It gutted me. My sweet, broken girl hadn't been given any reason to trust men, but from the first day we'd met, she'd chosen me as her protector. What if she needed to be saved from herself? I didn't know if this would be a good idea, but I couldn't deny her.

"You want me to stop at any time, you tell me. Understood?" I asked.

She nodded and placed her hand over mine. "I know it's you here with me. Seeing your face will keep me grounded. It's when I close my eyes that the darkness creeps in."

"How far do you want this to go, Raven? If you have boundaries in mind, I need to know them now."

She took my hand and slipped it under the hem of her nightgown. "I trust you completely, Josh. I don't know if I'll panic at some point, but don't stop until that happens. I need this. It's the only way I think I'll heal."

I ran my fingers back and forth across her stomach, slowly inching them upward. Cupping the soft mound of her breast, I swiped my thumb across her nipple. Her eyes went wide, and her cheeks flushed. The peak hardened, as did the other side. I didn't see panic in her eyes, so I explored a little more, taking my time and moving slow.

Getting to my knees, I straddled her thighs, pausing to see how she'd react. She watched me but didn't seem scared or nervous. I inched the hem of her nightgown up until I'd uncovered her breasts. Raven leaned up, letting me pull the garment all the way off.

"Still okay, sweetheart?" I asked.

She nodded and reached out a hand, cupping my cheek. I turned my face into her palm and pressed a kiss there before focusing on her again. She'd been okay with me touching her. How would she react if I put my mouth somewhere other than her lips? I leaned down, giving her time to move away or tell me to stop. My lips brushed the skin of her stomach, and I flicked my tongue against the softness.

Raven gasped and I glanced up, making sure it hadn't been from fear. Need burned in her eyes. I kissed my way up her torso until I took one of her nipples into my mouth. Giving it a tug, I sucked the hard bud. I gently bit down and lashed it with my tongue, making her cry out and buck underneath me.

"Oh, God! Josh!"

I drew back, not sure if she wanted me to keep going or stop. "Still doing okay?"

"Yes. Yes! Please… I… I liked what you were doing."

"Not scared? Anxious? Having flashbacks?"

Her eyes darkened a moment. "They never did anything like this. All I ever got from any of them was my pants yanked down and them taking what they wanted. This is different. Mostly because it's you, but also because you're trying to make me feel good."

I smile at her. "Only trying?"

Her cheeks pinked even more. "No, not just trying. It *did* feel good."

"We can stop right now if you want."

She shook her head. "I want to see how far we can go without me freezing up. Is that all right?"

I bent down to kiss her on the lips. "Sweetheart, for you, I'd do anything. Only thing I can't do is stop coming in the middle of an orgasm, but I can damn sure pull out if I need to."

"I want to try, Josh. I need to."

I kissed her again and settled my weight over her. I felt her hands on my back, and I vowed I'd do whatever it took to make this good for her.

Chapter Nine

Raven

The feel of Fox's body pressing mine into the mattress didn't scare me the way I'd thought it would. If anything, I found it comforting. He kissed me, soft and slow, taking his time as if he were savoring me. My nipples were still hard and brushed against his chest, sending little sparks of pleasure through me. A bit of apprehension lingered in the back of my mind, but I'd already promised to stay with Fox. I wanted to do this, not only for me but for us and the relationship we were building.

I'd always laughed at the romances where the hero and heroine took one look at one another and fell instantly in love. I didn't think this was love, but I certainly felt a warmth and fondness for Fox. Breaker may have rescued me from Balmoral, but Fox had saved me in every other way. I'd grown more in the two nights I'd known him, felt more at ease in the presence of a man than I had in what felt like forever, and I didn't know why. I also didn't really care about the *why* part of it all.

Fox was amazing, and he was mine. I didn't need to know more than that.

"Make love to me, Josh."

I felt him smile against my neck as he nibbled on me. "Thought that's what I was doing. I must be out of practice if you can't tell."

My brow furrowed. I couldn't claim experience, but shouldn't there be fewer clothes separating us? I tugged at his shirt, wanting it off. The stubborn man refused to give me what I wanted. Instead, he worked his way down my body. When he sat up and reached for my panties, my breath caught. He eased them over my hips and down my legs. My heart fluttered like the wings of a hummingbird as he parted my thighs and settled between my splayed legs.

"Josh?"

"I'm going to make you feel good, sweetheart. Trust me?"

I nodded. Of course, I trusted him. I would have never let him get this far otherwise. My cheeks burned as he spread me open, and I felt his tongue lap against me. I squirmed, but he held me tight.

"Want me to stop?" he asked.

"No. Yes. Maybe? It feels… odd."

He cocked his head and waited. I didn't have more to say about it. Odd seemed to cover it, well as good as any other word. It hadn't hurt. If anything, I'd go so far as to say it felt nice. I didn't understand why he wanted his face *there,* though.

"But not bad?"

"No. It's not bad." Fox licked his lips and blew across my pussy. My breath caught at the sensation. I felt my clit harden. "That's… that's…"

He flicked his tongue across the swollen bud, and I gasped, my eyes going wide. He did it again, and I couldn't stop the keening sound that slipped past my lips. *Oh, God!* I'd never known any part of sex could feel so good.

"Will you let me keep going?" he asked.

I nodded, not sure I could speak.

He licked, sucked, and teased me until I nearly sobbed. My body shook and strained. There was something just out of reach, a feeling I craved yet had never experienced. Frustration welled inside me, as I waited for release. I could feel it, so close and I couldn't quite get there. I didn't know what to ask for.

Fox sucked my clit into his mouth and gave it a

hard pull. I drew in a breath and felt like I was flying and coming apart at the same time. The sensations nearly overwhelmed me as I cried out, throwing my head back as my thighs clenched hard around him. My body trembled and I held back a sob from the intensity of the orgasm.

"That's it, beautiful. Come for me," he murmured, licking me again.

"Josh! I… what…" My chest heaved as I tried to catch my breath. I stared down at him in amazement. All the movies I'd watched, or books I'd read, hadn't prepared me for what he'd just done. Reading about an orgasm, or seeing one faked on TV, wasn't nearly the same as feeling it.

He levered himself up and sat on his knees, wiping his hand across his beard. "Now, do you still think sex is painful or scary? Or do you see what you've experienced so far wasn't sex? What those men did was all about control and inflicting pain."

"Yes, Josh. I understand the difference." I reached my hand out for him. "Will you take off your shirt? I don't like being the only one naked."

He stripped his shirt over his head, and I pushed up on my elbows to get a good look at him. Even though he had a lean build, his broad chest had definition, and I saw a hint of abs. He didn't look like the underwear models in magazine ads, or the buff actors on TV. Despite the fact I could tell he kept himself in shape, he wasn't a solid mass of muscle. He was… perfect. To me, anyway.

His hands went the waistband of his underwear and he paused. "You sure about this, Raven? We can stop. I'm okay waiting however long I need to. I told you the truth when I said I would be all right if we never had sex. I just want *you,* in whatever capacity you'll allow."

Tears pricked my eyes at how sweet he was. How could a man who looked so tough be so unfailingly kind? "I'm sure. I want this, Josh."

He nodded and removed his boxers, tossing them aside. His cock stood erect. Hard and ready. I sat up and reached for him, wrapping my hand around his shaft and giving it a stroke. He groaned and gripped my wrist, stilling my motion.

"Sweetheart, we already know I don't last long when you do that. If you want me inside you, better save that for another time."

I lay back again. A case of nerves hit me, but I shoved down the doubts. This was Fox. My hero. The man I wanted to spend the rest of my life with. He'd never hurt me and had proven that already. If I were ever going to give myself to someone, it would be him. I couldn't think of anyone I would trust more. I just wish *I* felt worthy of him.

He settled over me, his cock nudging my pussy. He braced his weight on his arms and leaned down to kiss me. His lips moved against mine, slowly, as if he wanted to savor the moment. Fox rocked his hips, sliding his cock up and down my pussy until I felt him start to push inside me. My breath stalled a moment, and I gripped his shoulder, my nails biting into him.

"You all right?" he asked, drawing back far enough to look at me.

"Don't stop." I tightened my hold on him as Fox slid in deeper. When he'd completely filled me, he held still, giving my body time to adjust. I might not be a virgin, but I hadn't been with anyone his size either. "So big."

He chuckled and kissed my nose. "You're good for my ego. Not big. Just average."

I shook my head. No, he wasn't average. He pulled his hips back, then drove forward. On the next stroke, he shifted so that he brushed against my clit.

"Remember our talk about how a cock can't hurt you by itself?" he asked, driving into me again.

"You're having this conversation *now*?"

He smiled. "It's all in how you use it. And I aim to make you scream my name, in a good way, before I'm done. I may not be as big as you claim, but I know how to use what I've got."

I clung to him as he took me hard and fast, his hips slapping against mine with every thrust. The bed rocked under us, and I felt that same incredible sensation from before building again. Sweat beaded on Fox's brow and along his body. The intensity of his gaze held me spellbound.

"Come for me, Raven." He growled, his strokes becoming erratic. "Come for me, baby. Please. I can't hold out much longer."

I wiggled my hips until he hit just the right spot and I came, calling out his name. I felt the heat of his release, and still he didn't slow. Fox kept stroking in and out of me, wringing one more orgasm from me.

"How do you feel about toys?" he murmured, pulling out and tumbling to the bed next to me. He drew me into his arms and held me close.

"Toys?"

"Vibrators and such. I'm thinking we need a small one for your clit. Being inside you is like nothing I've ever felt before. You squeeze my dick just right and I can't last long. I want you mindless with pleasure, so sated you can't move for hours. I feel like I failed you."

I curled against him, tracing patterns on his chest. "You didn't. That was amazing, Josh."

He kissed my forehead. "I'll make it better next time."

I sighed and closed my eyes. It seemed he was going to be stubborn about it. I didn't need it to be better. As long as he was the one inside me, the one touching me, nothing else mattered. I liked feeling this close to him, like we'd shared something special.

As I felt his release coat my thighs, my heart nearly stopped. "We didn't use protection."

"Can't get you any more pregnant than you already are," he said.

"But… what if those guards gave me something?" I leaned up to look at him. Fear filled me at the thought of hurting Fox in any way. What if I'd contracted something that couldn't be cured? "After the incident with the cowboys, I got tested and I didn't have anything. They didn't test me at Balmoral."

He cupped my cheek. "Easy, beautiful. I should have told you sooner. The doctor's office called. He had a rapid STD test run on the samples he took during your appointment. You're clean, and for the record, so am I."

I eased back down next to him, my heart still racing. I hadn't even thought to worry about Fox giving me something. It never crossed my mind he'd put me in danger. Even if we hadn't known each other long, he had too much integrity for something so underhanded as being careless with my health.

He stroked his hand up and down my back, and I closed my eyes, reveling in the moment. When Breaker came for me at Balmoral, I hadn't known what to think. He'd beaten the guard, but even still, I hadn't known for certain if I'd be better off by leaving. Then I'd met Fox. One look in his eyes and something inside me had settled. Calmed. I'd felt safe just sitting next to him, safer than I'd felt in such a long time.

"I'm sorry I didn't tell you about the call," he said. "I actually missed it and listened to the voicemail while you were sleeping. I stepped out of the room to make a call to Spider. He's calling Church in the morning. That's the room you went to before at the clubhouse. Will you be all right here by yourself while I'm gone?"

I tensed and tried not to panic. "Why do I have to stay here?"

He kept rubbing my back. "Church is for patched members and officers only. They won't let you sit in, and I'm not sure you'd be comfortable in the clubhouse by yourself."

"Who else would be there?"

"Probably a Prospect or two. Maybe some of the girls who come to have some fun. The old ladies typically stay home. Would you want to go hang out with Luciana? Or meet the other women?" he asked.

It would make sense to meet everyone. This would be my home from now on, and the thought of having friends made me smile a little.

"I'd like to meet them," I said.

"When the call goes out tomorrow for Church, I'll let Spider know. I'm sure Luciana can set something up. They could all come over here, or I could ask Luciana to pick you up."

"Are the women never allowed at the clubhouse?" I asked.

"More like they prefer to not be there unless it's a family event."

I snuggled closer. "I'd feel better staying close to you. Can you ask them to meet me there? I won't interrupt your meeting or whatever you'll be doing. Knowing you're in the same building will keep my anxiety at a manageable level."

He kissed the top of my head. "Then I'll take you with me. We'll figure it out. But, Raven, sooner or later, I'm going to have to leave you alone while I handle business. As much as I love spending time with you, I can't be with you every second of every day. You understand, right?"

I nodded. Didn't mean I had to like it, but he was right. When he needed to get back to work, I'd have to loosen my hold on him. I only hoped it didn't happen until I'd settled in more and figured out exactly how I fit not only into his life, but with his club as well.

"Get some sleep, Raven. Morning will be here all too soon. I don't know about you, but I'm exhausted."

"Tired," I murmured.

He kissed the top of my head again. "Sweet dreams, beautiful."

I could only hope. The nightmares left me feeling shaken for hours after I woke. I shifted and the stickiness between my legs made me shudder. How long would it take before I wouldn't associate it with bad things? I refused to let the guards beat me. They wouldn't make me afraid the rest of my life. I wouldn't let them.

I heard a soft snore from Fox and smiled. He'd fallen asleep so easily and I envied him a little. With a sigh, I closed my eyes and breathed in his scent. It didn't take long before sleep pulled me under too.

Chapter Ten

Fox

An insistent chirping sound tugged at me. I groaned and tightened my hold on the woman in my arms, not wanting to move. Sadly, the damn thing making noise wouldn't shut up. I cracked my eyes open and looked for my phone. My vision blurred and I felt for the annoying piece of technology along the top of the bedside table. Closing my fingers around the device, I squinted and managed to hit the button to silence it.

It was too fucking early. When Spider said ten o'clock for Church, I should have asked him to make it in the afternoon. Of course, I hadn't planned on staying up making love to my woman. I smiled and looked down at her. She curled against me, her breathing deep and even.

If the vote didn't go my way today, I'd seriously lose my shit. I hadn't asked for a single fucking thing. Not once. I gave to this club all the damn time. Had bled for them. Only thing I wanted was Raven. At least her dad seemed okay with me claiming her. Not thrilled, but what father would be?

Speaking of fathers… I wondered when a good time would be to talk to Raven about the baby. I didn't want to stress her over the situation, but if she wanted to keep him or her, I wanted to start working on the nursery. Or get us moved into one of the new homes. Assuming she would be all right with moving. Since this was the first place she'd felt safe in a while, it might hold sentimental value for her. If that were the case, I'd figure out a way to give us more space. I could always put a tiny house out back for when her dad wanted to visit. Enclose the carport and add a storage room on the other side.

Whatever it took to keep my woman happy.

I ran my fingers through her hair, not wanting to wake her. She had to be exhausted. I remembered what I'd promised her and picked up the phone to text Spider about Luciana and the others meeting Raven at the clubhouse. He'd probably have quite a bit to say about it, but I didn't have the mental capacity to get into it with him right then. I needed a shower and coffee. Lots of coffee.

"Raven, time to get up."

She groaned and burrowed farther into my side. Too fucking cute. I smiled and ran my hand up and down her arm. If it were up to me, I'd let her sleep the day away. I knew if I left without her, she'd either freak out when she woke to an empty house, or she'd be upset I hadn't taken her with me so she could meet the other women.

"Come on, Sleeping Beauty." I gave her a slight shake. "Time to shower and head to the clubhouse."

She sighed and opened her eyes, blinking at me a few times. "Shower?"

"Yeah. I got you all dirty last night." I waggled my eyebrows at her, making her laugh just as I'd intended. I let her go and rolled out of bed, yanking the covers off her in the process. She squealed and made a grab for them. "Nope. Sorry, sweetheart. Got to get up. Or stay home while I go to Church."

She bolted upright in bed and scrambled off the mattress. "I'm ready."

I let my gaze skim over her curves. "Not quite. You go with me like that, and I won't have a club left. I'll have to kill every last one of them for looking at my woman while she's naked. Want to shower by yourself, or want to join me?"

She swayed on her feet and yawned widely. "With you."

Taking her hand, I led her into the bathroom and started the shower. I had a feeling we'd be late to Church, but it would be worth it. Now that I'd had a taste of her, I wasn't sure I could wash her and not want more.

Once the water had warmed, I nudged her under the spray and followed her into the glassed-in enclosure. I shut the door behind me and took a moment to admire the view. She'd tipped her head back while the water soaked her hair. Rivulets ran down the slopes of her breasts and her belly. My mouth watered, remembering how good she'd tasted.

"I'm one lucky bastard," I murmured.

She heard me and opened her eyes, giving me a cautious smile. "I'm not too sure about that. I got the better deal."

I tugged her against me. "How do you figure?"

"I'm broken, Josh. Some part of me will probably *always* be damaged. Being with you has been amazing, and in just a few days I feel like I've come a long way. I'm just worried something will set me off, the nightmares will return, or I'll wake up one day and it will feel like I can't breathe and need to escape."

I cupped her cheek. "And when you feel any of those things, you tell me. I'm here for you, Raven, in whatever capacity you need. I'll make love to you, when you allow it, and I'll hold you when you think you'll fall apart. You're mine, but there's a flipside to that. It means I'm yours too. Use me however you need to, sweetheart."

As soon as I said the words, I caught their double meaning. I hadn't meant anything sexual. Didn't mean I'd turn her down if that's what she needed or wanted.

Even though Raven seemed to be doing remarkably well, far better than I'd thought she'd be this soon after escaping Balmoral, I didn't kid myself into thinking all was well. I knew she'd have demons the rest of her life. She hadn't needed to tell me. The fact she trusted me enough to share that part of herself, however, meant we were on the right path. She'd heal, even if she never became whole again.

"Do you think they'll like me? The other women?" she asked. "Luciana seemed nice."

"They're going to love you, and remember, they have dark pasts too. They aren't going to look down on you. They'll see your strength, just like I do." I leaned down to kiss her, my lips barely brushing hers before I pulled back. My cock started to harden, and I didn't want her to feel obligated to do anything. I took a step back, but she advanced.

"You don't have to do that," she said.

"Do what?"

"Run." She smiled a little. "The fact you're hard doesn't scare me, Josh. After last night..."

Her cheeks warmed. I pulled her against my chest again and hugged her to me. I knew I didn't deserve her. She was too sweet, and despite all she'd suffered, too innocent. Yet I didn't want to ever let her go.

"Not running, beautiful. I'm a badass biker." I grinned. "We don't run, unless bombs are involved."

"Will you tell me more about you? Not now because I know we need to go, but I want to learn all about the past and present versions of you."

I kissed her forehead. "Deal. Now, scrub up because if I put my hands on you, we'll be late."

She smiled and backed up, reaching for the soap. I shouldn't have offered to shower together. Even if I wasn't touching her, seeing her soap her breasts had to be the hottest thing I'd watched in a long time. Hell, I'd seen naked women every night at the clubhouse for as long as I could remember, but their images had blurred in my memories. All I saw now was my sweet, beautiful Raven.

After she finished, I took the soap from her and cleaned myself, trying not to stare as she washed her hair. I felt like a starry-eyed teen who had never seen a naked girl before. Except with Raven, I'd be struck dumb by her even fully clothed. I'd seen women who looked flawless. It was her scars, and all she'd survived, that made her shine brighter than all the others.

We got out and dressed. I pulled on my usual jeans and tee and shrugged my cut over my shoulders. Raven opted for denim shorts and a black V-neck tee. She put on a pair of sandals she'd picked up at the store yesterday and left her wet hair hanging down her back.

"You're not riding on my bike with sandals on."

Her nose wrinkled. "Why not? I was barefoot when I rode behind you the first time."

"And it wasn't safe. You could have gotten burned on the pipes. I still have the truck. We'll take that."

"Josh, I liked being on your bike."

I crossed the room and tipped her chin up. "And you'll get to go on more rides, but not today. Besides, I know you're pregnant now. I didn't know it when I let you ride behind me before."

"Are you saying I can't ride with you as long as I'm pregnant?" she asked, her eyes going wide. "Why not?"

I slipped my hands around her waist and hugged

her. "Because you're the most important thing in my life, Raven, and for now, so is the baby. If you decide we aren't keeping the baby, then I'll try not to get attached."

She rested her head against my chest. "You really want this baby, don't you?"

I sucked in a breath and contemplated lying my ass off. I didn't want her to feel like she had no choice in the matter. But I didn't want to start out with a lie between us.

"Yeah, I want the baby. Not enough to tell you to keep it. I'll be first to admit I can be an ass at times, and domineering, but I would never force you to keep the baby, Raven. The decision is completely yours and I'll support you no matter what."

"What if I see the baby and can't stand to look at them? What if they remind me too much of how they were conceived?" she asked.

She had a reason to be worried. It was quite possible that very thing could happen. Or she could look at the baby and fall completely in love with our child. And yes, I already thought of the baby as mine, simply because Raven was mine. They were a package deal in my opinion.

"Then we discuss adoption. It's possible someone from another club might want to raise them. I know Havoc and Jordan adopted some kids down at the Devil's Boneyard. If you don't want the baby, we'll make sure they have a loving home."

She sucked in a deep breath and blew it out. "All right. For now, can we plan on keeping him? Or her?"

I smiled and hugged her tighter. "Absolutely."

We left and drove to the clubhouse. The line of bikes out front was proof we were late, even if sex hadn't been involved. I led Raven inside, noting the three club whores huddled in the corner. I narrowed my eyes at them, wondering why the fuck they were here.

Luciana and Violeta sat at a table near the bar. I took Raven over and pulled out a chair for her. Once she'd sat, I got a drink for her from behind the bar.

"Where's Vasha?" I asked.

"Watching the kids," Violeta said. She cast a glare at the club whores. "Once we saw them, there was no way we were bringing the kids inside."

"Spider's chewing out your brothers right now," Luciana said. "They knew we were coming and left those skanks in here. He's pissed. Those three scurried outside, but once everyone went into Church, they came back like fucking cockroaches."

I kissed Raven's cheek. "You know where I'll be if you need anything. It's frowned upon for you to interrupt Church, but if someone's bleeding or the building is on fire, by all means barge right in. Stick with Luciana and Violeta. I'll be back soon."

I walked down the hall and pushed open the doors to Church. Considering Spider was supposedly reading everyone the riot act, it seemed a bit too quiet. Hornet and Freak both stared at the table, the latter with flushed cheeks. Those two must have been responsible for the club whores. I wondered if Spider knew those women had come back inside. Doubtful. Couldn't wait to see how pissed he got when he saw them.

"You're late," Spider said, leaning back in his seat.

"Sorry. Raven needed a hug and..." I sank into my chair and sighed. "She started to freak a little over the baby. I had to calm her down again."

"Baby?" Breaker asked, looking a bit green at the

thought. "Those fuckers got her pregnant?"

I nodded. "They did. She isn't sure how she feels about it. For now, we're planning to keep the baby."

"We?" Bear asked.

"And that brings us to why I called Church," Spider said. "Only Breaker and the club officers have met Raven. She's the one we pulled out of Balmoral. Hatchet's daughter. You may have seen her in the clubhouse that first night when Breaker brought her here. She immediately clung to Fox and has been living with him."

"Hold the fuck up." Hornet lifted a hand. "You're telling me you put your hands on some poor girl who's been raped and abused?"

I tipped my head back and counted to ten. Then twenty. When I thought I had enough control to not lunge for him, I scanned my brothers seated around the table. "Yes, Raven is living with me. No, I didn't force her to endure my touch. From the first night she was in my house, she's felt safer with me lying next to her at night. Anyone has an issue with it, I'll be happy to settle this outside."

Breaker cleared his throat. "I saw how she reacted to Fox. He got upset over how I'd found her and put his hand through the wall. Raven ran to him, worried he'd hurt himself. She held onto him and wouldn't let go."

"She's like Luciana and Violeta," Rocket said. "Only one person makes her feel safe, and it seems that would be Fox. I'm not sure I understand why we're here, though. You could have just sent a text to let us know Raven would be living with him for a while."

"It's more than that," Spider said. "Raven has agreed to be Fox's old lady. I called Church so we can take a vote."

"I'll cast mine right now," Rocket said. He lifted his hand. "I say give them what they want."

More hands went up around the table. I hadn't realized I'd been worried until I saw Breaker's hand go up too. Spider slammed his fist into the table.

"It's unanimous. Congratulations, Fox. You have an old lady. I'll have Luciana contact the woman who makes the property cuts. Raven should have it by end of the week. Now, if there's nothing else we need to discuss, everyone get the hell out and make sure you don't scare our newest family member."

I stood and hurried out of the doors, only to come to a halt at the end of the hallway. My heart hammered in my chest as I stared at the chaos in front of me. Violeta kicked a club whore in the stomach and legs as the woman curled into a ball on the nasty floor. Luciana slammed her fist into another's face. And my sweet Raven? She had a handful of another's hair and smashed her face into the table until blood sprayed everywhere.

"Holy shit," I muttered.

Spider came up behind me and grunted, taking it all in. "What the hell is going on out here?"

Joe ran over, his face pale and a slight tremor in his hands. "Pres. VP. I, uh… I tried to throw them out, but… I didn't want to hurt them."

I motioned for Joe to keep talking.

"CeeCee started mouthing off about how much she'd enjoyed your cock, and how she'd be riding it again soon. Talked about your woman being a cheap, ugly whore who'd never keep you satisfied." He gulped and looked at Spider. "And um… Rochelle said some shit about Luciana getting fat and how you'd be available again soon enough. It sort of went to hell from there."

I strode into the room and wrapped my arm around Raven's waist, hauling her back against me. I turned to the side to set her away from CeeCee, who collapsed to the floor with tears and mascara running down her face.

"Fox, I think she broke my nose," the woman whined.

I grabbed her hair and hauled her up to her feet. "I don't give a shit if she broke your nose. After what I just heard, I hope she loosened a few teeth too. You're gone, CeeCee. Don't ever come back here. You get me? I may not hurt women but push me and I will make your life fucking hell."

She cried harder and I tossed her away like the unwanted trash she was. I felt Raven's hands on my back right before her scent hit me. I reached back and held her closer to me. I should have known those bitches would start shit.

"Pres, your woman all right? Rocket, how's Violeta?"

"We're fine," Luciana said, shaking out her hand. "You should be proud of your girl."

I smiled. "Oh, I am. She was fucking fierce, wasn't she?"

Turning, I lowered my head and kissed Raven in the middle of the clubhouse. I didn't care who saw. She was mine, and I wanted her to know just how hot it made me to see her take down that whore. When I pulled back, a few of my asshole brothers wolf whistled and clapped. I flipped them off.

Breaker came up, a smile on his lips. "Welcome to the family, Raven. I'm really happy for you. Fox is a great guy."

Her cheeks flushed and her eyes brightened. "Yes, he is. The best."

Well, I wouldn't go that far. I only hoped she felt that way in another month, another year, or a decade from now. Assuming I didn't keel over before then. I planned to be around a long-ass time for her and our kid, or kids, but I knew bad shit happened and life sometimes fucked you over.

Fate was a fickle bitch. But if she tried to take me from Raven too soon, I'd dig my way out of hell to get back to my family.

Chapter Eleven

Raven

I couldn't believe I'd done that! I'd physically assaulted someone, and all because she said something I hadn't liked. I'd never been a violent sort of person, at least not toward others. The fact Fox hadn't been angry over the incident, and if anything seemed pleased by my reaction, made me feel a little less sick over it. The woman might have been mouthing off about Fox, but I'd gone too far when I broke her nose. At least, I thought so. Everyone else seemed happy about it. Even Luciana and Violeta had attacked the other two women.

"You're not angry?" I asked Fox as he drove away from the clubhouse.

"No. You were staking your claim, Raven. In my world -- now yours too -- that shit's important. Those women wouldn't have backed down if you'd asked them politely."

"You pulled Spider aside to talk. I thought maybe you'd actually been upset about it but hadn't wanted to say something in front of everyone. I didn't want to embarrass you."

He reached over and took my hand, lifting it to his lips. "Sweetheart, I was damn proud of you. As for Spider, I needed to get something from him. We're making a stop on the way back to the house."

We hadn't driven through the gates, so whatever it was I knew it had to be part of their property. Fox drove past the house and continued down the road. The houses became farther apart until we were nearing the end of them. I saw two that seemed larger than the others, both set farther back off the road. Fox pulled into the driveway of the first one and shut off the engine.

"Are we visiting someone?" I asked.

"No. This house is empty. When I picked out the house I have now, I didn't have anyone special in my life, and kids weren't even on my mind. Now that I have you, and we have a baby on the way, I thought we might need more space." He turned in his seat to face me. "We don't have to accept this house. If you don't like it, I'll tell Spider we're keeping the one we have. I'll just need to come up with a way to give us more room. I have a few ideas, but this seemed like a simpler solution."

I eyed the large home and wondered exactly how many rooms he thought we needed. As far as I knew, there was only one baby growing inside me. He'd mentioned the possibility of more kids, but we hadn't really had a discussion about it. Did he want a large family? Could I handle having more than one child? Having grown up without a father, and then my mom throwing me out, I hadn't had the best example of what a parent should be. What if I screwed up our kids?

"If you don't want to go inside, we won't," he said.

I could tell he wanted this house. Or more accurately, he hoped I would want it. He hadn't asked for a single thing since he'd let me move in. The least I could do was look at the house with him. I'd try to keep an open mind.

"It doesn't hurt to look, right?"

He smiled. "Right. Come on, sweetheart. Let's see if we even like this place. I haven't been inside it since they finished putting up the walls and made it livable."

I opened the door and got out, then followed him

up the walkway. The yard had been cut. A flower bed stretched along the front of the home, but only dirt filled the space. Someone had placed stones along the outer edge to form a border. Decorative pavers led from the front porch down to the mailbox. The home had beige bricks and a brown roof. Rustic wood shutters framed the windows. It would have fit into any suburban neighborhood and didn't look a thing like a house I'd expect a biker to have. Then again, I hadn't really known any before coming here. Maybe they all lived in beautiful homes like this one.

Fox pulled a key from his pocket and unlocked the door. He motioned for me to enter first, and the moment I stepped inside, I knew we'd be taking the house. The entry had a natural stone floor that continued into the kitchen to our left. A large family room on the right had dark hardwood floors. I saw three other doors on this level as well as French doors that led into what appeared to be a sunroom.

The brightly lit space called to me, and I had to see it. I pushed open the doors and stepped down into the room. The same stonework in the front entry covered the floor. Large windows encased the space on two sides. The third held mostly windows, but also had a large glass door that led out into the backyard. Since it didn't have a fence, I could see for what seemed like miles. In the distance, I saw a line of trees. I hadn't realized the club had so much property. Although, if he wanted children, we'd need to put up a fence.

"It's beautiful," I murmured.

"Come on. Let's see the rest of this place." Fox took my hand and pried me away from the sunroom. One of the other doors opened to a small bathroom with a standing shower, sink, and toilet. The other two were probably intended to be bedrooms, even though they were on the smaller side. Unless someone had thought to make one an office.

Fox walked back to the front entry and went into the kitchen, pulling me in his wake. The stone floor covered the room, just as it did the entry and sunroom. The walls were a pale, buttery yellow. The cabinets were a darker wood, and the counter tops boasted a smooth marble in a *café au lait* sort of tone. Brand-new appliances were in place, the tags still on them. I walked across the large space and opened a door on the opposite side. It led into a small side entry. I saw a door with glass in the top, letting me look out into the side yard. An open doorway showed a spacious pantry with a lot of shelves and room along one wall for a chest freezer. It even had an outlet already available.

"I haven't seen a laundry room," I said as I went back into the kitchen. Surely a house this size would have one? Or some sort of spot for a washer and dryer.

"Let's look upstairs."

Fox and I climbed to the second floor. All the doors stood open so we could easily peek into each one. One door stood off a ways from the other rooms. I went inside and saw a washer and dryer, along with cabinets over the top of them and a counter on the opposite wall that would give me space to fold clothes.

"This place has four bedrooms up here," Fox said. "And a big bathroom for three of them. Want to check out the master suite?"

Suite? Did he mean it was bigger than we had right now? I went inside and my jaw dropped a little. The room sat at the end of the hall and had two exterior walls. One wall had two windows and the other had one. The light made the room feel open and welcoming. A nook caught my attention and I saw someone had added a small sitting area through an archway to the left of the lone window. Just large enough for a bookshelf and two chairs. The perfect spot to relax at the end of the day. The space also had a window.

"The bathroom is amazing," Fox called out.

I left the little nook and went to see the bathroom. A large sunken tub looked big enough for four or five men the size of Fox. The shower had an open doorway, but as I stepped inside, I saw the drain and showerheads -- yes, plural as there were two -- were designed in such a way the water wouldn't seep out into the main part of the bathroom. The wall between the shower and the rest of the room had been made of glass blocks, letting in light but obscuring anyone's view.

Double sinks and a long counter sat under a mirror. The sinks were unlike any I'd seen before. They looked like large bowls on top of the counter, and the curved spout reminded me of a waterfall when I turned it on. The cabinets and drawers under the counter would give us plenty of room for towels and other bathroom items. I found the toilet hidden behind another door, which seemed a bit humorous since most bathrooms didn't hide the toilet. There were even his and her closets.

"I think this bathroom is the size of the bedroom at the house we have now," I said.

"No, I think it's bigger." Fox came up behind me, curling his arm around my waist. "Does this mean you like the house?"

I nodded. "But do we really need all this room?"

"Well, I thought we could make one of the downstairs rooms a play area for any kids we have. The other can be a guest room for your dad when he visits. That leaves three bedrooms to fill with children. If we're blessed with that many, or if you even want more than one. We can talk about it later."

"I didn't see a linen closet."

"There's enough room in the laundry for me to add some rolling storage carts or something under that counter. Or you could get decorative bins to put there. Hell, I could rip out the counter and put in a set of cabinets to match the ones over the washer and dryer."

He better not touch that counter. I liked the idea of not having to haul a basket of clean clothes to the bedroom, then dump it on the bed to fold everything.

"We don't even have enough furniture for this much space."

He kissed the side of my neck. "We can buy new things. Or leave the rooms up here empty for now. When you're ready to set up a nursery, you let me know which room to use and what color you want it painted. No reason to rush out and buy everything right away. We can take our time."

I turned in his embrace and faced him. "What about the cost?"

He smiled. "It's a perk of being in the club and being the VP. None of the patched members pay for the homes here. The club earns money off various things. Typically, whoever helps with a certain job gets a cut. When we decided to build houses here, everyone agreed a percentage of any incoming funds would be earmarked for the compound."

"So we don't have to buy it or pay rent?" I asked.

"Nope. It's ours if you want it to be." He rubbed my back. "The house we have now will be up for grabs if another brother wants it, or it will sit empty until someone else gets patched in."

I nodded, thinking it was too good to be true.

The home was beautiful. More gorgeous than anything I'd ever lived in before, even when I still stayed with my mom. And it could be ours? I almost wanted to pinch myself, certain I must be dreaming.

"So, do I tell Spider we want to move in?" he asked.

"I want it," I said.

"Then I'll make arrangements to have us moved in by end of the day. You and I are going to make ourselves scarce, and I'll have two Prospects box up everything and start moving stuff. We can start with a celebratory lunch and go from there."

He pressed a kiss to the side of my neck, and I leaned into him. Everything seemed to be happening so fast. I kept thinking I must still be at Balmoral, doped up on drugs and locked in a dreamlike state. None of this could be real, could it?

Fox led me back outside and helped me into the truck, then he made some calls on the way to the front gate. He rolled down his window and handed a set of keys to the guy standing guard. I hadn't had a chance to meet everyone, and I didn't know who he was. He seemed nice enough, and even gave me a little wave as Fox pulled out of the compound.

"Is this a date?" I asked.

Fox glanced at me before focusing on the road again. "Do you want it to be?"

Did I? I couldn't remember the last time I went out with someone in a date-like capacity. Certainly before *the incident*. "I think I would. We haven't really been on one yet, even though you say I'm yours and you're mine."

He pulled over onto the shoulder and turned toward me. "I didn't even think to ask. Do you want a ring?"

"Ring?" My brow furrowed as I tried to figure out what he meant.

"Wedding ring." He held up his left hand. "I'll wear one if you want me to. I'm having a property cut made for you, or rather Luciana is. It will look like the one she had on today, except the back of yours will say *Property of Fox*."

I thought about it a moment, mulling the idea over. "A ring might keep men away from me. I don't like it when strange men come up and talk to me. It usually doesn't end well."

Fox reached over and took my hand. "Sweetheart, no one is going to hurt you anymore. I won't let them. Anyone even thinks of touching you, and I will gladly rip out their spines."

I blinked at him, and the rather vivid picture he painted. Perhaps his urge to commit violence should have scared me, but since he wanted to hurt people on my behalf, I felt oddly special. Cared for. Maybe even… loved? No, he couldn't love me. He didn't know me well enough for that. In fact, there was a chance he'd never love me, but he treated me well.

He pulled the truck back onto the road. "We'll stop for rings before we go eat. Do you want to officially be Mrs. Josh Turner?"

"You mean actually get married?"

He made a humming sound. "I was thinking more along the lines of asking Surge to hack into the county clerk's office and make it look like we got married. The paper trail would show we're officially husband and wife, but without all the hassle involved with a wedding. Unless you want one."

Did I? The thought of standing in front of a bunch of people, all of them staring as I married Fox, made my stomach churn. No. Nope, I definitely didn't want to get married. Not if it meant having a wedding ceremony. But having someone marry us without all that other stuff? I would be okay with that.

"Can you ask Surge to do it?" I asked.

Fox handed me his phone. "Can you pull his name up in the contacts and put the call on speaker?"

"It's locked," I said, staring at the *Enter your Pin* screen.

"Six. Nine. Eight. Three."

I entered the numbers, wondering what they meant. Instead of asking, I scrolled through his contacts and found the name Surge. I connected the call and put it on speaker like he'd asked.

"I'm a bit busy, Fox," Surge said instead of using the customary *hello.*

"I don't even want to know," Fox said, as music blasted in the background through the small phone speaker. "Raven wants to be my wife. Can you take care of it?"

"Yeah. Not right this minute, but I will later tonight. By morning she'll legally -- or illegally -- be yours. Anything else?"

"That's it. Have fun with whatever you're doing," Fox said and nodded for me to end the call.

I handed the phone back to him and he shoved it into his pocket. When he pulled up in front of a small jewelry store, my palms started to sweat. Diamonds sparkled in the front windows. I hadn't realized he'd meant he would buy me a ring at a place like this one. I'd thought we'd get cheap bands somewhere.

Fox got out of the truck, and I had no choice but to follow. When we entered the shop, the lights flickered off all the gemstones in the cases. I couldn't remember a time I'd felt so underdressed. In my shorts and tee, I felt better suited to the discount store than an upscale jewelry store. The shop might be small, but there had to be a fortune in jewelry in the glass cases.

"Come on, beautiful. Let's get wedding bands."

Chapter Twelve

Fox

I'd thought women loved jewelry, the flashier the better. Except Raven. Not my sweet, beautiful, broken little Raven. She'd looked at the cheapest plain bands she could find. It had taken quite a bit of arguing to get her to accept a white gold band with four diamonds embedded in a scattered pattern across the top. Even then, she'd balked at the cost.

I'd opted for the plain matching white gold band. After I'd paid, we'd worn them out of the shop. Since I knew Spider, Rocket, and Slider had all frequented the shop before to buy their women special trinkets, I'd known the proprietor wouldn't have a fit over a biker walking through his door. The man knew we could afford whatever we selected, and we wouldn't try to rob him.

Raven kept running her thumb over her band as she stared off into space. She hadn't said much in the truck on the way to the restaurant, and I'd been parked, waiting for her to acknowledge we weren't moving, for at least fifteen minutes.

"Honey, you okay?" I asked.

She looked at me, her face paler than usual. "It was too much money."

I unfastened her seat belt and lifted her into my lap, wrapping an arm around her waist to hold her in place. "Raven, you're mine. My old lady. My wife. The ring on your finger didn't cost as much as you think."

Her brows rose. "It was over one thousand dollars!"

"Yeah, but those are quality diamonds in the band. Do you think you aren't worth the cost? Because let me tell you something… I could have bought out the entire fucking store, and it still wouldn't have equaled your value. Hear me? There's nothing more precious to me than you, Raven."

She snuggled against me, and I hoped I'd gotten through to her. Truth be told, I hadn't spent my money on much of anything over the years. A bike, some guns, but no super big purchases. My needs had been simple, and I hadn't seen a reason to blow money on stupid shit. Which meant I had more in the bank than she realized. Not millions or anything, but enough we'd be comfortable all our lives and could pass some down to our kids. I'd even let Knox talk me into investing about ten years ago. In another decade, those shares would pay out dividends of a few hundred grand a year.

"You ready to have our first date?" I asked.

"Yes and no," she mumbled against my shirt.

"What's the no part?"

"I don't like being in places where I feel like people are staring at me."

I could understand how she felt. I scanned the area and didn't see any reason we couldn't eat on the patio. I only saw one other couple out there. "So we'll eat outside. Or will that make you feel the same way?"

She lifted her head. "Really? We can eat outside?"

I nodded. "I'm sure they won't have a problem with it."

"That would be much better. Even though there are shoppers passing by, it wouldn't be the same as being confined inside."

Raven put her arms around my neck and pressed her lips to mine. It warmed me from the inside out, knowing she felt comfortable enough to instigate a kiss. My sweet girl had already started to heal, even if she didn't realize it yet.

I opened the truck door and slipped out from under her, then helped her out of the vehicle. I held her hand as we walked into the restaurant and waited for the hostess to acknowledge us. She looked up from her podium with a warm smile.

"Welcome to Santiago's! Table for two?" she asked.

"Yes, but my wife would like to be seated on the patio if possible," I said.

"Of course! Just follow me." She grabbed two menus and two sets of silverware before hustling through the main part of the restaurant and out a side door. She led us around the corner and seated us at a table in front of the restaurant. "How's this?"

"Perfect," I said, giving Raven's hand a squeeze.

I pulled out Raven's chair before claiming my own seat. The hostess set our menus and silverware down before clasping her hands in front of her.

"Marney will be your server, but in the meantime, what can I get you to drink?" she asked.

"Water's fine for me," I said.

"Same," Raven murmured.

"All right. I'll put in your drink order." The woman rushed off and I nudged Raven's menu, encouraging her to open it up and figure out what she'd like to eat.

"Everything I've eaten here is amazing, but I'm partial to their tacos. Order whatever you want. If you can't eat it all, we can take any leftovers home with us and snack on them later."

She nodded and perused the menu. I opened mine, even though I already knew what I wanted. I noticed the tension in Raven's body and had hoped to put her at ease. One day, going out wouldn't be so difficult for her. Until then, we'd keep trying. And if this was too much for her, then I could always take her to Spider's while the Prospects packed up our house. She seemed to have enjoyed being with Luciana and Violeta today.

She scanned the area, and I noticed the exact moment the blood drained from her face. I looked around, trying to figure out what had scared her so badly. A man stood on the sidewalk across from the restaurant, smoking a cigarette. The way he watched Raven had me clenching my fists.

"Raven, who is he?" I asked.

She jerked her gaze back to me and I saw the fear in her eyes. "Guard Simmons. I thought… I thought I saw him at the store yesterday, but when I looked again he wasn't there. I'd convinced myself he hadn't really been there."

"You should have told me."

"I'd planned to, but then we got home and…"

"And I'd asked you to be mine." I took a deep breath to calm myself and looked across the street again. The man had left. It seemed they knew where to find Raven, which meant she wasn't safe.

I took out my phone and sent a text to everyone in the club. They needed to know to be on alert. Well, more than they were supposed to be already. Now that I knew for certain at least one of the guards was here, I had a feeling the others would be closing in soon too. They had to be pissed they'd been fired. Even though it was no one's fault but their own, they'd blame Raven. Men like that always did. They never took responsibility for their own actions.

One of the guards from Balmoral found us. He's gone now, but I want at least three brothers here now. I included our location and hit SEND.

Marauder was the first to respond. *I'm down the street. Be there in a second.*

Iron and Shooter confirmed they were on their way as well. I'd have them fan out and keep an eye on all sides. I didn't want that fucker sneaking up on us, assuming it was just the one in the area. Which meant we needed faces and names.

I pulled up the last message I'd sent to Surge. *Send out faces and names of the three fired guards to the entire club. We need to know who we're watching for.*

I got a thumbs-up emoji that had me shaking my head. Surge sometimes reminded me of a kid. I had to remind myself he wasn't even thirty yet. At least he realized this took precedence over whomever was in his bed right now. He didn't realize the club knew he tended to prefer men, even though we'd seen him with the club whores. He and Slider had something going on for a while, before Slider claimed Vasha. They'd both kept quiet about their relationship, and I didn't know if they'd worried we'd give them shit about it. None of us cared. There were too many other things to worry about than who Surge wanted to sleep with.

"A few of my brothers are on their way here," I told her. "They'll make sure Simmons and the other two don't get anywhere near you, all right?"

I reached over and placed my hand on top of hers, giving her fingers a slight squeeze. Her eyes were glassy with unshed tears, and I hated that fucker had ruined what had been a good day. She should be happy right now. We were moving into a new house, she'd been accepted as mine by the club, and I'd even put a ring on her finger. Instead, the monsters who'd hurt her were now foremost in her mind. I wanted to gut the bastards.

"Sorry," she said, trying to pull herself together. I

saw the struggle as she gave her a head a little shake and looked down at the menu again. "I won't let them win."

I smiled. "There's my girl."

"Where are we going after this?" she asked.

"Wherever you want. If you feel safer at the compound, we'll go there. Or if you want to run some errands, see a movie, whatever… I'll have Marauder, Shooter, and Iron stick with us. They've accepted you into the family, Raven. They want to keep you safe as much as I do." I thought about it a moment. "All right, maybe not quite as much as I do. You're mine, after all. But they would give up their lives to keep you safe."

She nodded. "Let's hope it doesn't come to that."

No shit. If those punk ass guards took any of us down, we had it coming. Quite a few of us had served our country. I'd given four years of my life to the US Army. Yankee, Dread, and Shooter had also been in the Army. I knew a few of my brothers had been in the Navy or Marines. If the asshole guards had military backgrounds, Surge would have said something by now. Which meant they were bullies who needed to be taken down and didn't have a snowball's chance in hell of taking us.

Our server came out with our waters and to take our orders. By the time she'd rushed off and returned with chips and salsa, Raven seemed to have calmed a bit. I even noticed a hint of determination in her eyes. Looked like she was ready to fight back.

"I want new furniture," she said. "If that's okay."

I smiled and leaned over the table to kiss her softly. "More than."

While we ate our food, I kept an eye on our surroundings. I could see my brothers and knew they wouldn't let Simmons near us. But if all three guards showed up, there was a slim chance one of them could slip through.

By the time we'd finished and I'd paid the check, I wanted to get Raven out of there. Going furniture shopping wasn't the best idea at a time like this, but I couldn't deny her. As I helped her into the truck, Marauder, Shooter, and Iron all pulled up on their bikes, waiting for me to lead the way. The roar of a Harley coming from the opposite direction caught my attention and a man who appeared close to my age came to a stop. I didn't recognize him, but as I scanned his cut, I saw the stitching. It seemed my sweet Raven's daddy had arrived.

Hatchet swung his leg over the bike, leaving it running. He pulled off his helmet and approached. I couldn't see his eyes behind the dark lenses of his sunglasses, but I had no doubt he was taking my measure.

"Hatchet," I said, holding out my hand.

It took him a moment. I started to think he'd refuse to shake when he gripped my hand. Hard. I didn't flinch, wince, or give any indication he'd caused me any pain, even if the fucker did have the hold of a damn gorilla on steroids.

He flashed me a smile. "Good to meet you, Fox. Prospect at your gate said I'd find you here."

I nodded to the truck. "About to take your daughter shopping. She wants new furniture."

"What's wrong with the shit you have now? She doesn't want something another bitch has used?"

I straightened to my full height, which was still an inch shorter than Hatchet. "I've never had a woman in my house before. So knock that shit off. We decided to upgrade to a bigger house. With the baby on the way, and we may want others, we decided we needed more room. And I told her she can replace anything I have that she doesn't like."

Hatchet smirked. "I'm fucking with you. Now… where's my daughter?"

"In the truck. You sure you want to meet her the first time in a parking area?" I asked.

"Motherfucker," he muttered. "No. I probably shouldn't."

I heard the truck door open and shut. I felt Raven come up behind me and reached back for her. She pressed her body against mine.

"Looks like she took the decision out of our hands," I said. "Raven, sweetheart, you ready to meet your dad?"

She tensed, but I felt her nod between my shoulder blades. I tugged her around me and placed my hand on her hip, holding her against my side. She stared at Hatchet and fuck me if the big man didn't seem to tear up a bit as he saw his daughter for the first time.

"So beautiful," he mumbled. "I wish I'd known about you sooner, Raven. I'd have gone to hell and back to make sure I was part of your life."

"Mom never mentioned you," she said. "I got the feeling she didn't like you."

He snorted. "Understatement. I knocked your mom up in high school. She'd been slumming it with me, I guess. If I'd known she had you, I'd have stuck around. She told me she'd aborted you. I left town and never looked back."

Looking between the two, I could see the resemblance, although Raven definitely had more of her mom in her. The woman sounded like bitch, so Raven had to have inherited her demeanor from Hatchet. The overall shape of her face wasn't his, nor her coloring, but her eyes? Those were all Hatchet. She had his strength too, whether she realized it or not.

"Raven, would you mind if your dad came with us while we shop for furniture? If you'd prefer to spend more time with him at home, he can hang out at the clubhouse until we're done." I noticed the slight tightening around Hatchet's eyes, but he didn't say anything. He knew giving Raven the option was the best thing to do.

"I'd love to spend time with you, but it can be on your terms," Hatchet told his daughter. "I know I'm a stranger and need to earn your trust."

Raven pulled away and took a hesitant step toward her dad. Then another. Before I realized what she planned, she'd thrown herself at her dad. Hatchet wrapped his arms around her, his eyes closing, a mixture of pain and pleasure crossing his features as he hugged her for the first time. I hoped like hell he got the chance to do something about Raven's mom. The bitch needed to pay. If not for her, Raven would have never ended up at Balmoral. Hell, if Hatchet had known about her, there was a chance none of this would have happened to her.

Then again, I probably wouldn't have met her either. As much as I didn't want to think of my life without her in it, if it meant she'd have never been raped and beaten, then I'd prefer to have never met her. Anything to save her from the pain she'd endured.

"Guess that means you're going with us," I said.

Hatchet kissed the top of Raven's head before releasing her. She came back to me, leaning against my side. I gave him directions to the furniture store in case we got separated and helped Raven back into the truck. When we pulled up to the store, the four motorcycles keeping pace with us drew more than few eyes our way.

Shooter and Marauder stayed outside, making sure we weren't blindsided by the Balmoral guards. I still needed to give Hatchet the latest update, but it would have to wait for now. We let Raven roam the store, keeping her not only within sight, but within arm's reach as well. I noticed her checking out the living room sets and gave her the freedom to buy all new pieces for the house. Whatever she didn't want of mine, I'd leave behind for whichever brother moved into the place next.

Other than answering questions she had about what I liked or didn't like, I hung back a bit to give her some time with Hatchet. I could tell he loved it when she asked what he thought about a couch or the kitchen set. The two were bonding, and it warmed my heart to watch them. Would I have a day like this with my own daughter sometime in the future? Assuming we had a daughter.

My phone buzzed and I answered, seeing Spider's name on the screen.

"Hey, Pres. Everything all right?"

"Not hardly. You need to bring Raven back here. Now."

"What's going on?" I asked, quickly making my way over to Hatchet and Raven, who'd stopped to haggle the price of the bedroom set.

"Someone sent smoke bombs over the fence in three spots. I'm thinking it was the guards. They know Raven is here at the compound, or think she is. I'd rather have her in one spot, behind a locked door, with the perimeter watched at all times. I know we don't have the manpower to keep eyes on every inch of the fence line, but I think she's still safer here than outside the compound."

"On it," I said. I hung up and took Raven by the arm. "Honey, we need to go."

"But the furniture…"

I looked at the store clerk and tossed out a number a few grand under the total for everything she'd said she liked. He must have seen something in my face because the little shit didn't even try to argue, and he didn't make me add delivery. He handed me the paperwork, I signed, and got Raven the hell out of there. I explained everything to Hatchet and the others as I buckled Raven in. Her scared gaze met mine, and I stopped long enough to give her a kiss, hoping it would reassure her.

I sped through town and toward the compound like hellhounds were on my tail. Didn't even slow when I approached the gate. The Prospect threw it open as I barreled through.

The phone rang again, and I had Raven answer and put it on speaker.

"Take her to the new house," Spider said. "I had Archer pick up surveillance cameras while you were gone, and we have most of them installed. Just a few more and it will be finished. Already made sure the Wi-Fi worked."

"When the fuck did the house get Wi-Fi?"

Spider chuckled. "While you were gone."

Raven hung up and I drove straight to the new house, pulling into the driveway and shutting off the truck. I noticed my bike parked in the open garage and wondered who had brought it over, and when.

"Come on, sweetheart. Let's see what everyone's been up to. It seems we weren't the only ones who were busy today."

She took my hand, and we went into our new home.

Chapter Thirteen

Raven

I looked around the house and noticed they'd brought Fox's furniture over while we'd been gone. Everything had been packed and moved, including the dishes and the food he'd had in the fridge. One of the downstairs rooms held the guest room furniture, and I saw my dad had put his bag in there. How had they gotten all this done so fast?

"What do we do with all this when the new furniture arrives?" I asked Fox.

"We can have them move it back to the other house or store it somewhere in case anyone needs it. Why don't you visit with your dad while I check out the security system they've installed?"

I nodded and went to find my dad. It felt odd, realizing I had a father, and that he actually wanted me. Why had my mom lied all my life? Not just to me, but to him too? Had she hated him that much? Or maybe she'd hated both of us. The way she'd turned her back on me, I'd often wondered if it had given her the perfect excuse to get rid of me.

"Dad?"

He turned, a smile on his face and his eyebrows lifted. "I can get used to hearing that."

"Fox said he needed to check out whatever security the club installed. He suggested I spend time with you while he's busy with that."

"Let's go see if they set up the TV right. We can pick a movie and talk," he said.

I led the way to the living room and found the remote on the coffee table. I handed it to Hatchet and let him pick something. He flipped through the options and settled on *Halloween*. I eyed him.

"You like horror movies?" I asked.

"Mostly eighties slasher flicks. Although I can admit I like the Scream franchise too. Why?"

Smiling I leaned into him, putting my head on his shoulder. That was the moment I fully accepted him as my dad. Mostly because no one else in my family liked these movies except me. At least, that's what my mother had said. It had only been the two of us, and whatever boyfriends she'd had along the way.

"They're my favorite," I said. "Mom always wrinkled her nose and told me the movies were low-class and I shouldn't watch them. But I'm addicted to horror movies and shows."

Hatchet put his arm around me, and we settled in to enjoy the movie. Fox found us a short time later. I patted the couch next to me and he sank onto the cushion. My dad relinquished me to him, but I noticed he didn't get up.

"We have cameras that cover every inch of the outside," Fox said. "They installed an alarm system too, and it has a panic button that sends a silent alarm to the other officers and Surge. In addition to that, we'll have at least three brothers outside throughout the day. Everyone is going to watch the house in shifts."

"Until we catch those fuckers," Hatchet muttered.

"Right. And they're close. All three. Surge found them by searching camera feeds around town. When Simmons stood across from the restaurant earlier, the other two were nearby but out of sight. I have a feeling they'll strike together. The smoke bombs they tossed over the fence earlier were most likely a test, to see how we'd react and maybe get an idea of how many men are here."

"Smart, but are they smarter than us?" Hatchet

asked.

"Let's hope not. Surge is digging into their backgrounds. So far, there's no military connections that he can find. Doesn't mean they don't have some other sort of training. I'm hoping we'll have a full workup on all of them before nightfall. They won't strike in the middle of the day. Not after the stunt earlier," Fox said.

"I just want it to be over," I said.

"We're going to handle these men, Raven, and then we're going after Balmoral. Their negligence allowed you to be raped right under their noses, every damn night. I won't stand for it," Hatchet said. "They'll pay."

"I'll have to show both of you how to use the system. It can wait for a bit. I may have some popcorn in the kitchen. Anyone want a snack while we watch the movie?" Fox asked.

"You're going to watch it with us?" I asked.

Fox smiled. "Of course. Horror movies are my second favorite."

"What's your first?" I asked.

"Action flicks where they blow shit up." He shrugged. "I'm a typical guy."

Hatchet snickered next to me. When Fox left the room, my dad nudged my shoulder. "He's all right. Long as he protects you, and doesn't break your heart, I can live with the two of you being together. Even if it means you don't live as close as I'd like. I'd hoped to take you home with me."

"You can't kidnap my woman," Fox yelled out from the kitchen.

Hatchet lowered his voice. "Is that why they call him Fox? Because of his super hearing?"

"I heard that too," Fox shouted. "And it's

because I'm such a fox."

My dad snorted, then started choking and laughing at the same time. I smacked him on the back and glanced toward the kitchen, not sure if Fox was being serious or just trying to get a rise out of us. I'd noticed he could be playful at times, like scraping up all the cherry filling on his pie plate at the diner.

"You lying little shit," a voice bellowed from the back of the house. I craned my neck, not realizing anyone else was here.

Fox appeared with a bowl of popcorn and three sodas. He set everything on the table just as Spider strolled into the room. I didn't know if he had a key to all the homes here, or if Fox had left the door unlocked. Either way, the President entered the place like he owned it.

"Spider," Hatchet said, with a nod of his head. "Thanks for letting me come for a visit."

"Like I'm going to keep you away from your kid?" Spider leaned against the doorframe. "As for this fucker, he didn't get his name because he's a fox, as he put it."

"Pres." Fox's tone had a warning to it, and his cheeks had flushed a bit.

Now I really wanted to know why they called him Fox. I eyed my man and the President of the Hades Abyss. It was clear the two were close.

"Used to spend as much time with Fox as I could when he was younger, seeing as how his parents were gone. His dad was my best friend," Spider said. "Kid was a runt until he hit puberty, then he sprouted up and bulked up overnight. Before that, he was small and smelly."

"Hey!" Fox flopped onto the couch. "That was harsh."

Spider grinned. "And true! You were always into everything, and had this musk, like a fox. You ever smelled those things close up? They reek. So I started calling him a little fox. It stuck. When he patched in with the club, I knew exactly what we'd call him. I just never shared *why* with the others."

"Thank fuck," Fox muttered.

"Think most boys smell," Hatchet said. "It's why we have to work so hard to win over the girls after puberty. They still remember us as those smelly kids who ate too much and put bugs down their dresses."

I eyed my dad. "So how did you get the name Hatchet?"

He rubbed the back of his neck. "Probably not something you want to hear."

"I know why they call him that," Spider said, the humor fading from his eyes. "And he's right. You may not want to know, but I think you should."

I looked between the two men. "I'm so confused right now."

"When I deal with bad people, I'm not afraid of getting my hands dirty," Hatchet said. "I've been known to cut them up… with a hatchet. I'm not like the monsters in these horror movies. I don't kill innocent people, but men like the ones who hurt you. I'm all about making them pay for their sins and making them beg for mercy."

I swallowed hard, trying to picture my dad as such a brutal person. When his gaze clashed with mine, I saw the sorrow and pain there, but also a steely determination. I knew he hadn't regretted whatever he'd done in his past.

"For the record," he said, "they don't get any. I have no mercy for men who prey on the weak."

I nodded. "Good."

He gave me a slight smile and knocked his shoulder into mine again. "Glad you aren't freaked out and running from me. It would have sucked to meet my daughter for the first time and have her be so terrified of me she ran away."

"Not running," I said. I leaned into Fox. "I've been told I'm strong. I don't feel it most days, but I'm trying."

"You probably have a few hours until the guards will make a move. They're most likely planning things out right now. Hopefully, Surge will have more info on them before then. I told him to call in whoever else he needs. I know Shield has been in contact with him," Spider said.

"Do you think it will be over after tonight?" I asked. "Or will I always feel like I need to look over my shoulder?"

"We'll finish it before the sun comes up," Spider said. "Luciana, Violeta, Vasha, and the kids will be at my house until this is over. I'll be staying with them, and so will Rocket. Everyone else will be focused on keeping you safe, Raven."

"I shouldn't have sent the others home," Hatchet said. "If I'd known she was in danger, I'd have brought backup with me."

Spider smirked and walked to the front door, yanking it open. I heard the heavy tread of boots, then three men entered the house. Men I'd never seen before. Hatchet stood and swore.

"What the hell are you three doing here?" he asked.

"You really think we'd leave you to face all this alone?" one of them asked.

"Raven, this is Copper. The other two are Nitro and Snake." Hatchet pointed to each so I'd know who was who. I huddled a little closer to Fox. My dad might trust these men, but they were strangers.

"Raven still isn't used to men she doesn't know," Fox said, putting his arm around me.

"Not a problem," Snake said. "Thought I'd go help Surge out until closer to dark."

Copper snorted and elbowed him. "Yeah, I'm sure you'd love to *help* him."

The men all laughed, and Snake snarled at them before stomping out of the house. I had no idea what was going on. Why did they make fun of the man for wanting to give Surge a hand with whatever he was doing?

Copper must have noticed my confusion. He gave me a smile. "No worries, Raven. We're just yanking his chain. Everyone knows he thinks Surge is smart and sexy, a combination Snake can't resist. He's bisexual, so the help he's going to offer Surge is more in the --"

He got cut off when Hatchet knocked the wind out of him. "Enough. She doesn't need to hear all that."

"So they're both bisexual? Or is Surge gay?" I asked.

"They both like men and women equally," Fox said. "Slider is bisexual too. He's with Vasha. Seems she was his *one,* so they're committed to one another."

I scanned the men in the room. I remembered watching some show about bikers a few years ago, until my mom discovered what I'd been watching. It made me realize she must have kept tabs on my dad, otherwise, how would she have known he'd joined a motorcycle club? The men in the show hadn't taken too kindly to men who weren't straight. For that matter, they hadn't seemed to care too much for men who weren't white.

"It doesn't bother any of you?" I asked. "That they like men?"

"There are clubs out there who would have a big issue with it," Spider said. "Some who also wouldn't like mixed race members in their club, or anyone who wasn't the same race as them. We're not like that, and neither are the clubs we consider our allies. We try to stay open-minded. The color of someone's skin, and who they decide to love, doesn't make them any less capable of having our backs. A few might be uncomfortable with the fact a brother likes other men, but at the end of the day, we support one another."

"The Reckless Kings, the club I belong to, is the same way," Hatchet said. "The Devil's Fury, down in Georgia, has two brothers who are together, but they claimed a woman and her kid. They make it work. The Devil's Boneyard, in Florida, has a VP whose old lady is mixed race. And several clubs we know have brothers who are either not fully white or are another race altogether. Like Spider said, none of that means shit. It doesn't affect whether or not they can watch their brothers' backs, or if they're loyal. That's what matters at the end of the day."

I saw the men in a new light. They weren't only willing to risk their lives to save me, but they seemed so accepting of other people. And Fox had mentioned the Hades Abyss helping those who were less fortunate. I wished there were more people in the world like these big, tough men. They could just as easily crush those weaker than them than try to help them.

It made me proud to be part of the Hades Abyss family, and to be Hatchet's daughter. I hadn't felt pride in myself, much less my family, in a long time. My mother hadn't exactly been a prize. She'd looked down on most people and had been insanely jealous of anyone better off than she was. Instead of molding me in her image, she'd made me realize I didn't want to be anything like her. People didn't respect her. She didn't have true friends. She could keep her cold, heartless life.

The front door open and shut again. A breathless man appeared, his shirt half-untucked and his hair mussed. "We need to talk."

"Surge, figured you'd be busy for a bit," Copper said.

He waved him off. "Yes, yes. Snake came to see me, but Wire and Lavender ran across something and called. Those guards didn't act alone."

"What's that mean, exactly?" Fox asked, his voice going cold and hard.

"Raven's mom." Surge's gaze locked on mine. "She paid them."

My world spun and had I not been sitting, I'd have fallen. My mother *paid* the men who'd been hurting me? What sort of monster had given birth to me? I heard Hatchet roar and the front door slam. An engine revved, and I had a feeling he'd just taken off. I hoped he didn't plan on riding all the way to wherever my mother was living these days.

"How did she know?" I asked.

"She may have said shit to your face, but in her circle of friends she either toed the line or ran her mouth to someone who found her offensive. I'm guessing she'd have backtracked and tried to save face. It's clear she thinks highly of her reputation, and badmouthing her daughter wasn't the way to make friends in the elite social circles she's aiming for. After you left, she had to put on a big production about her baby girl missing," Surge said. "Gave the cops your prints and DNA. Balmoral found you in the system when they processed you as a patient. Your mother knew exactly where you were because they called her."

"Two days." I licked my lips. "I had two days of no one bothering me."

"Probably took them that long to find her," Surge said. "It wasn't just the guards, Raven. The doctor knew. We thought all this time that he'd tried to sweep the scandal under the proverbial rug, but he was saving his own ass when the nurse came forward about how you'd left with Breaker and why. He couldn't have anyone know that your mom had paid him too, to put her in touch with those men and to look the other way while they hurt you."

Tears gathered and slipped down my cheeks. "Why? Why would she do something like that?"

"I may know. No one here will like it, though," Surge said.

"So fucking tell us already," Fox said, lifting me onto his lap and holding me close. "Rip the damn bandage off, Surge."

He took a breath and dropped a sheath of papers on the table. He pointed at the stack. "Dug deep into your mom, Raven, once I found out someone paid the guards. Went back all the way before your birth. Your mom didn't come from a wealthy family, but they were well-off. And she'd been trying to get her hooks into some rich boy."

"But got knocked up by dad. I don't understand. She'd been dating him, or so he said."

Surge nodded. "She was. There are pictures of the two of them together. What your dad probably didn't know is that she'd been seeing someone else too. A college boy with a well-connected family. When she got pregnant with you, her plan went to shit. From what I've been able to dig up, I think your dad had been the only one she was sleeping with. Except I think the college guy must have found out about you before your mom had a chance to get the abortion she'd told Hatchet she'd get. He clearly never questioned whether you were his, which tells me there was zero chance it was possible."

Spider motioned for him to get on with it.

"The college guy helped your mom financially for a short while. Then a few months after you were born, he married a woman with a similar social standing to his. I think your mom hated you from that moment on," Surge said.

"She never really did give many hugs. She'd been a bit distant, but I thought maybe she just wasn't the emotional type," I said. "My childhood wasn't awful. It could have been a lot worse."

"Your mom thought she was in the clear after what happened with the cowboys. You left and she could live her life without a kid hanging around her neck. Until people asked about you. Apparently, no one knew she threw you out. She gave a sob story about you running away and tried to cover her tracks." Surge folded his arms. "Balmoral reached out to let her know you were in their care and had tried to kill yourself. I think you popping back up infuriated your mom enough she wanted you to hurt. So she paid the doctor off, as well as the guards. Her new husband-to-be is none other than Missouri State Senator Phillip Lewis."

"Please tell me the bitch is in Washington and not here," Fox said.

"They're at the Lewis family home, just outside Branson." Surge cracked his neck. "We have to be careful. She's too in the spotlight to go after her outright. Which means we need to handle her a different way. I know you'd like to gut her, Fox, and I'm sure Hatchet does too, but it would bring down heat on all of us."

"I'm going after Hatchet," Nitro said. "I'll get him calmed down and bring him back."

I snuggled into Fox, wondering if this nightmare would ever end. If my mom had landed herself a politician, would it ever be over? Or did she have enough power at her fingertips now to make sure no one ever knew what she'd done?

Chapter Fourteen

Fox

I knew I couldn't go after the woman, and Surge had a valid point… we could make her suffer in other ways, but I didn't like it. She'd done something horrible to her daughter. The ultimate sin, in my opinion. Not only had she thrown out Raven after she'd been raped and beaten, but the woman had the audacity to pay men to continue hurting her daughter every fucking night?

"I'd call Church," Spider said, "but I don't want to leave Raven alone. I think she needs you right now, Fox. I'll get the officers over here and a few brothers. If we need a vote, we'll figure out how to handle it when the time comes. At the moment, we need a plan."

"Wire had a few ideas," Surge said. "Are we going to wait on Hatchet?"

Spider shook his head. "Don't think we can. No telling how far he got, or when he'll cool off enough to come back. We'll fill him in when he gets here."

I pulled out my phone. "I'll text the other officers. Who else you want over here?"

"Other than Bear, Slider, and Knox, text Brazil, Yankee, Shooter, Gunner, and Cotton. We need as many of our ex-military brothers as we can get to deal with this shit," Spider said.

"On it." I typed up the text and sent it to all the men he'd mentioned.

"Everyone in this room needs to stay," Spider said. "Surge, I'll get you to conference in Wire when we're ready. If you need anything from your place, get it and come right back."

"Food," Raven mumbled. "We'll need food and drinks for everyone."

"I'll order some pizzas," Surge said. "One of the Prospects can bring over beer and soda from the clubhouse. Not sure you've got a spot big enough for all of us in one room, though. And yes, I do need a few things from my place. Won't take me long to gather it up."

"Sunroom," I said. "We don't have anything out there right now. Whoever brings the drinks, have them load two folding tables and some chairs into the back of a truck. We'll make the sunroom our Church for this particular meeting."

"It faces the back of the property. Not possible for anyone outside the fence to see in." Spider nodded. "That should work."

"We can't leave Raven in here by herself while we convene in the sunroom," I said. "I know women usually aren't allowed, but… I'd feel better if she were in the room with us. Either that, or I need someone to stay with her."

"I'm not a child," she mumbled.

"No, but you're the most precious thing I have," I said, and I placed my hand on her belly. "Both of you."

Copper took a step back. "Whoa! Hold the fuck up. She's pregnant? Does Hatchet know?"

I nodded. "Yeah, I told him. So it's not just Raven we're protecting. No fuckups tonight."

Raven cuddled against me. I could tell the news about her mother had emotionally wiped her out, and she likely needed a nap. I didn't like the idea of her sleeping upstairs while everyone was down here. With all the security, I didn't think the guards would be able to get into the house, especially on the second floor. Didn't mean it wasn't possible. I'd learned the hard way if something could go wrong, it usually would.

"Tired, sweetheart?" I asked.

She nodded and sighed. "How long before you have to start your meeting, or whatever you call it?"

I looked over at Spider, who eyed Raven with a thoughtful expression. "It will probably take an hour to get everything set up and get the food and drinks here. Maybe Hatchet and Nitro will be back by then. Take her upstairs, Fox. Let her rest or run her a hot bath. Whatever you need to do."

He winked at me, and I knew he damn well didn't think she needed rest, but something else. Considering my cock went half-hard at the thought, I had to admit if she were up for it, I'd be on board. But I'd give Raven whatever she needed. Sleep. Bath. My cock. It was all up to her.

I stood with her in my arms and went upstairs, trusting everyone to remain on the lower level. Our bedroom door stood open, with a row of boxes along one wall. I saw they'd at least written something on each to give me an idea of what items were inside. I saw one that had *towels* scrawled across it.

"You want a bath?" I asked.

"Will you get in with me?"

I kissed her cheek. "Of course, I will."

I eased her down onto the bed, shut the door, then ripped open the box to get to the towels. I set two out on the counter and rinsed out the tub before I filled it with hot water. It took me a minute to find the box with her bathroom stuff and I added a bit of her shower gel in an attempt to make it a bubble bath. The water foamed up a bit, but not as much as she'd have probably liked.

Stripping out of my clothes, I reached down to test the water. Hot, but just right. I shut off the taps and went to get Raven. She'd already removed her clothes and stood, coming toward me with her hand out. I wrapped my fingers around hers and helped her into the tub. Before I got in with her, I hurried to the bedroom door and made sure to lock it.

Raven sat in the center of the tub with her arms around her knees. I sank into the water behind her and pulled her against my chest. She relaxed against me, and I ran my hand up and down the outside of her thigh.

"Better?" I asked.

"Much." She sighed and closed her eyes.

I ran my hands along her arms, digging in a little to knead the muscles. I did the same to what I could reach of her legs, and felt her body start to relax. All the shit going on had me ready to put my fist through a wall. Raven had lived through it, and then had to hear just how little her mother had wanted her, how the bitch had been the reason she'd been repeatedly raped at Balmoral. I couldn't even imagine how she must feel right now. I may have lost my parents at an early age, but at least I'd always known they loved me.

"What can I do?" I asked. "Whatever you need, just say the words and it's yours."

"Love me?" she asked softly. Her body tightened and she tried to twist away from me, but I held her fast. "Sorry. I shouldn't have said…"

I banded one arm around her waist and reached up to cup her breast with my other, palming the soft mound. "Stop fighting me, Raven."

She went still, but I felt her chest heaving with every breath.

"Sweetheart, I have no idea what romantic love feels like, or looks like. I don't believe in the shit I see on TV or read in books. Life doesn't happen that way. But I do know I'd die for you. I don't know if what I feel is love. I only know that I can't imagine my life without you in it. Since you've moved in, I've looked forward to every day, and getting to spend time with you."

I stroked her nipple, drawing a gasp from her. "I love your body, and how responsive you are to my touch. I love the way you worry about others, or at least about me, even though your life has been pretty shitty."

I kissed the side of her neck and rubbed my beard on her shoulder. "I love that whatever house I'm in feels like a home just because you're in it. I love the thought of raising a family with you. I guess all that boils down to… I love you, Raven."

She made a soft sound and tried to twist in my grip again. I let her, and she straddled me, her palms on both my cheeks.

"I love you, Josh. I know some people will say it's too fast, that I'm too broken, but I don't care. No one has ever cared about me -- until you. The way you make me feel… it's almost too much."

I gripped her hair and tugged her closer for a kiss. My lips devoured hers, and my cock started to rise. I knew she could feel it when she wiggled, trying to get her pussy closer. Gripping her hip with my other hand, I helped her adjust. She sank down on me, and I groaned at how tight and incredible she felt.

"So fucking perfect," I murmured against her lips. "Ride me, beautiful. I want to watch you come."

She drew back and planted her hands on my shoulders. As she rose and fell on my cock, the water sloshed around us. I didn't give a fuck if we flooded the bathroom. I stroked her nipples, unable to look away as her breasts bounced with every movement. A flush crept up her body and settled in her cheeks. The heat of her pussy told me it wouldn't take much to make her come.

"Take your pleasure." I pinched her nipple, making her cry out and ride me harder. "That's it. Milk my cock, pretty girl."

She lost her rhythm a moment, and her eyes locked on mine. It seemed she'd liked that bit of dirty talk. I fought back a smile.

"You want me to fill you up, don't you? Want my cum in your hot, wet pussy?"

She nodded and kept moving. I reached between us to rub her clit with my thumb. I wrapped my finger loosely around my cock, so I could feel her pussy taking my cock with every stroke. I wished like fuck I could see her stretched around me right now.

"Come for me, Raven."

She faltered and sucked in a breath. Her eyes went wide, and I felt the heat of her release. Her body shuddered and she whimpered, clinging to my shoulders.

"Hold on, baby."

I stood with her in my arms, water pouring off us. I stepped out of the tub and over to the counter. I set her down and leaned back, looking at where my cock still filled her. I pulled my hips back and thrust into her, nice and slow.

"Hottest fucking thing I've ever seen," I murmured. "I love watching you take my cock."

"Please, Josh!"

"Please what? Please fuck you?"

She nodded.

"Please fill you with my cum?"

She nodded even harder.

"Oh, I will. I'm going to fuck you hard and deep. Going to fill your pussy up with my cum." I leaned forward and kissed her, nipping at her bottom lip. "Hold on to the counter."

She wrapped her fingers over the edge, her knuckles going white. I held onto her hips and drove into her. I took what I wanted, what I needed, and every gasp, the flush on her cheeks, and the dazed look in her eyes only made it that much better. I couldn't hold back the roar that burst from me as I came, my hips jerking as I slammed into her again and again. I felt the flutter of her pussy right before she started coming.

I rubbed her clit, letting her ride it out.

If we didn't have shit to take care of, I'd take her to bed and keep her there the rest of the day and through the night. I started to pull out and realized we'd make a mess all over the bathroom counter and floor. Keeping us connected, I lifted her and walked to the shower. I twisted the knob until the water came out warm, then stepped under the spray. Pressing Raven to the tiled wall, I kissed her, not ready to let her go yet.

"I know you went through hell to get here, but I feel like the luckiest bastard on earth because you're mine." I cupped her cheek. "But if I could take away everything that happened to you, even if it meant we never met, I'd do it in a heartbeat. I'm sorry for what those men did to you. And even sorrier your mother is a piece of shit who sold you out. Whatever it takes, they'll pay the price for having hurt you."

"I love you, Josh," she murmured, leaning forward to brush her lips against mine. "I'd like to believe we're meant to be together. Which means we'd have found one another regardless."

I pulled out and helped her wash, knowing the others were downstairs waiting on us. By the time we'd finished, and I'd soaked up the water on the bathroom floor, I heard Spider shouting my name up the stairs. I pulled on fresh clothes and admired Raven as she dressed. Her cheeks flushed and she gave me a smile when she caught me.

"Come on. Time to get back to the mess downstairs. We need to handle those guards and your mom once and for all." I reached out and took her hand. Together, we went down to the sunroom.

"It's about time," Spider grumbled, but I didn't miss the wink he gave Raven. I also noticed Hatchet and Nitro had returned.

Hatchet came over and hugged Raven, kissing the top of her head. "Sorry I ran. Everyone caught me up on what happened after I left. I wish like hell I'd checked in on your mom at least once all those years ago. I'd have known about you and fought like hell to be part of your life."

"It's okay, Dad." Raven hugged him back. "You're here now."

Spider clapped his hands together. "All right. Everyone grab a drink and some pizza, and let's figure this shit out. Preferably before those assholes make a move."

Chapter Fifteen

Raven

Spider hadn't wanted me to hear their plans, and I understood why. Didn't mean I agreed with him, and apparently my dad and Fox didn't either. Fox had tugged me onto his lap, and Hatchet pulled up the seat next to him. I'd eaten a slice of pizza while I listened to them make a plan for dealing with the guards and my mother. Even though it hurt to hear what she'd done, it made me realize I'd missed all the signs before. She'd never wanted me.

"They aren't going to come into this house with all the bikes and trucks outside," I said.

"That's the point, baby girl," Fox said, rubbing his hand up and down my thigh.

I frowned. "But… how are you going to catch them? Don't you need bait or something?"

"No!" Hatchet banged his fist on the table. "You're not offering yourself up to those men."

The Raven of the past year would have flinched and tried to make herself small. But I wasn't that same, scared woman. I'd gotten stronger in the short time I'd been with Fox, and I knew these men wouldn't hurt me. It was time for me to take a stand. It wasn't fair to ask these men to protect me if I wasn't willing to do more than hide.

"No one here will let me get hurt," I said. "If it lures them out, wouldn't that be better than sitting around waiting?"

"Raven, you have to think about the baby too." Fox pressed his hand to my belly. "What if we didn't reach you fast enough? They could make you miscarry or snatch you and run. I don't even want to think about what they'd do to you. They blame you for them losing their jobs."

I leaned back against him. "You'd think whatever my mother paid would more than compensate them."

"We're not using her as bait," Hatchet said, glaring at everyone around the table.

Sighing, I knew they weren't going to agree. At least, my dad and Fox wouldn't. I saw the look on a few of the other men's faces. They didn't like waiting for something to happen. Or maybe they agreed those men would never make a move as long as I was so heavily protected.

"Spider, you know I'm right," I said. "Fox and my dad aren't being objective about this because they're worried about me. I get it, I really do, but I can't sit here and do nothing. I can't fight. Can't do strategic planning. But I *can* be bait to lure them in."

Fox's hold tightened on me, and he growled. "Raven."

I patted his arm. "You'll be there to keep me safe. The entire club will be, as well as Dad and the men who came with him. Besides, if they can't get to me, they may go after the other women to use them as leverage. You know it's me they want."

"She's right," Spider said. "I know neither of you wants to hear that, but it's the truth. Luciana, Violeta, and Vasha aren't anywhere near as safe as Raven right now. If they can't get to the woman they want, they may take one of the others. Or worse. One of the kids."

My stomach knotted at the thought of them getting to the kids. I'd never live with myself if something happened to a child because I'd been hidden away. I had to make Fox and Hatchet see reason.

"I know the two of you love me, and you want to

keep me in a bubble, all safe and tucked away. But you both know it would devastate you if a child got hurt because of your actions." I turned in Fox's lap so I could see both him and my dad. They shared a glance, and I had a feeling I'd finally gotten through to them. "Please let me do this."

"There will be conditions," Hatchet said, addressing the men around the table. "I just found out I have a daughter and got to meet her. I'm not about to lose Raven because something goes wrong."

"They won't come for her unless she's alone," Surge said. "And I've found a bit more info on them."

He tapped on his keyboard. "Mark Simmons. Divorced, twice. No kids. No military training. A bit of scandal several years back with an underage girl, but it got swept under the rug. Parents were paid off.

"Tom Larson. Married. Father of two boys. No military training. Church deacon. On paper, the guy looks like a fucking saint. Unless you know where to look. He's done some porn films, dark shit. Even though he wore a mask, it's definitely him.

"Derek Keates. His father owns Balmoral. Never married. No kids. He joined the Army right out of high school but didn't make it through boot camp. He washed out. My money is on him being the strategist. He's smart. If he's touched Raven, he made sure he was never caught on camera. The other assholes weren't always so careful, at least not where Raven is concerned. Raven told us they were hurting the other women. I don't know if her mom offering up money opened the door and they just enjoyed themselves so much they decided to hurt more women, or if they'd already been abusing the patients."

Surge slid some pages down the table, and I saw all three men's faces staring up at me. Bile rose in my throat, and I swallowed it down. Larson and Simmons had been the ones who visited me the most. They always worked the same shift and seemed to have more hours than the third man. But I knew Keates, and I'd never forget him. I couldn't stop the tremor that went through me. Just looking at his picture made me break out in a cold sweat. The nights he'd been on shift were always the worst.

"Raven?" Fox rubbed his hand up and down my arm. "What's wrong, beautiful?"

"Keates." My hand shook as I slid the picture closer. "He's evil. Far worse than the other two."

Hatchet took the picture and studied it. The way everyone stared at me, I knew they needed me to clarify why I thought Keates was evil, why the others weren't so bad in comparison. I didn't know if wanted to relive those moments. No, I *knew* I didn't.

"Keates liked pain and humiliation. Or rather, he liked inflicting it. He didn't rape me as often as the other two, mostly because he didn't work the night shift as frequently. And he never got off on that alone. He liked hurting me in other ways. If he had been with me every night, I probably wouldn't have survived."

Fox kissed my shoulder. "You don't have to tell us. I can tell it hurts you to think about it."

I shook my head. "You need to know what you're up against. Keates would make me strip. Then he'd take his time hitting me, cutting me, and taunting me with threats to let the men on the next ward have some fun. I never thought about it before, but the nurses never batted an eye at the marks. I think he hurt me when he knew someone would be working who didn't care."

"What men?" Hatchet asked, his hands fisting.

"The ones locked up for being criminally

insane," I said softly. "They've raped, murdered, and who knows what else, but they were deemed not mentally fit to stand trial. That scared me more than any of the guards touching me. Those men… I saw them once. They were savage, and I knew if Keates made good on his threat, I'd not survive it."

"He beat you?" Fox asked, his voice low and deep. "Cut you?"

I nodded. "Shallow cuts. He said they'd hurt more."

"So we need a plan…" Spider leaned forward bracing his arms on the table. "Raven, I have a feeling they're watching the compound. They may or may not know which house you're in. I'm going to need you to run from the house, toward the clubhouse. It's the only way I think they'll see you for certain. Dart toward the gate but stop far enough from it they couldn't reach you."

"What the fuck, Pres?" Surge asked.

Spider held up a hand. "I'm going to have men watching from the clubhouse, and the surrounding homes. We'll have plenty of brothers in place to keep her out of their clutches."

"Just run?" I asked. "That will be enough?"

"If they're as desperate as I think, it should draw them out," Spider said.

Hatchet leaned forward. "So we're clear, anything happens to her, I don't give a shit if you're the President or not. I will beat the fuck out of you for putting her in danger."

Spider's eyebrows lifted but he didn't say anything. Fox ran his hand up and down my thigh, and I noticed he didn't leap to Spider's defense. It seemed he would go along with my dad if things went bad.

"Raven, put on something comfortable," Spider said. "I'm going to work out the details with this crew and get a message out to the others."

I stood and paused a moment. "Don't hurt them. I know my dad shouldn't have said what he did, and Fox should have stood up for you, but they're worried about me. Their defiance comes from love."

Spider smiled faintly. "I know. It's why I haven't ripped into them just yet. Before my Luciana, I'd have already been pounding on them. Now that I have a woman of my own, I can understand where they're coming from. Now get out of here, girl."

I rushed from the room and ran upstairs. I didn't see anything wrong with the clothes I'd put on, but I'd need shoes that would allow me to run. After I put on socks and tennis shoes, I went back downstairs and sat in the living room until the club needed me.

A snuffling sound at the door drew my attention. I stared and waited, wondering if someone had gotten locked out. When I heard scratching, I knew it had to be an animal pawing at the door. I peered out the window and saw the cutest puppy on the porch. It must have belonged to one of the men in the sunroom. Or maybe one of the guys they said would patrol the area? I didn't see anyone, though.

I unlocked the door and opened it, reaching down to pick up the puppy. "Come here, cutie. Let's find your daddy."

A hand closed over my arm and yanked me off my feet. I yelped and dropped the puppy. Looking up, my gaze collided with Larson's. Everything in me went cold, and I knew I'd screwed up. Spider had been wrong. They weren't outside watching the compound. They were already here, and now they had me. I opened my mouth to scream, but Larson muffled me by placing his hand over my lips.

"Now, now. None of that, Raven. You know we don't like it when you scream." He smiled, the sight chilling me.

He dragged me off the porch and I saw Simmons and Keates waiting in the shadows. I didn't know how they'd gotten past everyone and inside the fence, but I knew this was really bad. No one knew they had me. How long before Fox and my dad realized I'd gone missing? Tears pricked my eyes when I thought about them finding my body. I knew these men wouldn't keep me alive. They'd hurt me and then leave me for dead.

I scanned the area, hoping to see one of the Hades Abyss members. A few lumps on the ground drew my eye and I had a feeling they were the men who'd been guarding the house. How had these assholes gotten the drop on them?

Keates reached out to stroke my cheek. "Be nice and quiet, otherwise, you won't be the only one we take with us. You aren't the only woman here. Understand?"

I nodded. I'd do whatever they wanted, as long as they left the others alone. I'd only met Luciana and Violeta the one time, and hadn't had a chance to meet Vasha, but I couldn't let these men hurt them. As long as I remained compliant, they'd take me elsewhere before they started in on their fun. At least, that was my hope.

They tugged me away from the house and into the dark. I noticed we weren't heading for the main gate and started to panic. If we didn't leave the compound, they could still go after the other women.

"You got me fired, you little bitch," Larson said, his breath hot against my ear. "My wife got pissed and demanded to know why. That asshole doctor told her I'd been raping the female patients. She kicked me out! If I didn't worry that freak would pay someone to take me out, I'd have made sure to take him down with me."

Surge hadn't discovered that. My heart slammed against my ribs as they dragged me farther from the house and toward the tree line. I could see the house getting smaller the farther we walked, and with no lights out here, I knew no one would be able to see us. We had to be nearing the back end of the property, but I'd look like a speck to the men in the sunroom.

"To make it look good, the doc fired me too. Asshole has too much on me or I'd retaliate," Keates said. "My dad is mad as hell. Says I must have fucked up big. The old bastard cut me from his will and severed all ties with me. I think you owe me, Raven."

As we got closer to the trees, I saw four stakes in the ground with rope, and a camera on a tripod. Fear slithered through me as I began to realize what they intended. I *owed* them. Whatever they had planned, they were going to find a way to use it for financial gain. If they took a video of them hurting me, Fox and my dad would lose their minds. The only payment these men would get would be a sound beating, and possibly death.

We stopped next to the area they'd prepped, and my legs started to shake. Keates noticed and grinned.

"Your man thought he was so smart, him and his club. We've been under their noses all this time. Simmons stayed in sight around town, and Larson and I made an appearance when you were eating out. The rest of the time we've been here, watching and waiting."

Simmons stepped closer and ran his hands over

me. He licked his lips and leaned in closer. "Can't wait to get a taste of you again, Raven. You were always my favorite."

"People pay a lot of money for snuff films," Keates said. "Of course, everyone argues none of the ones out there are real. I know different. Congratulations, Raven. You get to be the next girl to die, but not until after the three of us have a bit of fun."

I couldn't hold back the tears anymore. "You'd kill your own baby?"

He froze, as did Larson and Simmons. The three looked at one another, and Simmons shrugged. "Ain't mine. I'm sterile."

"I got snipped after my wife popped out the last brat eight months ago," Larson said.

Oh, God. That meant the baby belonged to Keates. He'd mostly beaten on me, but he'd raped me too. I'd hoped it didn't belong to him. Out of the three, Keates was the least likely to have a soul.

Keates moved in closer, his breath fanning my face. "You saying my brat is in your belly?"

I nodded slowly. "If you've been watching me, you know I went to the clinic. I found out then."

His gaze skimmed down my body, and he pulled out a knife. I tensed and braced myself. Would he stab me? Try to cut his child from my body? He sliced through my clothes. Keates roughly shoved his hand against my belly, and I flinched.

"Doesn't feel like there's a brat in there," he said.

"Believe what you want," I said. "But there's a baby. If Simmons and Larson can't have children, it means the baby is yours."

He sneered and stalked away from me, pacing along the tree line. He muttered under his breath, and I couldn't hear what he said. Larson held me tighter and

Simmons finished cutting my clothes off me. Once they had me naked, Simmons and Larson wrestled me to the ground and tied my hands and feet to the stakes, leaving me spread-eagle.

Keates hunkered down next to me. "Guess I can't kill you just yet. Maybe a kid is what I need to get back in my father's good graces. Doesn't mean we have to completely abandon our little film."

"Do we still get to fuck the bitch again?" Larson asked.

Keates smiled and I whimpered, wishing I could get away. "Oh, yes. The two of you can have her once I'm done. If it's my spawn in her belly, I get to take her first. After that, I don't care who gets her. We'll go until we can't film anymore. Then I'll take her home and tie her to the bed, where she'll stay until she gives my kid to me."

I cried openly, wishing I could have kissed Fox one more time, or hugged my dad. Were they looking for me? If they found me, after the men had started their film, would Fox still want me? He'd heard what I'd been through before, but he hadn't witnessed it.

Keates winked as he stood. "Get ready for some fun, Raven. We have all night. No way those fuckers would think to look for you on their own property. They'll be scouring the city, and we'll be right here under their noses."

Sobs wracked my body as he turned on the camera. I heard the clink of belts and started screaming, thrashing as I tried to break free. I couldn't go through it again. I *wouldn't.* I knew I wouldn't survive.

Chapter Sixteen

Fox

It took longer than I'd have liked for everyone to get into place. I went to get Raven and stopped when I saw the front door stood open.

"Who the fuck went outside?" I yelled over my shoulder. Anyone who'd left the sunroom had gone through that door and cut across the backs of the houses.

"No one," Hatchet said. He fisted his hands. "Not a single fucking one of us opened that door, which means Raven did. The question is why."

Oh, fuck. That meant she was gone. Out there somewhere alone. Had she thought we meant for her to run now? I pulled out my phone and called Archer, since I knew he had gate duty.

"What's up, VP?" Archer asked when the call connected.

"You seen Raven?"

"No, sir. All quiet up here. Everyone's been checking in. No one's said anything about seeing her." There was a pause. "Except I haven't heard from the men at your place. They weren't really checking in regular like the others, though."

I hung up and faced Hatchet. Shit. "She's gone. I don't know how or when, but I think those fuckers got her."

I texted out an SOS to the entire club, letting them know Raven wasn't in the house any longer. I ran outside and scanned the area for any trace of her. It looked like the grass had been flattened just off the walkway. I followed what I hoped was a trail, and noticed it went off into the dark, toward the back of the compound.

"Think they took her this way," I said. Hatchet stuck close as we looked for Raven. And then I heard her scream.

"I'll text Surge to check the camera footage," Spider said. "And I'll make sure the damn alarm system alerts someone when the fucking door is opened."

We broke off into a run, and I hoped like fuck we made it in time. When they came into view, it felt like someone had ripped my guts out and stomped on them. They'd taken off her clothes and tied her down, and two of them had started undressing. The other, already naked, knelt over her.

"That one's mine," Hatchet said, his voice ice cold.

I nodded and focused on my girl. I'd failed her, but I'd be damned if I let them hurt her more than they already had. We caught their attention when we were less than three yards away. The one kneeling over her stood. Hatchet launched himself at the man, both of them tumbling to the ground. While he pounded on that one, I went after the other two. My fist connected with Simmons' jaw and I immediately turned on Larson.

I punched and kicked the two men until I'd taken them both to the ground. I hauled my foot back and nailed Larson in the ribs before grinding my boot into Simmons' groin. He squealed like a little bitch, and I drew my foot back, striking him in the balls. From the sounds he made, I'd probably made his testicles rupture. Served him fucking right.

My brothers ran toward us, and I let them handle Larson and Simmons. Hatchet had made a bloody mess of Keates. I knelt next to Raven and started to untie her. Once I had her free, I shrugged off my cut and yanked my shirt over my head. I helped her put it on before I lifted her into my arms.

"I've got your cut," Knox said. "Surge caught them on camera heading this way. More of our brothers will be here in a minute. The three left to guard the house were knocked out."

I nodded and carried Raven back to the house. She hadn't stopped crying and hadn't spoken a word to me. My heart felt like it had been ripped from my chest. How the hell could I ask her to stay with me now? I'd claimed her, made a home with her, and then I'd let those assholes get their hands on her. I hoped like fuck they hadn't done anything other than tie her down. If they had, I knew she'd never forgive me. Hell, I wouldn't forgive myself.

"I've got you, Raven," I murmured as I walked into the house. "I'm so fucking sorry."

I felt my eyes burn from unshed tears as I climbed the steps and went to our bathroom. I couldn't let her go. Instead, I kicked off my boots, tossed my phone onto the counter, and stepped into the shower. Didn't matter I still had on my jeans, or that she wore my shirt. I twisted the knobs while holding onto her, and let the hot water run over us. Unable to remain standing, I sank to my knees and cried as I held her.

"So sorry. So fucking sorry," I murmured over and over as I rocked her.

I felt her nails bite into me as she gripped my bicep. I didn't care if she drew blood. I deserved nothing less.

"Josh?" Her voice was soft and low.

"I'm here, Raven. I've got you."

"You still have your pants on."

I smiled and tried to pull myself together. "It's okay. They probably needed to be washed anyway."

She shuddered and twisted in my arms. I eased my hold on her so she could face me. Somehow, I ended up on my ass with her in my lap.

"How did they get you?" I asked, needing to know where the security had failed. I could watch the camera footage later, but I needed to hear it in her words.

"I heard a puppy and went to let it in." Her cheeks flushed. "I shouldn't have opened the door. I knew better, but… I didn't see anyone else out there. They were waiting in the shadows and grabbed me."

"I didn't see a dog," I said. I smoothed her hair back. "I'll have someone look for the puppy. Make sure it's okay. Honey, I… I need to know. Did they…"

I couldn't bring myself to say the words. My sweet Raven understood what I wanted to ask just the same and snuggled into me.

"They didn't get a chance to do more than cut my clothes off me and taunt me with everything they planned to do to me. You got there before they could do anything else." She let out a shuddering breath. "I know who the father of the baby is. Keates. I told them I was pregnant and the other two said they couldn't have kids. He'd planned to kill me until then. He wanted to use the baby to gain favor with his father."

"You won't have to worry about any of them anymore," I said. "Your dad took care of Keates. I'm sure he'll handle the other two as well."

"You didn't want to?" she asked, lifting her head again.

I didn't want to lie to her, even if it didn't paint me in a favorable light. "I do, but I want to be here with you more. You need me, Raven. And I need to have you in my arms right now."

"I was so scared no one would notice I was

missing. It was stupid to open the door."

"We'd boasted how hard it would be for them to get inside undetected. You felt safe, and you should have been. We'll find out how they got inside and make sure no one else can slip in without us knowing about it."

She shivered and I realized the water had already started to cool. I stood and removed the shirt, letting it fall to the tiled floor. Then I helped Raven wash. I ran my hands over every inch of her body, wanting to not only wipe away their filth, but replace the memories of their hands on her body. When I'd finished, I shut off the water and stripped out of my clothes, leaving the soggy mess in the shower. I grabbed a stack of towels from the box just outside the door and wrapped one around her before tucking one around my waist and carried her to the bed.

Raven curled into a ball when I placed her on the mattress. As much as I wanted to help her dress, and put on dry clothes, I also needed to hold her a little while longer. I lay down beside her and pulled her against my chest. Spider found us, entering the bedroom quietly.

"She okay?" he asked.

I nodded, looking at the woman who'd fallen asleep in my arms. "But she almost wasn't. If we'd have been one minute later…"

"I fucked up," Spider said. He sighed and ran a hand through his hair. "Even though the plan we had seemed solid enough, I was so focused on Luciana and what those men would do to her, I lost sight of everything else just long enough that those men took your woman. Had I not been worrying about my woman and daughter, maybe I'd have thought to ask you to check on Raven. It's time, Fox."

"What does that mean exactly?"

"You know what it fucking means. I'm too old for this shit, and I have a family I want to spend time with. I'm not even asking the club. After tonight, I'm handing it all over to you."

I'd known it was coming, but I'd hoped he'd remain President another year or two. The man was in his seventies, and I couldn't blame him for wanting to step down. He might not look his age, but he wouldn't live forever. I didn't begrudge him wanting to spend time with his wife and kid. Wouldn't be long before Marianna was a teenager.

"All right. Any ideas on who will be VP?" I asked.

"Rocket." Spider shoved his hands into his pockets. "He's not much younger than you, and he's more than proven himself, especially since he claimed Violeta."

"You know the club will have to vote on it. You may not be giving them a choice about me being President, but we can't just move up Rocket and not expect some fallout."

"Doubt anyone else wants it, but we'll take it to a vote. It will be the last thing I do when I hand everything over to you. We'll call Church tomorrow and take care of it."

"The men? Did Hatchet handle them?" I asked.

"He incapacitated them long enough to get his tools. Then he made sure they were in too many pieces for anyone to find them, or at least all of them. I've assigned a few brothers to clean up the mess. Still need to deal with the bitch who sold her out, but we can do that later."

"Thanks, Pres. Let Hatchet know he's still welcome to stay here? I don't want to leave Raven alone."

"On it," Spider said. "Night... Pres."

I smiled and flipped him off. He chuckled as he walked out of the room.

Raven stirred, then settled once more. I stroked her hair and breathed in her scent. I'd nearly lost her. Even if it took the rest of my life, I'd make it up to her. Never again would I take it for granted she'd be safe. I should have known better. And they'd lured her out with a puppy of all things.

A light knock sounded on the door, and I looked over my shoulder. Hatchet stood in the doorway, his hands in his pockets and a haunted look in his eyes.

"She's fine, Hatchet. Come see for yourself."

He entered the room and stopped by the bed, looking down at his daughter. "I made sure they won't hurt anyone ever again."

I nodded. "Spider told me."

"I saw him ripping the VP patch off your cut. Something going on?" he asked. "I know it's not my club, but if you're in trouble... Well, you're my son-in-law, even if you're older than me."

I couldn't help the laugh that escaped my lips. "Shit. That will be fun to explain to the kids. And no, I'm not in trouble. Spider has decided it's time for him to retire. I'd imagine he's having the President patch stitched onto my cut before he gives it back."

"Huh. How about that?" He grinned. "My little girl is the old lady to the Hades Abyss President."

"I have a feeling she'll sleep until morning. It's been a hellish day," I said.

He nodded. "It has. I, um, told Spider I'd like to handle Raven's mom. I'll crash here tonight. When Raven wakes up, I'll probably be gone. Tell her I'll come back soon as I'm done. I need to make sure no one else is going to come after her."

"Be careful, Hatchet."

"I will. See you soon… Pres."

He walked out, shutting the door behind him. It would take a while to get used to people calling me that. I wondered what Raven would think about it. I'd tell her when she woke up. Until then, I'd hold her and watch her sleep. I had a feeling I'd be awake all night, too scared to close my eyes in case she disappeared.

"I love you," I murmured, kissing her brow.

Epilogue

Raven -- Two Weeks Later

Luciana, Violeta, and Vasha shared the table with me while the kids played nearby. The clubhouse had been scrubbed top to bottom before family day. The men were scattered around the room talking and drinking beer. Things had calmed considerably, especially since my dad had returned. He'd taken an extended leave from the Reckless Kings in order to spend time with me, but I knew he'd have to go back sooner or later.

"What's it like?" I asked Luciana.

"You mean having Spider home all the time? Or him not being President anymore?"

"Both," I said.

She smiled. "It's nice. He's more relaxed, and he's even been sleeping in. I wish he'd stepped down sooner."

"What about you?" Vasha asked. "What's it like being the old lady of the new President?"

"Fox has been busy, but he still makes time for me." I pressed a hand to my belly. We'd had a long talk the other day and decided to keep the baby. Even if Keates had been the sperm donor, it didn't mean the baby would grow up to be evil. "He went to my first OB-GYN appointment yesterday and plans to attend every single one of them. They said the baby seems healthy. I'm not far enough along to tell the sex yet, but Fox and I have been discussing names."

"What did you decide on?" Violeta asked.

"Grayson for a boy and Harlow for a girl," I said.

Luciana leaned in and dropped her voice. "What happened with your mom? Or the doctor? Spider won't tell me anything."

I smiled, remembering the story my dad had shared when he'd returned. I only wished I'd been there to see it all happen in person.

"My dad went to see her. Turns out, she'd told quite a few lies to her fiancé. The senator listened as my dad told him how my mom had lied about getting an abortion, how she'd thrown me out of the house after those cowboys raped me, then made arrangements with the doctor and guards at Balmoral. Dad said the man looked horrified and couldn't get away from her fast enough.

"And the best part? Surge provided proof of her bribes and what exactly she'd paid for. As far as society is concerned, Mom had a nervous breakdown and is getting the care she needs."

"Where is she really?" Violeta asked.

"At Balmoral. She's gone from designer dresses to a straitjacket. The senator didn't want the scandal involved with Mom being arrested. He's paying for them to keep her for the rest of her life, and she's to remain sedated."

"And you're okay with that?" Vasha asked, a frown marring her face.

I shrugged a shoulder. "She can't do anything from Balmoral. I think the senator will protect his image at all costs, which means he's not going to let her slip away. He'll be keeping a close eye on her."

"And the doctor? The one she bribed?" Luciana asked.

"Surge and some of his friends handled it, even though my dad wanted to rip the man apart. They've drained the doctor's accounts and left an anonymous file with the police. They picked him up and he'll be spending a lot of time in prison, where I'm assured he'll get special treatment."

I smelled Fox before his arms came around me, and I felt his beard brush my neck. "What are you gossiping about over here?"

"Just reassuring the ladies Mom won't be an issue anymore, or the doctor."

"Come dance with me," Fox said, helping me from the chair.

"Dance?" I couldn't remember the last time I'd gone dancing.

Fox winked and pulled me into his arms. Someone turned up the music right as a slow song started. I pressed my cheek to his chest and swayed with him in the middle of the clubhouse. Despite everything I'd been through, I'd managed to get my fairy-tale ending. Oh, Fox might not be a prince, but he was my hero just the same.

I'd gone from being an orphan after my mother threw me out, to having a father, a husband, and a baby on the way. Counting all the men and women in the Hades Abyss, I also had a rather large extended family now. And since my dad was part of the Reckless Kings, I'd been assured I had a lot of adopted uncles waiting to meet me. I even had a puppy! Fox had located the one the guards had used to lure me from the house. Since no one had reported him missing, we decided to give him a home with us.

"What are you thinking about?" Fox asked.

"That I'm lucky."

He stopped and pulled back to look down at me. "What?"

I waved my hand at all the people surrounding us. "I have all these people in my life, the love of the most amazing man I've ever met, and I finally got to meet my dad. I love you, Fox. Our lives may not be perfect, but… this is a pretty amazing happily-ever-after. Don't you think?"

He smiled. "Yeah, I guess it is. But then I've known from the moment I took you home that my life would never be the same. I think I fell for you a little when you rushed over to make sure I hadn't hurt my hand."

I felt a hand on my shoulder and my dad spun me around, taking me into his arms and dancing me away from Fox. He glowered at my husband. "Stop hogging my daughter."

Fox laughed and walked off.

"As much as I love having you here, you can't stay forever," I said. "Just give me a few days' notice when you plan to leave so I can prepare myself. I'm probably going to bawl my eyes out when you leave."

My dad held me closer. "I'm just a day's ride away. Nothing can keep me away now that I have you in my life, Raven."

"You know, in all the talking we've done, you haven't said whether or not you have an old lady back home. Do I have a stepmom I haven't met?"

He snorted, then full out laughed. "Hell, no. I don't know a single woman who wants to put up with me."

"Really? No one?"

He stopped dancing and glowered. "Don't even. I'm happy with my life the way it is. I have you, and a grandbaby on the way. I don't need a woman under my feet complicating shit."

"Hmm." I smiled and liked the flash of fear I saw in his eyes. Oh, he had every right to be worried, because now that I knew what happiness felt like, I wanted everyone to have it too.

Challenge accepted. I'd find the perfect woman for my dad, when he least expected it. I just needed the right damsel in distress and his instincts would take over.

Life would be interesting with the Hades Abyss and Reckless Kings as part of my family, and I couldn't wait for the adventure to begin.

Harley Wylde

Harley Wylde is the International Bestselling Author of the Dixie Reapers MC, Devil's Boneyard MC, and Hades Abyss MC series. When Harley's writing, her motto is the hotter the better -- off the charts sex, commanding men, and the women who can't deny them. If you want men who talk dirty, are sexy as hell, and take what they want, then you've come to the right place. She doesn't shy away from the dangers and nastiness in the world, bringing those realities to the pages of her books, but always gives her characters a happily-ever-after and makes sure the bad guys get what they deserve.

The times Harley isn't writing, she's thinking up naughty things to do to her husband, drinking copious amounts of Starbucks, and reading. She loves to read and devours a book a day, sometimes more. She's also fond of TV shows and movies from the 1980's, as well as paranormal shows from the 1990's to today, even though she'd much rather be reading or writing. You can find out more about Harley or enter her monthly giveaway on her website. Be sure to join her newsletter while you're there to learn more about discounts, signing events, and other goodies!

Harley at Changeling: changelingpress.com/ harley-wylde-a-196

Changeling Press E-Books

More Sci-Fi, Fantasy, Paranormal, and BDSM adventures available in e-book format for immediate download at ChangelingPress.com -- Werewolves, Vampires, Dragons, Shapeshifters and more -- Erotic Tales from the edge of your imagination.

What are E-Books?

E-books, or electronic books, are books designed to be read in digital format -- on your desktop or laptop computer, notebook, tablet, Smart Phone, or any electronic e-book reader.

Where can I get Changeling Press E-Books?

Changeling Press e-books are available at ChangelingPress.com, Amazon, Apple Books, Barnes & Noble, and Kobo/Walmart.

ChangelingPress.com

Printed in Great Britain
by Amazon

82468499R00190